CHAPTER ONE

"Damascus Road."

"Walk together children, don't you be weary. Walk together children, don't you be weary."

The preacher led the solemn parade of mourners, swaying greatly with girth, as he walked down the aisle. The ancient floorboards and joists, hand-planed eighty-five years before, creaked beneath the weight of the procession.

His voice boomed as he repeated the gloomy invocation over and over with authority until he stood directly behind the little pink coffin at the head of the church.

"Walk together children, don't you be weary."

The Right Reverend Doctor Joshua Jackson was a big black man, with size 15EE feet and an overly round belly that testified to God's own truth that he didn't miss too many meals. But then, everybody here, weeping in the pews, already knew that.

They liked it that way.

A skinny preacher just didn't have the lungs to fill Grace Baptist. It was the difference between Mariah Carey and Aretha Franklin.

They tried a skinny preacher once about fifteen years ago, just before Reverend Jackson took over.

He wasn't bad.

His name was Howard Beasley, and he came highly recommended by the Black Baptist Convention. He had even cut his teeth as an apprentice minister in Dallas, which, back then, was the Broadway of Southern-stylistic preachers,

He was a handsome man, with good hair and a thin mortician's mustache.

And when he shook his head for emphasis, his hair fell back and forth tidally in a thick black swoosh like Cab Calloway.

But his collar was always too loose, and his pants were always too baggy in the back.

And, more importantly, he never seemed to catch the spirit.

The ghetto dowagers who sat in the balcony liked a preacher who could catch the spirit. And they didn't even mind if he danced a little.

The dowagers constantly complained that they couldn't see Rev. Beasley when he stood behind the pulpit, and that they didn't like the scratchy sound the microphone made when he spoke into it.

After all, as they often reminded the church board- to whom they had willed their estates -their dear departed Rev. Wright "didn't need no micaphone to preach."

Not long afterward, the church gave young Rev. Beasley a friendly pat on the back, a celebratory dinner, and a one-way bus ticket back to Dallas.

When Joshua Jackson showed up for his audition, the board liked him right away.

His jovial man-child's face; his high-water pants; his white socks; his incessantly sweating brow. The head deacon walked over and squeezed his arms with both of his hands.

"Big boy!" the old man marveled. "Lawd if you aint a hog-headed sonofagun. Woowee!"

"Good lookin!" one of the elder matrons, whispered. "Looks like that Luther Van Dross."

"Mmmm mmm," another seconded. "And I hear he's single."

The young preacher just stood there grinning like the Buddha-elect himself, as the diminutive deacon orbited about him, shaking his head in happy disbelief.

As they ushered him into the church, his silhouette filled the giant doorway and cast a long shadow down the aisle right toward the pulpit.

A good and propitious sign that he followed as he walked.

Right to the place he was meant to be.

That was many years ago. And getting here was a hard journey.

Damascus Road.

Reverend Jackson had come up the rough side of the mountain.

From Cabrini Greens in Chicago.

He was a fine student as a boy and had even won a scholarship to the University of Chicago. But on the day Joshua Jackson was to give his valedictory, his father had a stroke as he and his wife walked to their reserved seats in the auditorium.

And even as Joshua ran off the stage and held his father's hand, wiping the foam from his mouth, he knew he would have to turn down the free ride at U of C. It would now fall to him to go to work and help support his family.

That night, Joshua prayed to God for a long time.

A passionate and heart-felt prayer. Of thanks. That He had spared his father.

After putting in ten hours a day on a hospital maintenance crew, young Joshua Jackson went to night school at the community college, before going to his second job as an overnight security guard at a law office.

But there, at least, in between doing his rounds, he could read and sleep and dream the dream that had kept him going all these years.

The dream of Jesus and Job. Moses and Martin.

The dream of prophets who knew that woe is the price of faith.

But Joshua was willing to pay it. With sweat equity.

So he worked. And worked. Paying the rent. Buying the groceries. Even giving his momma a few extra dollars a week for the two things he knew she couldn't live without. The two tiny vices of an otherwise sainted woman of the Lord.

Marlboros and a Powerball ticket.

Joshua sweated for three years, simultaneously earning a minimum wage and an associate's degree in Social Work.

His father was slowly beginning to re-learn how to walk and talk. And his siblings were getting old enough to pitch in a little here and there when they could.

He figured he would only have to work another two years before they could pick up the slack, and he could go back to school full time.

But on March 17th, 1995, God parted the seas of poverty for eight people in the Chicago area.

And Eloise Jackson was among them.

Joshua's momma and seven others hit the number and won a share of the five million dollar Powerball jackpot. For the next twenty years, she would get a check every month with the neatly printed sum of 5,391 dollars and 15-cents.

It wasn't a fortune. But it was right on time.

Joshua reapplied to the university but had missed the scholarship window.

The counselor at the Bursar's office said that the only financial aid he could find was a thirty hour-a-week job in the computer lab. At the information desk.

He apologized profusely and promised to look harder as he saw the tears welling in Joshua's eyes. But when the young man rushed over and gave the counselor a giant bear hug, he realized they were tears of joy.

And just as hard as he had worked before, Joshua worked hard again.

When he finished his undergraduate studies magna cum laude, God Himself gave him another scholarship. To the Trinity School of Divinity at Duke University.

Three years later, with a new doctorate in theology and a weary Chevy Impala named Old Betty, the Reverend Doctor Joshua Jackson drove to Augusta, Georgia; the first stop in what would become a yearlong vision quest of faith.

He came to Augusta on a whim. He had about a thousand dollars saved up and figured he could work his way through the South, the way the little white kids did through the hostels in Europe. But what he both knew and did not know was that Europe was a world away from the South.

When Old Betty's transmission seized, and the engine threw a rod, Rev. Jackson couldn't afford to fix it.

He was lucky that it gave out downhill near a church, so he could coast it into the parking lot where it over-heated in a hissy-fit of steam.

A small hot river of green radiator fluid ran slowly, terminally, down the curb into the sewer grate. He knew there was nothing he could do, especially at night on a Saturday, so he crawled into the backseat and went to sleep.

The next morning, he heard the sweet sounds of chorale music gently invade his dreaming. He could tell even with his eyes closed that this was a white church.

Probably Presbyterian. Maybe Methodist.

White folks didn't like too much shouting when they sang, he remembered.

And they favored pump organs with pipes as tall as steeples. He knew this because he had been a guest speaker at one of the Southern Baptist Churches in Durham, not far from Duke.

It was a big honor.

The church was well heeled, and many politicians, including a sitting senator, called it home.

The congregation kind of adopted him, and every fourth Sunday, he was invited to add what the deacons called a little "hot sauce" to the ministry.

"Just a tetch, now," they would say.

He didn't mind giving the white folks that little dose of color.

For him, preaching the black idiom for a white church was like theatre, a cartoonish homage to George Jefferson on a tirade.

A black church would see the condescension and inside joke of it all.

But here, among the friendly white folks, it was harmless satire.

He would prowl around the stage obliging the stereotype, Bible in one hand, hankie in the other. He would growl his R's with righteousness and shake his fist with the gesticulated librettos of conviction.

And when he slid on one foot like James Brown, the love offerings, which he got to keep, went up 50%.

Besides, the sermons here were televised, and that meant so was he.

Rev. Jackson figured ultimately, the show was good for everybody. And long overdue. Black and white churches had always been segregated. Especially in the South.

The third chapter of his dissertation was dedicated to the fact that it took the Southern Baptist Convention 125 years after the Civil War to finally condemn slavery.

In a close vote.

But the Reverend truly believed in the saying "let change start with me." He wanted to let the white folks know that at least one black person wasn't still holding a grudge.

Faith would be the clemency for fear.

As he listened to the hymn being sung in the church behind him now, he chuckled to himself.

He remembered that Sunday when Senator Terry Bradford had come to the church in Durham. Senator Bradford was what the Reverend's daddy liked to call a Ritz Cracker, one of the rich ones with a good name.

He could still hear his daddy imitate Andy Griffith in those television commercials. "Goo-ood cracker."

But the Senator was a religious man and a friend of the black community. He was about eighty years old and spoke his mind, whenever and where ever the Spirit moved him.

That Sunday, he was so genuinely moved by Rev. Jackson's sermon, that he stood up from his seat on the front pew and implored the young preacher to lead them in a chorus of that "old Negrah spiritchal, 'Andy.'"

Rev. Jackson flipped through the hymnbook in his head and politely told the Senator he couldn't remember that particular song.

"You know," the Senator insisted. "'Andy!'"

Rev. Jackson grinned with modest embarrassment. "'Andy'... hmm. Still doesn't ring a bell."

"They sing it at every Negrah church I ever been in. I just love that song. I swear I do."

"Can you remember how it goes?" Rev. Jackson asked.

"Hell yeah, I can!" the Senator boomed. He held his arms before him like a conductor. "Andy walks with me.... Andy talks with me.... Andy tells me I am his own!"

As the Senator waved his arms and closed his eyes and opened his mouth wide with singing, Rev. Joshua Jackson nearly broke his ribs as he doubled over in laughing.

And as he opened his eyes and laughed aloud at the memory here, he became vaguely aware of police lights behind him in the parking lot.

A patrolman was conferring with two neatly dressed youths, who appeared to be junior ministers at the church Sunday school.

Reverend Jackson could hear words like "vagrant" and "dangerous" being used by the men.

"Officer, I can explain," the Reverend said as he stepped out of the car. "I am a minister."

"You gonna need a minister, if you don't git back in that car, right about now, boy!" the cop shouted, pulling his baton, as the others cowered behind him.

Reverend Jackson was suddenly conscious of how he looked and smelled in the early heat of the day. "But I can assure you, officer, that... ooph!"

Before the preacher could finish his words, the cop poked him hard in the solar plexus with the end of his baton.

"I done told you once, git back in that car! Now, you can listen to me, or you can listen to Mr. Headache Stick. Gimme yer dayum license. If you got one." The cop slapped the baton hard in his hand.

"If you aint, you best git to prayin for a miracle. Reven."

Holding his gut and catching his breath, Rev. Jackson surrendered his license and slowly got back into the car while the cop went to his car to check out the tags.

Above the static of the police radio, he could hear the choir singing the words of the dismissal song.

"MAY THE LORD CAUSE HIS FACE TO SHINE UPON-ON YOU!"

The policeman walked back over to the Reverend's car.

"All rightee, Mr. JoSHUa Jackson. You wouldn't be no kin to that trouble maker, Jesse, now would you?" he laughed. "Well, it's your lucky day. Seems you aint wanted nowhere, so I gotta let you go."

"As I told you. I am a minister. A Reverend Doctor, sir, trained at Duke."

"Duke? Duke what? Duke of Earl? Duke Ellington?" the cop laughed.

"Duke University."

"Uh huh. Well see, this here aint Duke. And unless you got permission to be here, you gonna have to do your preachin' somewhere else."

Joshua looked at the Junior Ministers, who were shaking their heads. The crowd was beginning to file out of the church.

He took note of the harsh startled looks on their faces as they studied him.

Inside, the choir continued to sing.

"AND GIVE YOU PEACE! AND GIVE YOU PEACE!"

"In about one minute, Reven, you're gonna be trespassin'." the cop warned him.

"AND BE GRA-... AND BE GRACIOUS! UNTO YOU! AND BE GRA-CIOUS!"

"My car is broken. Can you at least call a tow truck?"

"Sure, I could," the cop laughed. "But see, me myself, I'd suggest you git to pushing son, cause if we tow it, we gonna put you in jail till we get the impound fee. Twenty dollars. A day."

"THE LORD BE GRA-CIOUS! GRA-CIOUS UNTO YOU! AH-AH-AMEN! AH-AH-AMEN!"

And as the Reverend Doctor Joshua Jackson listened to the harp-like cascades of the refraining Amen's and the ebullient lifting of hearts inside the church behind him, he pushed his car alone, a quarter mile down the street and across the tracks into the parking lot of a liquor store. On the dark side of town.

Where he now wished he had gone before.

Instead of the Holy House of God.

CHAPTER TWO:
"She looks like a Beaulah to me."

Joshua made a deal with the store manager to let him keep his car parked in the back. For five-dollars a day. It was a lot cheaper than a hotel, and the weather was warm enough that sleeping in the car wasn't uncomfortable.

He could use the bathroom at the back of the store, and there was a hot plate he could plug into an outside socket.

Every day, the preacher went out to look for work.

Anything to help him get back on his feet.

But for many days, even after he had learned where all the labor pools were and what corners to stand on for the construction pick-ups, he still had a hard time getting a job.

It seemed nobody wanted to hire him. He couldn't figure out why, until an old carpenter named Mr. Shenks pulled him aside and bent his ear.

"Listen here son," the old man said. He snapped his words briskly, punctuating them with an occasional elevation in his voice. "Bossman don't particular want to hear abouts no smartass Yankee nigga from Chi-town, see. 'Specially no sweet-mouth nigga with a education."

"Say again, sir?"

"You heard right, preacher-boy. This aint Illinois. Aint no unions here."

"Hmmm."

"You got any kinfolk hereabouts?"

"Down around Tupelo."

"Sho you right. All the black folks I ever did meet from Chicago came from Mississippi."

"The Great Migration."

"Now you talkin', son. See, the white man, he don't forget nothin'. He remember his pappy tellin' him about all them colored folks turning they back on the South and headin' up North. Now, alls of a sudden, here come all these niggros back down to the South again. But, see, aint nothin' here changed. Same as it ever was."

The young preacher breathed a heavy sigh and shook his head. "So what you're saying is that I'm not gonna find any work down here."

Mr. Shenks stroked his dark, leathery face with his long adroit fingers. "Not if you keep sayin' you from Chicago, you aint," he winked.

"What am I supposed to say?"

"Just tell him you from Missipp."

"I can't lie."

"Such a thing as bein' too mannerable, boy."

"I may not have a church, but I'm still a preacher."

"Well, you aint rightly lyin'. If yo peoples is from Mississippi, you from Mississippi."

"You've got a point."

"Sho you right!"

After that, getting work was easy.

The old carpenter even let Joshua live with him until he could save enough money to go in search of his calling.

He also helped him buy another car, an immaculate 1975 Deuce and a Quarter, with less than thirty thousand miles on it.

"She looks like a Beulah, to me," Joshua grinned.

"She's slow, but she's sho," Mr. Shenks told him.

"It looks almost new."

"The old gal say she'll take five hunert dollar fo' it."

"You're kidding. It's beautiful!"

"Sho you right! That old widow-woman drove it two places, once the week. Church. And the marketplace."

"Why is she selling it?"

"Her eyes about like marbles. The cataracts is got her."

"I'm sorry."

"Don't be! That means I gets to take her where she needs to go!" Mr. Shenks smiled.

"I see," Joshua grinned.

"Sho you right!"

The day he was to leave, Joshua pulled out a few hundred dollars to give Mr. Shenks as repayment for his kindness.

The old man politely pushed the money away and told the young preacher to join him on the stoop in front of his house.

"Son, the only thing I want from you is to take a humble word of advice. Can you do that?"

"Yessir."

"Eighty-fo' years is taught me one thing, boy. And that is, aint nothing new under the sun," Mr. Shenks said, as he rested his elbows on his knees, looking Joshua straight in the eye.

"Just like you was homeless, so was Jesus and his kinfolk. But somebody helped them, just likes I helped you. Now, what you got to do is pass that blessin' along. That's all I want from you. Can you do that?"

"Yessir. I believe I can."

"Then, I believe God is with you. You gonna be a fine preacher. Mebbe one day I'll even get to see you preach."

"I would love that."

"You take care of yo'self, boy. If you need anything, you know where I live."

"Thank you, Mr. Shenks."

"No thanks needed. Now, you best git to where ever you's goin'. It's been my pleasure."

The two men gave each other a long hug and never saw each other again.

Except in their fond thoughts.

In memory of the old man, Rev. Jackson created the Shenks Harbor Oak Mission in the basement of the church, to give homeless people room and board as well as job skills training.

He promised himself that Grace Baptist would never turn away anyone in need like that church in Augusta had done to him.

But he found that few in his community shared that vision.

CHAPTER THREE:
"He could see in the distance what looked like a Trail of Tears."

The black churches in Atlanta were little more than faith factories, bigger even than Philips Arena where the Hawks played basketball.

But then the preachers were bigger stars than any of the players in the NBA.

They wore seven-button ghetto-fabulous suits and gator-belly shoes. Their nails were manicured and delicately painted with white tips.

The Sins of Angels

They drove up in Bentley's with gold-plated spinners on the wheels, while most in the congregation took the bus, clutching their dog-eared Bibles like fat wallets filled with promissory notes from God.

One of the biggest was the World Savior's Chapel, which had its own TV studio, satellite uplink, and Lear jets.

Reverend Jackson attended a workshop at the church once.

They were feted with surf and turf, rare aperitifs, and complimentary gold pinky rings emblazoned with a crucifix of tiny diamonds.

The waiters looked like something out of an absurd Jamaican courtroom with their colonial costumes, white powdered wigs and dark skin.

Outside, through the mirrored glass, he could see in the distance what looked like a Trail of Tears.

A long line of worshippers made their way slowly to the campus from the bus stop down the road.

The afternoon weekday services were about to begin, five of them, simultaneously with a shotgun start.

Each one was presided over by an associate pastor who made in a month what Reverend Jackson made all year.

He could imagine this same line making its way inexorably here three times a week, as their tithing covenant demanded, shivering in the cold, sweating in the heat, soaked in the rain.

They were greeted at the pearl-painted gates by security personnel talking into their cuffs like palace guards.

Reverend Jackson never went to World Savior's again.

He considered it a sin the way even the smallest neighborhood churches in Atlanta locked their doors at night and let the homeless and needy sit like garbage along the closed iron gates and curbs.

Under his stewardship, Grace created a day-care center, a detox outreach program, and a computer lab for kids and the elderly.

Soon the church began receiving large grants from corporate sponsors and the government.

A visit from the First Lady solidified its pedigree, and the President named Grace Baptist one of the Shining Lights of the American faith community.

The Reverend eventually donated the old Deuce and a Quarter to the church.

It still ran like it was brand new.

But these days, he drove a big, red El Dorado with a white top. The church bought it for him as a gift. It was a bit ostentatious for his taste, but he soon forgave them their collective vanity, persuaded by a comfortable conspiracy of thick leather seats, power windows, and cold air-conditioning.

And as he became more and more fond of the Cadillac's sweet embrace, he took to calling her Big Momma.

He was still a bachelor, but never lacked for an invitation to a home-cooked meal. Nor was he shy about asking for seconds.

The Sins of Angels

He was known to favor fried chicken and ham, yams and yeast rolls, Texas Pete, macaroni and cheese, and, of course, cobbler of any genus fruit.

After prayer meetings on Wednesday, the elder crones would chuckle amongst one another, as the younger holy sisters, who were single, tripped all over their white nurse's shoes to bring him supper plates when he retired to the church study.

By all accounts, Rev. Jackson was a good man.

He didn't have a penchant for Rolex watches or diamond Cartier crosses worn about the neck. And, most importantly, he didn't fuck every woman in a big hat and a red dress who sat on the front pew.

He was ingenious, innovative, and filled with the legitimate spirit of Christian fellowship.

Reverend Jackson quickly made a name for himself in the city's elite circles of power, accepting appointments to many civic and corporate boards of directors.

Politicians in need of the black vote curried his favor, because he could hand deliver voters by the busload. And as his belly grew, so did the congregation. Indeed, the crowds had come to fit the old pews the same way he fit his old suits.

Barely.

And tonight they were standing shoulder to shoulder in the lobby. And the garden. And out into the street.

CHAPTER FOUR
"Atlanta was dangerous."

Tonight, they needed to hear Rev. Jackson's big booming voice. They needed him to shake the windows like old Rev. Wright used to. To tell them that God would set things to right.

They needed him to tell them that the soul of the little girl in the pink coffin was no longer in pain.

And that the man who murdered her was already in hell.

Cliché' Baker was the little girl they had all come to mourn.

She was one of those black kids who had gotten their Afro-centric sounding name courtesy of a racist practical joker.

Her mother was still sedated in the maternity ward of Germantown Hospital, when a couple of pediatric interns walked in and very helpfully suggested a few names they had heard.

One was Chlamydia. The other was Cliché'.

The groggy new mother liked the first one more, but picked the latter. It was easier to spell.

So that's what was put on the birth certificate.

The family had moved to Atlanta from Philadelphia after Cliché's older brother got shot with a no-name bullet fired from an AK-47.

The slug weighed 16 grams and sounded like a tiny propeller as it tumbled end over end, 1800-ft.per second, from a drive-by shooting two blocks away.

It had whirled through backyards, across streets, past cars, and through the monkey bars at Mallary playground before it ripped through the tendons in Erique's left arm.

Despite the surgeon's best efforts, the boy's arm looked like a shark had taken a big chunk out of it just below the elbow. To this day, part of the bullet remained lodged in the cartilage of the joint.

He could still bend it. But he could barely squeeze his fingers, and over time what remained of the muscles in his arm had atrophied into a useless twig-like appendage.

Cliché's mother had wanted to remove her children from the danger of the city, and had often read about the black Mecca of Atlanta in Jet and Ebony Magazine. Keith Sweat and TLC lived there. And so did Whitney Houston and Bobby Brown in the old days. So did Ludacris, TI and Jermaine Dupree.

It was the land of the Bankhead Bounce and Outkast. Magic City and Freaknik.

It was Black Hollywood.

The new Motown.

But like all black people who move there, it didn't take long for the Baker's to realize that the Mecca was little more than a mirage. A perilous illusion, like the flowering bud of a Venus Fly Trap.

The only way a poor black person could even catch a glimpse a rich black person was at forty miles an hour as they were chauffeured past them on Peachtree Street, in what appeared to be the same low-rider Maybach with smoked black windows and gold trimmed pimp wheels.

And rich black celebrities didn't live anywhere near the 'hood. They built monuments to themselves deep in the woods of suburban Alpharetta or Fayette County.

Or they lived next door to the rich white folks in Buckhead.

At least, until they blew out a knee or couldn't sell any more rap CD's.

Then, they went bankrupt, and their homes were sold in foreclosure for a dime on the dollar. Indeed, the streets here were littered with the celebrities of yesterday, who were the broke, crack head felons of today.

And Atlanta was dangerous.

Far more than Philly ever was. There were times when more people were murdered per capita here than even New York or Los Angeles.

But Atlanta was also a beautiful city, with a skyline of soaring pyramidal shapes and colorful lights that seemed to levitate the clouds as they passed above the cityscape.

The best view of the city was from the Techwood project.

That's where the Bakers were now living. On borrowed time.

The city was about to raze all the housing projects to make way for the new gentrification developments the council was pushing through. These were designed to give the best view of the city back to the rich folks who were now pouring back into the neighborhoods.

In the meantime, the crime was out of control. And that was okay with developers. Violence was the new way to block bust communities.

And the only people to blame were the people who lived there. And most of them were trying to move out just as fast as they could.

There was gunfire on the hour here, just like in Philly. It was the same kind of audible graffiti that the drug dealers used to mark their territory.

And parents here, just like in Philly, kept the windows closed even in the summertime, without air conditioning.

But that didn't keep out the bullets or the prowlers or the rapists.

Still, the Bakers were lucky. Erique found a job at the black movie theater, and he got to dress up in a flyy tux, which made him very popular with the local girls.

And he could get people into the movies for free, which made him very popular with the local hoodlums. Who, in turn, kept him and his family safe from harm.

Cliché' had been accepted into the magnet program at Hill Elementary and was already reading on a ninth-grade level.

The little smart-asses who were jealous of her called her Hubble, like the telescope, because her glasses were so thick.

But Cliché' didn't care. She was a teacher's dream, and they looked out for her. She was a good girl with a genuine zeal for learning. Her counselor had already recommended skipping her two grades.

That way she could take part in the Atlanta University's Future Doctors program before it ran out of money.

For a little girl who could barely see past her arm's length, Cliché' knew her way around the city better than some taxi-drivers.

She had memorized most of the MARTA schedules and made friends with a lot of the drivers. Rarely did she have to spend a token to take a bus or train anywhere.

The drivers just enjoyed her company.

Her favorite was Fat Smitty, the subway conductor.

He was a short fat white man, with a jellied gut that shook through his shirt with every vibration of the train.

But his heart was just as big and soft, and he always let her ride in his cabin, with the windows open. The cool underground air would blow through her hair and make her eyes blink hard even behind her thick glasses.

He would tell her the stories of how the subway tunnels were blasted out of solid granite with dynamite.

"Fire in the Hole!" he would bellow, as they sped past the places along the tracks where sticks of TNT had chewed into the hard rock like sets of bad teeth.

In fact, before he worked as a conductor, Fat Smitty worked with the construction crews that helped shore up the walls of the tunnels, a quarter-mile deep into the earth.

And no matter how many times he drove her through them, pointing out the places he had worked, Cliché's face stayed wide-eyed with wonder.

"Fire in the hole!" she would yell over the ringing rails, as they sped past the blast sites.

"Fire in the hole!" he would laugh back at her.

The Sins of Angels

She loved to ride the subway into suburban Dunwoody, where she could browse through the Starnes bookstore.

It was a huge place with thousands of books, but it was unlike any library or bookstore Cliché had ever been to before.

Here, guitarists played live acoustic music, and couples came on dates to sip imported coffees and look into one another's eyes in the soft light.

The store had a section just for kids, and Cliché liked to lie on her stomach in one of the little niches off the beaten path, where she could read in the silence and privacy that she loved but lacked back at Techwood.

Often, she would stack books in a little wall around her, and lie there in deep fascination as she consumed everything the store had to offer. The clerks all knew her and gave her free sodas and cookies to munch on while she devoured their books.

Many times, it would be nightfall before she left to go home. When she did finally leave, she liked to linger stubbornly along the aisles, fondling the leather-bound tomes with her fingertips as she dawdled slowly by.

Most nights, she would walk out in the company of an old man she called Professor Paul.

His full name was Paul Heinriche. He was an emeritus English professor, who also sat on the Governor's Poet Laureate Commission, having been a recipient of the honor himself.

Nowadays, he spent much of his time here, sitting alone in the children's section.

The Sins of Angels

He had recently lost his wife to leukemia.

It had been a long and painful journey of days.

The golden feast of words that had brought so much richness to his life had suddenly become a thin gruel that could not possibly assuage the agony of witnessing the agony in his wife's dying eyes.

But coming here, he discovered, was good grief therapy.

At first, he had looked to the great works of literature for succor and solace. But slowly, almost involuntarily, he had found himself drawn to the laughter of the children.

He took vicarious pleasure in watching them and their parents, as they thumbed through the many picture books and stories.

He liked Cliché' because she stood out from the others.

She was fearless in her hunger for knowledge.

Most of the kids were scared of the grizzled old man in the wrinkled old suit in the corner. But Cliché' was different. The first time they met, she had encountered a word she could not find in the dictionary. She looked around, saw him, and had thought nothing of bouncing over to ask him what the difficult word meant.

When he told her and explained its Latin derivation, she smiled with such a bounty of gleaming white teeth that he had laughed out loud. It was the first time in months.

From that day on, they had cultivated a close friendship.

Usually, he would walk her back to the subway station, unless she left early.

On the last day he saw her alive, he had fallen asleep with Coleridge in his lap and woke to find that she had left a note on the book. A one-word question printed neatly between the lines on a crumpled piece of composition notebook paper.

"Thanatos?"

CHAPTER FIVE
"Comforting voices rose up like bright solar flares."

Three days later, attracted by a small brush fire, Cobb County police found Cliché's corpse in a flood plain by the Chattahoochee River.

She was naked, but sexually unmolested. Her body was untouched by the still-creeping flames. Her clothes were found nearby, folded neatly, but in cinders beneath a burning bush.

Along with her charred and melted glasses.

The fire marshal surmised that the thick lenses had set the fire, acting like a magnifying glass in the harsh sunlight of the afternoon.

A black metal hangar had been twisted around the little girl's neck, forcing her tongue to swell and protrude grotesquely from her mouth. She had also been stabbed repeatedly in a pattern that was not clear until her body had been washed on the stainless steel gurney in the medical examiner's lab.

A similar pattern had been detected in the burned brush by a Luma Light, the device used to search for latent blood particles.

Police warned the mortician that he would be charged with a felony and lose his license if he ever revealed to anyone the evidence carved into the little girl's body.

Only the investigators and the killer were privy to exactly what that evidence was.

To make sure no one else could examine the body, a Georgia Bureau of Investigation detective stood watch outside the embalming room where Cliché' lay dressed in her favorite pastel blue pinafore.

"I went to the spot where they found little Cliché' Baker," Reverend Jackson wept. "It was sunset. And there was...."

His voice choked up, and he could not continue for a long moment that ached with a hard, spiny pain, that was amplified by the hundreds of people who were in the church, feeling the same thing.

He shook his head wearily, like a fighter who cannot stand up for the next round.

"The world is not safe," he sighed. "Not even for angels."

His broad shoulders slumped, wearing the heavy yoke of hopelessness and pity. His eyes were glazed and wandered across the canvas of faces looking to him for direction and salvation from their own misery.

There was Cliché's mother and brother. Professor Paul. Fat Smitty. The mayor and his city council. They were all looking to Rev. Jackson for the unction of God's good word.

But they could tell that he needed help too. And as he steadied himself against the oaken pulpit, comforting voices rose up like bright solar flares from the congregation.

"It's all right, Rev."

"Take your time."

The old deacon who had hired him brought him a sweating glass of cold water and whispered softly in his ear. "Bring it on home, Big Boy. We're with you, son."

And taking strength from the many, Reverend Jackson's eulogy suddenly poured forth with the boiling lava of righteous anger.

"Beloved!" he roared. "As I looked out upon that glowing, spectacular sunset, painted with the colors that only God's hand can blend, I thought of my Bible."

The comforting words erupted again in enthusiastic paroxysms and the intrinsic litanies known to all who were raised in the black church.

"Well!"

"Speak on it!"

And as they cracked the whip of words, Reverend Jackson drove himself even harder, and he broke into a hot sweat, pounding his fist on the pulpit, shaking the giant Bible sitting on a pedestal nearby.

"We all know how dirty and nasty and filthy the Chattahoochee is!" he said. "Big Billy?" he yelled, pointing to a man in a mechanic's uniform standing at the back of the church. He was the only one here as big as Rev. Jackson himself. "You and me done sent a lot of catfish to the great beyond, aint we?"

"Sho'nuff Rev."

"Uh huh.... But see, not even me and Big Billy'll sink a line in that water."

"No, sah!" Big Billy shook his head. "Sho won't."

"You gots to have a iron belly to fry up some channel cat out of the Chattahoochee. That's how dirty that water is."

"All right, now."

"Mmm hmmm. Well, I looked out over that nasty river! And in the cleansing brilliance of the sun, the Light of the Lamb, all I could think of was Revelations, Chapter 22, Verse one. 'And he sheweth me a pure river of water of life, proceeding out of the throne of God and the Lamb."

"That's right, now! That's right!"

"Tell the story!"

"Preach it, Rev! Preach it!"

The preacher's voice rose and shook the windows like Old Reverend Wright's used to, all the way up to the dowager's in the balcony, who fanned themselves and panted with the vapors.

"And it is written in the Book of Life!!!"

"What's written, Rev?"

"C'mon, now! Tell the truth that God love!"

"It is written, Beloved, that 'Blessed are the dead which die in the Lord.'" Each word was a salvo in a rising crescendo of conviction and faith. "And blessed is this little one here!"

The congregation was crying and shouting with joy and sorrow and tears and laughter. And Reverend Jackson loosed his tie, wiped his brow, and tapped his foot like a race horse ready to run.

"You see! This little girl will lead us! You! And me!" he said pointing his thumb hard at his own chest. "She will lead *us*, like Harriett Tubman! To Freedom! In the arms of God!!"

Cliché's family began sobbing uncontrollably. The church nurses ran over to her mother and held her in their loving arms.

The Reverend looked down at them confidently from the pulpit.

"Oh, no, no, no! If you must cry! cry tears of joy, Mother! Yes! Weep! In the Good News, Brother! For, she! She is saved!"

The preacher was almost laughing. Hysterically.

The spirit had moved through his big body and his big heart, from his big shoes to his big Buddha face. And his countenance shone with the invisible brightness of someone filled with the Holy Ghost.

And then, just as suddenly as the sermon had begun to rage, it began to recede. Tenderly. Thoughtfully.

"If we are lucky," he said with gentle authority, "we will go, to where she is. It don't matter how."

"No it don't, Rev!"

"Uhn uhn!"

"You see, it don't matter if the boat sinks, and we all drown. We all goin to the same place. It don't matter if the tire blows, and the car hits a gas truck. We all goin to the same place. It don't matter if the jet crashes into the mountain side. We all goin'...."

"...To the same place," the congregation said in unison.

The reverend paused for a moment and took a deep breath, as he looked down at the little girl in the casket. "And it don't matter if the devil hisself kills us in the night. Because, we all goin'...."

"To the same place."

"Amen, Beloved. Amen."

One of Cliché's classmates, a little girl with a sweet voice and tears running down her cheeks, sang "His Eye Is On the Sparrow," as mourners lined up to follow the coffin and the pall-bearers out the door.

Police cars and fire trucks from all over the metro led the cortege out of the city and onto the highway.

At the city limits, the police stopped traffic to all but the hearse and the limousines carrying relatives and only the closest friends.

Above, the news helicopters hovered in place, using steady-cams with long lenses to follow the small procession until it disappeared from sight.

At the family's request, the burial place was to be kept a secret. To keep it from turning into another ersatz shrine for the grief junkies to make spectacles of themselves.

Like they did at the grave of little JonBenet Ramsey.

CHAPTER SIX
"Perhaps these were the true stigmata."

Back at the church, Reverend Jackson continued to shake hands and hug the weeping and emotionally drained members of his congregation.

He felt good to them as they wrapped their arms around the liquid heaviness of his mass. He fed every one of them with his over-sized presence.

31

But even as they feasted in the embrace of his sympathetic magic, he starved in the emptiness of their desperation.

As he stood, finally alone, on the steps of Grace, Reverend Jackson thought of Jesus. Dying on the cross. The iron spikes tearing through the tendons of his wrists and feet. Hungry for a miracle of his own.

He could see Jesus staring through tears into the voracious eyes of so many who had mortgaged their souls on a soon-to-be-dead man.

Reverend Jackson sat down exhausted on the clean marble stoop. He suddenly felt what Jesus must have.

Ephemeral. Bankrupt. Betrayed.

Perhaps these were the true stigmata.

He took out his pocket bible and began to search frantically for the magic "opensaysamees" of truth. But his eyes were blurred, and his head was light, and the words murmured absently like his heart.

He tried to pray, but as he closed his eyes, the sounds of the city invaded his thoughts.

Blocks away, he could hear the drug dealers' cars, with their thousand watt bazooka bass speakers beating like angry jungle drums. Here, the natives were always restless.

And tonight, so was he.

Suddenly gunfire erupted loudly down the street.

Passersby and children paid it no mind, much like passersby and children in Bosnia, Rwanda, Columbia, and too many other Third World countries on the planet.

Reverend Jackson opened his eyes and abandoned his prayer.

He looked at the small stone sculpture of Jesus in the church garden, and for the first time in his life, he doubted, like Thomas.

Jesus couldn't save himself, he thought, embarrassed for the thought.

How was it that His apotheosis came to be?

Who promoted him to CEO and President of Acquisitions for Heaven?

Did God really need a middleman?

No one gets to the Father but through the Son?

Are we not all the sons and daughters of God? Wasn't pitiful little Cliché' Baker?

At that moment, a group of teenagers bouncing a basketball walked by. "What up, Rev?"

Reverend Jackson looked up, startled, and smiled weakly at the youngsters.

He watched them walking and jiving together in their new expensive sneakers and their signature outfits.

Polo. Nike. Tommy.

He squinted as he read the giant labels, shaking his head at the need of black people to continue to be slaves of something. Anything. Even fashion.

In the old days, he thought, black people were branded by their masters.

Now the masters branded their clothes.

And as a people, he thought, it was beginning to seem that blacks aspired to do nothing more than buy new outfits or waste hours in the mall looking for more new outfits. Even if they didn't have more than a few bus tokens to spend.

How is it, he wondered, that things that mattered like academics and spiritual enrichment had become so anathema to the black culture.

Even now, at this very minute, the church's state of the art computer labs were completely empty, while the basketball courts were filled from dawn to midnight with hordes of kids who "got next."

Kids who knew by heart the lyrics of every rap song ever written. Despite not knowing how to read.

He had never seen a child cry over the crucifixion of Christ.

But they all wept like babies over the murders of rap-felons like Tupac Shakur and Notorious Big.

The templates for raising future generations were all broken now, he thought. The children have become feral and savage. And the ones who might be able to rise above the tumult were too often "gone too soon."

Of all the educational programs and services the church provided for the community, maybe five children had taken advantage of them on their own, and most of them only came by to play computer games or listen to music in the CD-roms.

The overwhelming majority of the children who came to the learning center did so against their wills, by order of a court judge, as some kind of a plea bargain to keep them out of juvenile detention.

While, the press considered the initiatives of Grace Baptist Church a huge success, deep in his heart, Reverend Jackson thought of them as miserable failures.

He could see the very decline of civilization staring numbly at him every Sunday.

Single mothers struggling on welfare, packed the pews, dressing for church like it was some kind of fashion show. Their finger-waved hair sculptures were steepled high against the laws of gravity, obstructing the views of everyone behind them.

Their necks and ears were heavy with 10-karat ghetto gold that made their earlobes blister and cheap yellow diamonds sold on installments at the local pawnshop, which eagerly accepted food stamps in lieu of actual money.

Sixty-cents on the dollar, of course.

Their children sat uneasily next to them, fading in and out of fitful sleep, the result of poor carbo-loading from the potato chips and sweet-tarts they had for breakfast.

The young men, those few who showed up, could be divided into two categories: gays and rogues.

The homosexuals were generally discreet and often had a penchant for singing in the choir or playing an instrument. The rogues, however, thought nothing of hitting on the women in the congregation, and more than once the deacons had to kick someone out for finger fucking in the balcony.

Reverend Jackson continued to stare at the sculpture of Jesus.

Was He going to burst into the halls of Congress and save affirmative action and protect civil rights?

Did God really look like Jerry Falwell and Ralph Reed and their mob?

And if He wasn't going to save the black race, who was?

Puff Daddy? Snoop Doggy Dogg? Or some other cartoon of ghetto angst?

Reverend Jackson got up and locked the doors of Grace Baptist Church just like he did every night. He walked past the El Dorado and got in the old Deuce and a Quarter. He found the keys neatly tucked in the visor and cranked her up.

Beulah hummed patiently and warmed quickly.

Reverend Jackson pulled the car slowly out of the driveway.

He drove down the street, through the stop sign and into the path of a speeding transfer truck.

When the paramedics extricated him from the mangled wreckage, his eyes were wide open. And unseeing.

Just like those of the people he had left behind in the world of the living.

CHAPTER SEVEN
"Syzygy."

The man sat in front of a large clean desk, swathed in the palpable, pulsating blue aura of a computer screen. It was clear he was in the room all by himself.

What looked like a determined grimace could be seen on his face, despite the fact that the wide-angle lens of the surveillance camera was at least thirty feet away from him.

His right arm moved swiftly, but subtly, in precise phasic intervals.

The FBI special agent in charge of operations ordered the technical director to enhance the pixels on this part of the screen. And though the picture was now slightly diffused, it was nonetheless obvious that the man was masturbating.

With purpose.

By now, several security guards had come into the control room, gathering around the screen, laughing, pointing, and making lewd comments that passed for play-by-play.

"I'm turning Japanese, I think I'm turning Japanese," one of them sang, squeezing his eyes into slits and bucking his teeth, the presumed physiognomy of self-gratification. As he sang, he pretended to stroke himself *capriccio* in time to the man in front of the computer.

A few seconds later, to the prurient cheers of the guards watching, the man climaxed with a deep moan. Involuntarily, his foot kicked one of the table legs, dislodging a paper clip that fell between two plugs in an AC outlet. It only took a millisecond for the circuit to arc and shut off. But that in turn triggered a silent flashing alert in the facility's master control room.

Such alerts were not uncommon and would have been ignored had it not been for a smoke alarm that lit up moments later. The blue-gray wisp was barely more than a serviceable drag off of a cigarette, but it was just enough to ionize the sensors of the smoke detector in the vent.

The ostensible reason security guards were now replaying and laughing at the videotape.

Sitting at a vast bank of closed circuit TV screens, the guards had kept only a peripheral eye on lab F-17. Nothing much ever happened there.

In fact, nothing at all.

The room was stark and pretty much empty, with stainless steel cabinets and static-free black composite floors. A single chair and desk made of the same plastic material sat in the center of the room.

That's where the computer and the man had stared each other down day after day for years, in what appeared to be an almost still-life portrait of deep computer geek concentration.

Many times the guards had even tapped on the monitor, just to make sure that the line-feed wasn't malfunctioning and somehow stuck in a terminal freeze-frame.

Often, the only movement that could be seen in the room was the man's fingertips, which moved in a blur across the keypad.

Indeed, the chief of security had argued against the FBI installing the hidden camera here.

There were so many other places in the facility much more rife for sabotage and data-theft than F-17, the office of Ed Lee, chief support technician for the Syzygy project; the same man now furiously trying to wipe the semen off his pants.

Syzygy was one of several top-secret computer designs being developed simultaneously by the Defense Department at the Lyndon B. Johnson Nuclear Research Laboratory in Albuquerque.

Ed Lee had been sought after by the brain trusts in each of the various projects, because of his peerless genius with code writing, artificial intelligence theory, and quantum computer mechanics.

The director of Syzygy had stolen him from another team, promising him autonomy, four-day work weeks, and a limited interface with the DOD bureaucrats, who flew in weekly from Colorado Springs to check on the projects' status.

The Johnson Lab was one of the military's top priorities.

They were spending billions per year on building new super-computers here.

But that funding was now in jeopardy, thanks to the increased needs of Homeland Security, which the military types referred to facetiously as "Homeland Mall Security."

But what that department lacked in clout, it more than made up for in priority funding, including money that used to go to Syzygy.

Ironically, the IRS was already on the cutting edge of the super-computer technology. And indications were that if DOD didn't produce a better system soon, the whole project would be scrapped in favor of a Treasury Department clone.

But the military's ace in the hole was Syzygy. And Syzygy's ace in the hole was Ed Lee.

He alone convinced the project managers to switch gears and take a completely different approach to the problem of super-computing. Teleportation.

The Sins of Angels

In an e-interview with the department's intranet newsletter, Ed likened his job to Jeff Goldblum's role in the movie "The Fly."

"Teleportation is real," he wrote in the department's newsletter. "Scientists in several countries have been working on it for years. It's certainly not teleportation on a complex organic scale, but it is teleportation on an atomic level. It takes advantage of what Einstein called the 'spooky action' of atoms to understand one another.

"To be honest, in many ways, this spooky action appears to be less a function of teleportation than atomic telepathy. So-called 'entangled' atoms appear to be, for lack of a better explanation, psychically linked. That may be how they can emulate one another even when they're far away.

"But what we do know is that by replicating the quantum states of data atoms onto these entangled atoms we can create an invisible circuit that can link together untold streams of information.

"Right now, rather primitively, we link 150 computers together with wires to form one giant super-computer. Maybe we can crunch a terabyte per second with that.

"But with teleportation, the possibilities are endless and almost instantaneous.

"Still, it is not without risk. Remember when the fly got into Seth Brendel's teleportation pod? The result was catastrophic. The same thing could happen here.

"Presumably, some weak force or particle could be corrupted in the process, and the result might be a similar parthenogenic mutation not unlike a bacillary Brendel-fly… a super-virus whose epidemiology could not be reversed.

"My job is to stop that from happening; to make sure there are no bugs in the pod."

Decades before, as a 16 year-old freshman at MIT, Ed had written a paper on what was then a hypothetical prediction of electron deviations for nano chips.

He contended that without corrective micro-optics, electro-magnetic distortion could force data to "drift" into peremptory paths consistent with artificial thought, but on a level more appropriately defined as artificial epilepsy.

Ed's professor was unimpressed.

He was an Austrian national, who despite having spent the last forty-five years in America, still spoke with a thick German accent and insisted that his students refer to him as "Herr" Werner.

During World War II, he was a civilian engineer working for the Nazi's on their Messerschmitt-B163 Comet rocket fighter.

His expertise was in fuselage design, and his job was to lower the drag coefficients for the fighter, which could fly at a top speed of 600-mph.

He often told his students with an air of fond lament that the Germans would have won the war, if it weren't for the fact that Herman Goering thought the new technology was *"verrukt,"* or crazy.

Prop planes were cheaper to make and easier to fly, he reasoned, consigning the jet research permanently to the drawing boards and himself to the annals of warfare as one of the greatest fools in the history of battle.

Eventually Herr Werner was transferred to help build and maintain the first generation computers at Dachau, the ones that generated the coded numbers that would later be tattooed on the arms of the inmate slave laborers.

He was captured by Allied Special Forces toward the end of the war and was given the choice of going to prison in a Russian gulag or going to work on the cheap for the U.S. Army Air Corps.

Wisely, he chose the latter and became a data analyst, in an army of ex-patriot German data analysts. Eventually he would help design and build the first Gemini space capsule for NASA.

These days, he still kept his hair in a Fifties buzz-cut and wore what appeared to be Marines-issued black horn-rimmed glasses.

His suits too were black, accented with a skinny black tie; but his shirts were invariably bright white and sharply pressed, just like his socks.

He favored industrial strength brown wing tip shoes, which were always highly polished, even though they had to be at least a decade old.

Herr Werner could work a slide rule faster than most of his students could use their calculators.

He was clearly brilliant.

The problem was, he had spent too many years feeding punch cards into computers the size of gymnasia and had never adapted to what he considered theoretical "komputer science fiktion."

Despite the thick eyeglasses teetering heavily on the bridge of his nose, Herr Werner could no further see into the future than Herman Goering.

Unable to support his argument with any quantifiable proof, Ed received a "generous" C-minus on the paper and promptly dropped out of the university.

After that, he went on to work a variety of dead-end jobs across the country, from repairing computers to writing software in spam sweatshops. He never stayed more than a few months in any one place. Sometimes as little as a few days.

But his thesis remained on file at MIT. That's how the government eventually tracked him down and offered him a job at the Johnson Lab.

CHAPTER EIGHT
"Nerds in Armani Suits."

The work he was doing was heads and shoulders above anything being done at the top research schools in the world, including Harvard and Oxford.

There were maybe two other people on the planet who could truly understand it beyond the conceptual gist.

And both of them were making millions of dollars a month as the founders of Intellimax, a company working on a supercomputer of its own. To lease to the Defense Department.

Of any country.

It was a gentlemanly sort of extortion.

Businesses had learned that in a global economy, patriotism belonged in the liabilities column of the spreadsheet. Proprietary technology was no longer the government's eminent domain under the aegis of "national security."

NAFTA had made it possible for American companies to take advantage of foreign labor, offshore banking, and, inadvertently, international patent law to protect their products from being stolen by the United States government.

Faced with a legal mountain it could not climb, the military had already set aside the funds for the Intellimax contract, even though it was understood that the technology would never be used.

With the possibility of an infinite number of backdoors and Trojan Horses, the integrity of the computer would be untenable. So, writing it off as the cost of doing business, DOD was prepared to buy the system and shelve it in the giant warehouse of things never to see the light of day.

Unless Syzygy came through first.

The military did not like having a gun put to its head, especially by the new breed of entrepreneurial egghead, who was more than willing to pull the trigger.

It had become embarrassing to sit in on the endless procession of Requests for Proposals and not have a clue as to what made the new technologies work, even as they were being explained.

The Pentagon's credo had simply become "buy the shit before someone else does."

The "NIA's," or Nerds In Armani Suits as they were called, would talk in a hip lexicon of cyber-semantics and abbreviated Instant Message slang that might as well have been Navajo wind-talking to the Old School

Generals, who suddenly found themselves surrounded in what was quite literally a virtual Alamo.

And the nerds were closing in like Santa Anna.

After the dot-com bust, the smart Silicon Valley boys had to adapt quickly to find a new source of venture capital. And taxpayer dollars would do just fine. The conga line started at Defense, where they got it from both ends, like a cheap whore.

Trying to prevent the pitchmen from talking above their heads, the military began to hire expensive consultants to translate the geek-speak. It was a perfect symmetry. Because the translators and the pitchmen truly spoke the same language.

Money.

In fact, most of the time, they were working together, like street hustlers working the corner on a three card Monte game. While one flipped the cards, the "winner" would raise his loot and yell, "I won, I won!" drawing in the suckers.

It was a profitable arrangement.

Both on the corner. And at the Pentagon.

Intellimax was poised to break the bank, until a researcher with the Defense Intelligence Agency stumbled upon a hand-written term paper in the archives at the MIT computer science library, titled "Breakdown at Ten Trillion bytes per Second."

To the government, Ed Lee was a gift from God.

CHAPTER NINE
"Numbers. Random. Meaningless. Numbers."

By all accounts, Ed was a lonely, monosyllable of a man, who came to work on time, wearing the same battered Adidas sneakers and no-name corduroys everyday for the last two years. You could set your watch by his celestially infrequent deviations.

At 12:22 pm without fail, he would leave the lab for approximately 13 minutes, roughly the time it took to walk the 157 steps to the cafeteria down the hall, stand in line, pick up his food, pay the cashier with exact change, and walk the 157 steps back to F-17. At 2:22 pm, he walked the 68 steps to the men's room, where he stayed for 3-minutes, before walking the 68 steps back.

The exact number of steps was known, because Ed counted them. With an old click-counter he kept in the palm of his hand.

Security guards had x-rayed the device long ago, and knew it to be a harmless peccadillo in the hands of another harmless peccadillo.

They often let him pass through the metal detectors without checking it in the little plastic basket, where other employees had to check their keys and cell-phones and pagers and laptops. Ed's pockets never held more than a few loose coins and some dollar bills. And he always left his keys in the ignition of his 1973 Volvo station wagon.

He had a high-level security clearance, which meant access to sensitive schematics and programs, many of which he had written.

Government psychologists had given him the standard battery of personality profile tests, but even his Rorshachs were flat-line. His only personality flaw was that he had no personality.

But in his line of work, that was considered an archetype. His risk-coefficient was one of the lowest ever scored at the lab.

To the psychologists, Ed Lee was the perfect computer chimp.

It was true that he had a photographic memory, and an IQ that spiked above 200. But he showed little comprehension of the value of the facility's intellectual properties and secrets. Especially to the outside interests and governments that might be willing to buy them. He was like an autistic savant, except that he spoke less.

The shrinks liked the way he nibbled on the rubber eraser of his pencil when problem-solving. They adored the calculator he wore on his belt, and the little one on his watch. And, of course, they loved his car.

He was the poster-boy of all the geeks the government kept in the cellar, tap tap tapping on their computer keys, a minimum of 20-taps per minute, a maximum of 504. A maximum only one person had ever recorded. Ed Lee.

After reviewing the masturbation video, the FBI agent wanted to terminate Ed on the spot, revoking all of his passwords and privileges immediately.

But the psychologists who also watched it-- snickering --disagreed, saying that an FBI agent jacking off at his desk would be bad. But for a person with the limited social skills of an Ed Lee, it was perfectly normal behavior "in context."

47

True it was shocking, they said, but it was ultimately a minor foible of the socio-sexually-impaired. At least he wasn't whacking off in the coffee pots like some of the other pitiful wretches they dealt with.

The shrinks said they were only sorry that they had not thought to look for some statistical predictor. But then again, they argued, people like Ed Lee are hard to profile, living as they do in the asymptotes of the bell-shaped curve, the prediction-less purgatory, between the sane and the insane.

However, the agent countered that he, for one, had seen a few profiles like Ed Lee's. On the walls at Quantico at the FBI's School of Behavioral Analysis. Serial Killers 101.

It was for this reason that Ed Lee was summarily terminated with two weeks severance and escorted off the premises by a machine-gun toting guard.

Besides, his bosses were well aware that the project was almost complete, and that by firing Ed, it would make it all but impossible for him to legally challenge their complete ownership of any and all programs he had designed. And his NDA had sealed the deal.

It was as their lawyers called it, "a W-2." A win-win.

His passwords were deleted, and all access to the mainframes was denied.

The incriminating video was transferred to disc and kept as evidence in the agent's safe.

Several weeks later, the FBI agent received a phone call from the technicians who were brought in to clean out Ed Lee's hard drives.

With great difficulty, they had hacked into hundreds of hidden encrypted files in his office computer.

But after running thousands of programs to try and de-code them, it was determined that they were apparently simply full of numbers.

Page after page of random integers, single-spaced, paragraphed, and neatly punctuated. One page of ones. Two pages of twos. Three pages of threes. All the way up to 345 pages of 345's.

The techs didn't know what to make of it. But the agent had a hunch.

He had recently had dinner with an old friend from the academy who had told him a frightening story about a child-killer on the loose in the South. It sounded like urban legend. But it was real.

There was a strict mandate to keep this information secret, he had said, sweating like the glass beer bottle in his hands. The killer had struck in dozens of cities from Atlanta to Albuquerque. Dozens.

He liked to taunt the police and always left clues written in blood or carved into the bodies.

Numbers. Random. Meaningless. Numbers.

The agent knew that Ed Lee was most certainly a pervert, proclivities unknown. But the numbers. They had made no sense at all. Until now.

But there was a problem. The files could be construed, albeit liberally, as intellectual property of a personal nature that had been breached and searched illegally.

Yes, they were stored on a DOD computer, presumably giving the government slam-dunk provenance. But the courts were now stacked with left-leaning renegade judges who liked to legislate from the hip, especially on matters of privacy and the Fourth Amendment. They were always looking for a good case.

If it turned out that Ed Lee was, in fact, a suspect in the child killings, this lynch pin of probable cause evidence could be thrown out by any one of them.

So, after talking to the U.S. Attorney's office, the agent had the supervisor call Ed back in to download and retrieve his files.

At first, he balked, saying they were meaningless, but eventually he relented, and within an hour, he was back inside the room putting his files on a memory stick.

Just before Ed left the building, though, his former department head asked to inspect the contents of the stick, as was permissible under the termination clause. The agent watched from the surveillance room, hoping that Ed might make a run for it, but he didn't hesitate to cooperate, and began to call up the information on the screen himself.

"What's all this?" the supervisor asked.

"Just some numbers," Ed Lee said softly.

"Numbers? To what?"

"Nothing, really."

"So, what's the frequency, Kenneth?" the supervisor asked sarcastically.

"What?"

"The code. What's the code? What does all this mean?"

"There's no code," Ed said calmly. "Look for yourself. It's just doodling, really. As you know, the rooms are designed to keep distractions to a minimum. So I just improvised playing around with the numbers."

Ed was sincere enough that the agent was beginning to think his hunch was way off base.

"You gotta be a couple brews short of a six-pack," groaned the supervisor, shaking his head. "I see now why your damn keystrokes were off the chart. You're a fukn gold-brick."

Ed turned to look at his old boss.

"I had the highest output of anyone in this department. Including you. I loved my job. And I would never hide pertinent information."

The supervisor took a deep breath and sighed heavily.

He had seen Ed Lee's dedication to his job for the last two years and knew in his heart that he was telling the truth.

"Well... then I guess you won't mind if I make a copy," he said, almost as an after-thought.

But suddenly, the agent noticed, Ed's body language began to change. He shifted in his seat a little bit. His shoulders squared. And more importantly, he looked down and to the right.

Not in a pronounced way. But in a subtle, controlled manner. The agent had seen that kind of body language before. In fact, they taught courses on it at Quantico. Neuro-lingual kinetics. The subconscious physiology that is the liar's equivalent of a drunk trying to walk a straight line.

Ed Lee had something to hide.

Slowly, yet deliberately, he covered the mouse with his hand and quickly pulled the stick from the computer.

"Actually, I would mind your making copies. They're my numbers. Just a little game I play with myself."

The supervisor snickered. "And we all know how much you like to play with yourself, don't we Ed?"

Ed grinned painfully. "Can I go now? Or are numbers suddenly a crime?"

The FBI agent smiled to himself.

The supervisor made a sour face and looked Ed hard in the eyes, before moving out of his way and letting walk him out of the building.

CHAPTER TEN
"3:14."

Nineteen minutes and 37 seconds after 10am, according to the bright red LCD's on his watch, Ed Lee was arrested by an FBI SWAT team that had been waiting in the bushes at his house.

He was charged with two known murders involving children in Albuquerque. And was a suspect in at least 43 other unsolved child murders across the South. DNA from minute traces of dried semen found on his desk were already being matched to a hair found at the scene of one of the two local murders.

Ed Lee was taken in a long caravan of black Chevy Suburbans to a detention chamber in the basement of Saint Joseph's Presbyterian Hospital.

The hospital had an underground sally port where he could be unloaded beyond the reach of long-distance camera-lenses. Everybody agreed this was the safest place to secret him from the media, which after a tip from one of Ed's neighbors, were now camped out at all the usual spots for the walk-down of a suspect: the federal building, police headquarters, the courthouse, the local jail, the magistrate's office.

The press was not yet aware that Ed was a homicide suspect.

If they had known that he might be linked to scores of murders, it would have been a hundred times Camp OJ, with enough cameras and reporters to cover every possible building in which the FBI could have hidden him.

So, using provisions from the Patriot Act, prosecutors decided to have a federal judge seal all warrants and motions immediately and delay his arraignment indefinitely, without the benefit of counsel. Ed Lee was now officially an "enemy combatant."

The floors and walls of the holding cell were padded with the same kind of foamy rubber that was used on the surface of the track at the athletic field of the University of New Mexico.

They were painted salmon-pink to elicit an adrenaline response of muted rage in whoever was placed there. Two observation turrets were built into the tall corners of the room, where psychiatrists and other doctors could study the patient inside.

Tonight, that was Ed Lee, along with a dozen investigators from the Justice Department, Homeland Security, and the National Security

Agency, all of whom were brought in to assess the scope of the serial killings and to determine whether they could be linked to terrorism.

The Bureau's victimologists did a cursory review of un-solved child murders during the time when Ed Lee was known to be crisscrossing the country.

They found that the number of deaths and disappearances that he could be linked to, at least peripherally according to the profile of the crime, could reach easily into the hundreds, perhaps even a thousand or more.

Many of the presumed victims had never been found. Some were skeletons. Some were fragments of skeletons. Others were corpses that had been ravaged by animals and the elements, to the point where decomposition made it impossible to determine the cause of death.

And while it was true that some of the children did indeed have numbers carved into their bodies, the profilers conceded that it was also possible the numerology might be symbolic as well.

They began to cross-reference the numbers of the wounds inflicted, along with their geometry and even the number of salient landmarks at the scenes, all of which were in isolated wooded areas.

Investigators surmised that the number of the victims was also likely to be germane, though it was doubtful that could ever be estimated accurately without Ed's help. And Ed wasn't talking.

Evidence recovery had already gone through his home, confiscating anything that could be deemed important to the case, from steak knives and handwriting samples, to underwear and shoestrings.

The carpets were luma-lighted for invisible traces of blood, then were rolled up and loaded into the crime scene vans for closer inspection of the fibers. Also loaded into the vans were countless reams of printer paper filled with countless numbers.

Back at St. Joe's, Ed's personality had begun to shift dramatically from that which he projected back at the Johnson Lab. Suddenly, he seemed much more narcissistic and took a measure of perverse delight in the attention he was now being given.

He often smiled to himself as he let the detectives play good cop/bad cop. He nodded politely at the one who buttered him up like cold toast. He called him "1.49." And he pouted woefully at the one who screamed at him in frustrated paroxysms of anger. Ed called him "1.7."

Quietly noting the theatrics from one of the turrets was Dr. Gerald Harris, the FBI's top forensic psychiatrist for the Southeastern District.

Harris was based out of Atlanta, but he happened to be in Albuquerque for a continuing education retreat being held at the Greenhouse Winery.

The course was an update on the use of electron microscopes to peruse cellular anomalies in schizophrenic lesions.

It was held in the biggest conference room the winery had, because wine-tasting classes always followed the last lecture of the day.

The Sins of Angels

The doctor was into his third snifter of nubile yet petulant chardonnays when he got the text that he was needed at the hospital.

Harris was a star within the FBI's criminology division. As a rookie agent, fresh from Jefferson Medical School's Department of Psychiatry, his first assignment was to consult with the Fulton County District Attorney's office on a review of the Missing and Murdered Children's case in Atlanta back in the early 80's.

He was one of a handful of renegades who did not believe Wayne Williams had murdered all 29 of the "official" victims, though he gave short shrift to the popular parallel theory that the Ku Klux Klan was responsible for the rest of the killing spree.

Harris engendered admiration and notoriety from the police ranks for his conclusion that Williams was no more than an inferior copycat, a media hanger-on and attention junkie guilty of maybe one or two of the killings.

But when the murders appeared to stop after his arrest, the FBI had not wanted to throw APD's highest profile case under the bus.

So the alternative theories never became public.

Harris' audit also never left the Russell Federal Building. But it did officially redeem the detectives who had firmly believed that a child serial killer had been allowed to escape capture.

It was well known to the police that Atlanta had become a hunting ground of sorts for serial killers, almost like a sporting venue.

The Sins of Angels

Hookers were routinely murdered in numbers that far exceeded statistical probability. The various methods of homicide, which included strangulation by hand or garrote, stabbing, shooting, and beating, indicated that many predators were at work simultaneously.

The local police had gotten to the point of denying that their Serial Killer Task Force even existed, much the way the Pentagon denied the existence of the Delta Force.

But the young doctor knew how to play the game and didn't make waves. He quietly rose through the ranks as a top researcher and departmental academic, authoring analyses on a gamut of pathologies ranging from paraphilic violence and child abduction to sexual mortification and profiles on serial killers who preyed on children.

When the agents heard he was in Albuquerque, they sent four squad cars and a rolling roadblock of police motorcycles to pick him up and whisk him straight to St. Joe's.

After reviewing Ed Lee's computer files and listening to the ceaseless volley of cloying and invective from the detectives, Dr. Harris left the observation turret and went down to the room himself. There, he sat quietly, unannounced, in a dark corner so as not to disturb the interrogation.

After a time, he began to notice that Ed occasionally doodled on the desk in front of him with his index finger.

At first, it looked like he was drawing a capitol A.

But as Dr. Harris mirrored the outline with his own finger, it dawned on him that he had seen this image before. In ritualistic graffiti.

He had also seen it in an antique bookstore, in a dusty tome called the "Mysteries of Symbology."

He recalled marveling at how absurd it was that secret writing had changed so very little over the millennia. From glyphs on temples to spray paint on walls. And he wondered silently why an insatiate child killer would be making the sign of a pentagram.

Now that Dr. Harris had discerned it, the five-pointed star became more and more definable as Ed traced it over and over, even when he made eye contact with the agents who were interviewing him.

Then something remarkable happened.

Ed interlocked his fingers, pressing them over his mouth and below his nose, as though in serious thought. After that, he moved them slightly away, pushing his middle fingers together in a point. Next, he contorted the fingers behind them so that they stuck out in two different points. The thumbs were now pointing upward at a sharp angle.

Dr. Harris blinked his eyes hard and wondered why this digital origami looked so familiar to him.

It took a few minutes, but finally it came to him. It was on the MARTA subway.

He had watched with curiosity as the indigenous thug life idly twisted their fingers in a similar fashion, speaking in the silent vernacular of the gangs of Atlanta.

Harris knew that Ed Lee wasn't flashing a gang sign. But he also knew that it was almost certainly *some* kind of a sign.

He was aware that legend tells of blood enemies using the secret distress sign of the Masons to appeal to their brethren to come to their rescue, their ineffable allegiance to one another superseding any and all other causes.

Time and time again, these gestures staved off beatings, arrests, and even executions. But the pentagram was not that sign.

Harris took out his Blackberry and searched the Internet news groups for "pentagram." 381-thousand hits came up in .29 seconds. He refined the search with "ritual." 56,109 hits. He added "murder." 7108 hits. Then "children." 6411 hits.

By the time he added "Biblical" the number was down to 666, a Boolean coincidence that sent a shiver down his spine.

When he added the word "numbers," the hits dropped to 536.

The first of these referred to the writings of Aleister Crowley, the heroin-addled charlatan, who was considered by many to be the father of the modern occult.

Alternately listening to the detectives and surfing for possible clues on the Internet, Dr. Harris quickly rifled through the blogs and web articles, searching out the more arcane essays.

They all shared the same trite philosophical gibberish involving God and "magick," blood and cleansing, children and virtue.

The numerology could not easily be explained.

It was late. After 3:00 am. But Dr. Harris was wide-awake.

Maybe it was the chardonnay or the jet lag, but his mind was racing, as though his thoughts were hyperventilating in his brain.

He had a feeling in his gut.

So he took out a wallet-sized travel clock that he had in his brief case.

His wife had bought it for him to take on trips out of town. He set the alarm and placed the clock furtively on a table next to the bottled water that was brought in for the detectives. Then, he continued to watch and listen to the interrogation that was wearing itself down fast like a sprinter trying to run a marathon.

Ten minutes later, the alarm went off with a loud buzz.

The detectives jumped in their seats, but the doctor remained still. As did Ed Lee. Who instantly wore a different look on his face. He suddenly stopped doodling with his finger, and his demeanor became serene.

He closed his eyes slowly, as though lost in a nostalgic reverie. His gaze was pointed to the clock. And the blinking red numbers on it.

"3:14."

Ed closed his eyes and breathed deeply, like someone in deep meditation.

"Hey! Wake up, shit-head!" the bad cop bellowed in Ed's face. "MUR-der! Dead KIDS!" he yelled loudly in a sarcastic cadence. "Re-MEM-ber?! And somebody turn that fukn alarm off! Now!!!"

Ed kept his eyes closed, but smiled lightly, and sighed with a weary amusement.

"Do you pray, 1.7?" he asked softly, as Dr. Harris pressed the mute button on the alarm.

"What?"

"Do you pray?"

"Absolutely. I'm praying right now that I watch you get a nice big shot of the Good-bye Juice."

"Of course. Well, to me, that number is a prayer." Ed opened his eyes. "As sacred as your Lord's Prayer. It is the prologue to divine truth. Even you should know that. You are a Traveling Man, are you not?" he said with a wink, casting a glance down at the agent's Masonic ring.

"What the... !!" the agent yelled with a timbre of disbelief attached to his indignity. "For Christ's sake, you'd better not be a god-damned Mason! I'll kill you myself!"

"Beware, Mason," Ed suddenly sneered. "Lest *you* die at the hands of the just."

The detective involuntarily drew back for a brief instant as Ed continued.

"There are many who've taken great delight in killing off members of your esoteric brotherhood," he said, condescending sharply.

"Did you just threaten me, you son of a bitch?"

"*A daemonibus docetur, de daemonibus docet, et ad daemons ducit,*" Ed smiled provocatively.

Dr. Harris suddenly looked up from his furtive work. Ed had not threatened the agent. But he had in no uncertain terms warned him.

In fluent Latin.

He wrote the words down as best as he could remember them. It had been many years, but Latin was a language that was hard to unlearn. He shuddered at the translation before him.

"It is taught by the demons, it teaches about the demons, and it leads to the demons."

The back-and-forth limped on for the next hour and a half. Ed was becoming increasingly unresponsive, bored by the redundancy of the questions. He was no longer entertained. And the detectives had all but run out of their uninspired material.

Ed looked at the red numbers on the digital clock. 4:59.

"It's almost 5," he smiled. "I'll make you a deal, detectives. A simple one. Appertaining to your intellect. If you can tell me what the number five means, I'll tell you what you wish to know. But at 5:01, if you can't, I will not speak to you again. You get one chance. And one chance only."

"Is that a confession?" the agent asked greedily.

"Perhaps," Ed shrugged. "Perhaps not. Think of it as a challenge. But think quickly. Because you don't have much time left."

The investigators looked at the clock and then at each other, completely puzzled, muttering aloud, with absurd non-arithmetic theories.

"It's like the SAT's," one of them whispered. "Yeah, it's a trick question... a '5,' and two zeroes... add them up."

"No, transpose them."

"What?"

"Why?"

"Shit!"

The agents started scribbling numbers furiously, whispering loudly. Dr. Harris noted their collective agitation spiking, the side effect of the salmon-pink walls, which had done a slow burn on *their* endocrinology, not Ed Lee's. They were hungry, sleep deprived, and clearly confused to the point of being almost incoherent. They were everything they had hoped their suspect would be.

"All I get is five, fifty, or five-hundred! What the fuck?!" one of the detectives whispered to the others.

"Shit! Me too!"

"Damn it! We've only got a few seconds left!"

"Five is the number of metamorphosis. It is the ancient symbol of alchemy."

The investigators didn't even ask who had spoken. Simultaneously, they turned in an unkempt fury of hopeful stares, looking every bit like the wild-eyed disciples in the portrait of The Last Supper.

Ed studied the man in the corner intently as he spoke, nodding ever so slightly.

Dr. Harris continued.

"It is the square becoming the circle and the circle becoming the square. The Vitruvian impossibility."

"1.65," Ed murmured absently as he stared at Dr. Harris. "How did I not see you before?"

"I'm afraid you're being generous," Dr. Harris said with a muted grin. "I'm nowhere near that handsome."

Ed's eyes opened with surprise.

"You will not find the perfection of phi on my face," Dr. Harris continued.

And just like that, the smugly confident smile on Ed Lee's own face had evaporated, as though someone had just said checkmate. To his life.

The detectives shared the same stunned look on their faces as they watched the doctor do flawlessly what he was brought here to do. He stood up and emerged from the darkened corner of the room.

The agent closest to Ed automatically yielded his seat, so the doctor could take first chair next to the man whose mind he was now closing in on.

CHAPTER ELEVEN
"They pushed Pythagorus like the rock of Sisyphus."

"May I?" Dr. Harris inquired politely.

"Absolutely, Dr...."

"Dr. Harris. Gerald Harris."

For just an instant, and almost against his will, Ed closed his eyes and held his breath with the same resigned bravery of someone about to be guillotined. Dr. Harris' was the face beneath the executioner's mask.

"I know of you," he said with a trace of admiration. "Your work is brilliant. Now I know why you never put a picture of yourself in any of your books."

"Because then I wouldn't have been able to sit here unrecognized."

Ed chuckled out loud. "Sun Tzu."

"The element of surprise," Harris grinned, playfully raising his eyebrows.

"Bushido psychology," Ed said, shaking his head in mild disbelief. "What next?"

"The terms of the deal, I trust."

Ed paused for only a brief moment. "Of course."

From the turrets, muffled shouts of relief could be heard through the soundproofing. The agents in the room low-fived each other beneath their chairs, while a court reporter was brought in to record Ed's deposition.

"Just one question..." Ed interrupted.

"How did I know?"

Ed smiled, conceding that he had been outfoxed.

Dr. Harris smiled back, and seizing upon the empathetic mirroring, he pressed his hands in front of his face as he had seen Ed do, then he manipulated his fingers slowly into a crude but articulated pentacle. Ed's eyes were transfixed on the sign, and, once again, he responded in kind.

"Doctor, you astound me," he said, speaking through his contorted fingers with genuine flattery.

"I got lucky."

"I got cocky," Ed responded. "'Govern your tongue before all other things....'"

"'...Following the gods.' I minored in math at Penn State," Harris grinned. "They pushed Pythagoras like the rock of Sisyphus."

Ed smiled broadly. Genuinely. "I think I like you."

"Thank you."

"Of course, if I had known you were here, I would have given you a sufficiently harder clue to crack."

"Then I'll be the first to admit, that I'm glad you did not know I was here."

Ed smiled at the polite parry. The doctor continued.

"I have to be honest, Ed. Until tonight, I thought that the Pythagoreans were a myth. I had no idea that they really existed. Certainly not in modern times."

"Only a few. By design."

"How do you mean?"

"There is a place in mathematics where only a select handful can dwell without madness setting in. It's a place where the algorithms become spells and the numbers tessellate."

"Like the pictures where the stairs climb and descend at the same time."

"Precisely. Numbers also can be described as climbing and descending at the same time. Consider the square root of a minus number. It cannot exist, and yet it must. It is both 'imaginary' and essential. Then there's the number nine, my personal favorite. It reproduces itself in the sums of its multiples."

"Nine times two is eighteen," the doctor affirmed. "And the one plus the eight is nine."

"Like a single-cell organism, it seeks rudimentarily to create more or itself," Ed continued.

"I have to admit that I never thought of it like that before," Harris conceded.

The politesse between the two men was an exercise in civility, made remarkable by the fact that one of them was a prolific and unrepentant child killer. It made the detectives uncomfortable, even angry. Most tried to bite their tongues. Many could not.

"I got a number. How about 666? I'll bet you've got that tattooed on your fucking head, somewhere," one of them muttered aloud.

"Ah, the Beast Number," Ed smirked spookily, almost laughing.

"Why do you find that number funny, Ed?" Dr. Harris probed.

"Because it's nothing more than a numerical parlor trick: the squares of the first seven primes; the sum of the first three 6th powers; the total of the numbers on a roulette wheel, for crying out loud. It's glib, no doubt. But certainly not apocalyptic. Puerile at best, not unlike the infantile geometry of our Masonic friends," Ed grinned, looking back at the agent simmering in the shadows.

"You know, Doctor, back when you were a student, people used to think that prime numbers were the rarest of sequences. Now, they know they don't even come close to repfigits."

"What?"

"Repfigits. More precisely, repetitive Fibonacci-like digits. They're also called Keith numbers"

"What are they?"

"No one really knows. All we do know is that there are only 71 of them below a value of 10 to the 19th power."

"Extraordinary."

"More than you know. Sanskrit mystics may have used them linguistically to cast spells."

"Numbers?"

"More like harmonics. '*Maatraameru.*' In our language it's called prosody.

"Prosody like poetry?"

Ed grinned. "There's no difference in poetry and numbers, Doctor. It's all patterns and symmetry. You just have to know how to speak it. It is the divine idiom."

By this time, the detectives in the room had ceased trying to keep pace with the conversation with their notes.

As the two men played their verbal game above the rim, the rest of the room sat as silent spectators, not quite sure what to make of the powder-puff compliments and complex arithmetic being gently jousted back and forth before them.

One of them muttered just below his breath, "I didn't know there'd be fucking math."

"Math, detective, is the only thing there is," Ed interjected without looking away from the doctor.

"What about our own human sentience? The cogito ergo sum?" Doctor Harris asked.

"The great Cartesian lie."

"How so?"

"Because if it's true that 'I think therefore I am,' it is equally true that I dream therefore I am. That I hallucinate therefore I am. Ask a schizophrenic what reality is. Ask yourself... every time you have a nightmare."

The doctor nodded slowly, not sure what to make of the syllogism.

"The only thing that is constant in the known universe is the certainty of numbers."

"I can agree with that."

"Some believe that millions of years ago, there was another civilization on this planet, more advanced than our own. Today, there is no trace."

"Which is precisely why many would dispute that claim."

"Excellent point, Dr. Harris."

CHAPTER TWELVE
"Have you ever seen an interdimensional map?"

"Do you know what 'precession' is, Dr. Harris?"

"To a general extent."

"The earth spins like a wobbly top," Ed said, moving his hand back and forth to illustrate the image. "And every few million years, the axis shifts, changing the topography, moving the oceans, polar caps, and mountains, which would cover any trace of human civilization, especially one that may have been annihilated by the cyclic intrusion of the asteroid belt. It happened on Mars. It happened on the tenth planet. And it happens here."

"There are only nine planets, Ed. And Pluto's in doubt."

Ed smiled. "I should have said the erstwhile tenth planet."

"An interesting hypothesis."

"It's far more than that, doctor."

"What's the proof?"

"The proof is a sculpture."

"A sculpture?"

"Made of Martian rock."

"Have you seen it?" the doctor asked, trying not to betray his growing skepticism.

"I've held it," Ed said, raising his hands. "I actually touched a piece of Mars."

"Really?"

The technicians in the observation turret glanced over at the Voice Stress Analyzer, which detected no sign of deception. "Crazy sonuvabitch," one of them said, shaking his head. "He actually believes what he's saying."

"There are places, Dr, Harris, that have been untouched by cataclysm, since the beginning of the planet's existence. Numerically, using a perfect cube, the Pythagoreans were able to calculate the locations of the best of these. These places are where the statue and other artifacts are kept."

"Which Pythagoreans?"

"The Original sect."

"From the time of Plato?"

"From the time of Triceratops."

"You're kidding, right?"

"They were not called that, of course. Nor were they from this planet, originally. But in our time and our reality, Pythagoras is the one who is credited with the re-invention of their ancient theorems. He was an Orphic shaman who understood that within every human body, there is locked an immortal soul. A soul that is quite literally dying to get out of this chrysalis," he said, gesturing to his body. "To follow what is rightfully called the 'stream of consciousness.' Which is a life form all its own."

"Pythagoras was a shaman? I thought he was a philosopher."

"He was both. But as a shaman he could shift the awareness of his mind between dimensions. Today, they would call it channeling. That's how he was able to access the mathematical postulations of the Originals."

The VSA monitor once again confirmed that Ed Lee was either not lying or believed completely that he was telling the truth. In the room, the agents were starting to fidget nervously, still waiting for the pay-off.

Dr. Harris noticed this. "Ed, I assure you that I want to talk to you more about all of that, but let's turn back to...."

"Why I did it?"

The doctor nodded.

The agents starting low-fiving each other again furtively and couldn't help breaking into wide smiles.

"'Why' is something I can better articulate in numerics. 'How' and 'where' are a lot easier. So, I'll start there."

"Fair enough."

"First, let me say, I take no joy in my task. For each of them, quite simply, it was their turn, their fate, as ineluctable and predestined as any strong or weak force in nature. No different than my own fate."

"It is not my job to judge you, Ed."

"And I appreciate that, Dr. Harris. I really do. The numbers I inscribed on the children are sequential. Always three digits, or three symbols, though sometimes repeated depending upon the epiphany for that particular child."

"Epiphany?"

"That's what it is. Each of them resonates on a frequency commensurate with the numbers assigned to them. They show themselves to me. Like an epiphany."

"How could you tell their 'frequencies'?"

"That is my gift. It is limbic and unerring. The same way a diviner can find water under the ground, I can find the children. I was eight, when I found the first, a three year-old named Devon Zimmer. I initiated her with the highest honor, the first of the living numbers. 314. The next was Josh Phillips. He was 151. Then there was Trudy Simmons. Her number was...."

"267."

"Right. You see it now."

"Pi," Dr. Harris sighed. "I thought you said pi was a prayer. A Holy number."

"It is. But for the children, the numbers are an epitaph. An infinite epitaph."

"So you would have never stopped killing?"

"Not even if I have to come back from the dead."

And as the fiber-optic video-cameras hidden in the walls and light fixtures recorded the confession, the tech monitoring the recording devices muttered to himself, "You're gonna get your chance, asshole. You're gonna get your chance."

"You and the FBI prejudicially call them 'victims.' I call them what they are. Initiates. They leave this world as unclean children. But enter the next as the higher, untouched souls they should have been. Before they were touched by an angel."

"The angel of death, you prick," snapped one of the agents. "This is bullshit, doc!"

Dr. Harris looked at him sharply, but by now, Ed was nearly oblivious to anyone's presence but the doctor's.

"People think of angels as spirit emissaries, flown here from heaven on gossamer wings. There are so many fantasies about them that they've become part of the modern lexicon of our culture. We think they are here to intervene. But actually they're here to interlope. They are trespassers. And they trespass against us."

"You are a man of numbers, Ed," the doctor prodded gently. "As such, you know that the laws of science are much more demanding than the laws of so-called truth. '*Res ipsa loquitur,*' that which speaks for itself, is not enough in your domain."

"Nor your own, I trust."

"You're right. The evidence of science must be seen and quantified and replicated in order for one to believe. So, how is it you came to believe in angels?"

Ed took a deep breath and steadied his gaze toward the doctor. "You, as I, have read the works of Heisenburg, Oppenheimer, Capra."

"Frank Capra's angel didn't murder little kids, you fucking ghoul," one of the agents burst out.

"Fritjov Capra," Dr. Harris corrected, looking around with great agitation.

At that point he ordered everyone but the stenographer out of the room with Ed and himself. The game was above the rim again, but this time, there would be no heckling from the guys on the bench.

"All right, continue, Ed."

"It was Heisenburg himself who said that on an atomic level, the act of observing the experiment, by its very nature, changes the experiment."

"Agreed."

"He further said that atoms are there. And yet they are not there. Real. But not real. These theoretical paradoxes are abundant in our universe. The way light is both an infinite wave and a fixed particle."

"I suppose."

"It is at the intersection of these paradoxes that we find the things that are not there. Such is the way of angels. There. But not there. We cannot see them for looking. And yet dare not look for seeing."

"So where are they?"

"They are as much here, as you or I. They're in this room, right now."

"Can you see them?"

"The very same way Michelangelo said he saw one in the stone, before he set it free with a chisel and a hammer."

"He wasn't being poetic?"

"Quite the contrary. He did see the angel. And he did set it free."

"Please, continue."

"If atoms are both things and not things, both here and not here, then it stands to reason that anything made of atoms is both here and not here. That includes you and me and everything in our dimension. Angels, unlike us, simply have the ability to use and un-use their 'here-ness'... to travel in, out, and through our dimension. They are the living equivalent to an enharmonic interval in music. Two notes occupying the same place on the same scale at the same time."

"Like C-sharp and D-flat."

"Yes. They are like chameleons that can change dimensions instead of colors."

"Proof, Ed. Where's the proof?"

"Some proof needs must be circumstantial and hypothetical. Theory is often ahead of the mechanisms needed to confirm it. But let me illustrate. May I borrow a pen and paper?"

"Absolutely not!" a voice boomed from the speaker beneath the observation turret.

"How about a magic marker and paper?" the doctor offered.

"That will do. Have you ever seen an inter-dimensional map, Doctor Harris?"

"I can't say that I have."

"I guarantee that you have. In elementary school. Watch."

Ed took the paper and drew a straight line across the middle. "This is the first dimension." Then he drew a perpendicular line intersecting the first. "This is the second dimension. Now through these, I'll draw the third axis...."

"The Z-axis," the doctor said, shaking his head at what should have been obvious.

"The third dimension," Ed corrected. "Just as I use third grade algebra to prove tri-dimensionality, angels have similar roadmaps to even more complex intersections of reality. Hyper-dimensionalities."

"It's a competent but academic, argument. A debate team polemic."

"I understand the mandatory constraints of your vision," Ed said, looking at the smoked glass of the main turret. "But in your scientist's heart, you know what I say is valid."

"So Ed, you believe that most angels are dark angels, whose purpose is to harm us."

"Not to harm us, but to annihilate us. To be touched by an angel, is not to be blessed. It is to be cursed… infected with the original particles of sin that corrupt our souls with the seminal ingots of vice. All the evils of mankind can be traced to the angels. It is they who deliver the children to me unwittingly. They are the incubi. The progeny of darkness."

"They're children, Ed."

"Yes. But they are also angelic carriers. They are the mothers, the fathers, or actual incarnations of the future Hitlers, Mao Tse Tungs, or Stalins. Just these three murderers killed maybe 100 million people between them. They were children once too. Imagine what the new and improved versions will do, if people like me don't find them first."

"And kill them."

"Yes," Ed said matter-of-factly. "And kill them. With prejudice."

CHAPTER THIRTEEN
"Precisely whose God?"

"But again the proof, Ed. Where's the empirical proof that these infectious angels even exist, besides in the minds and the dogma of the people addicted to faith."

"Addicted to faith. An excellent analogy. In your job, you have to be critical and objective. But most people are not. They take it on their faith that angels exist, without studying the very existence that we presume to have so much faith in. It's easier to believe than to know. Que esse verdi."

"To seem rather than to be."

"We, as humans, do not reckon our own reality with such vapid truth. So why do we allow the angels the easy proof of divine altruism."

"I don't know."

"Because we believe that God loves us, amen, slam-dunk. That's all the proof we need. And that anything from heaven is from God. So it, or they, must love us as well."

"Simple enough."

"Right. But here the transitive property of elementary arithmetic does not apply, and worse still, what if the entire premise is erroneous. What if God does not love us? What if He eschews us? What if," Ed said pausing, "we are the fungus on God's feet? Then what?"

"Then he sends the flood, or the plague, or something."

"He's been there, done that, and gotten the t-shirt."

"You've got a point, but...."

"Do you remember the tale of Soddam and Gomorrah?"

"Of course."

"Do you remember, who destroyed them?"

"God."

"Wrong. Angels. On the loose. Just like they are today."

"How come we can't see them?"

"*You* can't see them. But many others can. There is a painting of Pope Leo repelling the Huns. Over his shoulders are the angelic incarnations of Peter and Paul, wielding swords. Two angels. The Huns were thousands upon thousands. And yet they turned and ran. Why is that, doctor?"

"They feared the wrath of God."

"Precisely *who's* God? The Huns were not Christian, so why would they fear the Pope's God?"

"I don't know."

"And now I ask you, Dr. Harris, where is *your* proof that Pope Leo served the God you know at all?"

The doctor thought hard before conceding. "I have none."

Hours later, Ed Lee was charged with the murders of the two children in Albuquerque.

But despite the fact that he admitted to killing 15-hundred more, providing agents with a plethora of locations and other incriminating details, the Justice Department abruptly suspended any further investigation.

The books were cooked, and the outstanding cases were quietly ordered purged from the unsolved list. Everyone agreed with the NSA spin-meisters that the risk of telling the truth outweighed the value of the truth.

CHAPTER FOURTEEN
"Life here was a hospice."

All of the known pictures of Ed Lee, including the laser-disc copy of the masturbation incident, were confiscated by the FBI.

The media never got a chance to photograph him. Since he pled guilty, there was no trial. Just a quick series of hearings, scheduled after-hours in a shill game of federal courtrooms. All of which barred cameras.

In a sense, Ed Lee had become his own prophecy.

Real. And not real. Here. And not here.

However, one newspaper kept an artist stationed in Federal District court for a week and got lucky. With a simple charcoal sketch from memory... after the original was snatched away by the U.S. Marshals.

It ended up on the Internet in a brief un-sourced blog about a child-murderer who wrote in numbers and believed he was an agent for the angel of death.

Absurdly, in a matter of days, hundreds of websites written in numerical code began to pop up like mushrooms in a sewer. Chat rooms followed, devoted to people who believed they could communicate numerically with one another.

Dr. Harris informed Ed of this, during one of his many follow-up visits with him.

He was being held in a special solitary confinement wing of the Atlanta Federal Penitentiary, a setting where, on the surface, he seemed out of place, but was in fact vastly more qualified to be here than any of the other criminals.

Often, during the drive to the prison, the doctor would listen to NPR on the car radio. He enjoyed the soothing, dispassionate voices of the newsreaders. To him, it was intellectual tryptophan, soporific and soothing. He could actually feel the dopamine surging into his bloodstream. It had the identical effect of an intravenous morphine drip.

It was a welcome change from the venomous and vitriolic vomit that typically filled the airways from of the right-wing radio talk shows. Harris reasoned that his limited tolerance for that kind of programming was an occupational hazard.

Back when he worked on the Olympic Terrorist Bombing Task Force, the problem got so bad, that he began to hear the voice of the bomber Eric Rudolph in every caller.

He would listen to their harangues and silently add Rudolph's whispered telephone warning as a subliminal postscript at the end of every sentence.

"That president Clinton is a dang fool, and her husband aint worth a crap either… (Rudolph's voice whispering creepily) *There's a bomb in Centennial Park.*"

Harris carried the thankless burden of knowing what the rest of the general public did not. That most of the callers would actually fit the very same profile as the Olympic bomber himself.

What an odd commentary, he thought, that those very same 18-49 year-old white males were the Holy Grail of desirable demographics in every platform of advertising.

They were the most facile of consumers and were quick to buy anything. From deep-fried Chicken McNuggets to foaming-at-the-mouth ideology. It simply didn't matter.

He reached down to his car radio and turned up the volume on the morphine drip, continuing down Moreland Avenue in what had become a weekly hypnotic ritual, not unlike sensory deprivation.

The trip took him through the heart of Southeast Atlanta, a forgotten slum on the outskirts of the city.

It was a mix of dirt-poor blacks and whites who found themselves mired together in the quicksand of brutal poverty that came when the local textile mill closed up shop and moved to Mexico.

And that was ironic given the fact that the streets here now looked just like those Harris had seen in the slums of Tijuana.

Especially with so many Hispanics moving into the area.

It never ceased to amaze him how poor children always seemed oblivious to the abject nature of their condition. Not even the stifling heat of the Atlanta summers could chase them out of the streets.

They played basketball with juice crates for goals, football with empty milk cartons, and baseball with broomsticks and rocks.

The fire hydrants had long ago been shut off illegally by the fire department to keep them from playing in the water. And the tar from the asphalt was so hot that their sneakers often left footprints in the street.

Yet they laughed as loud and played as hard as any of the rich kids you could find on a well-manicured Buckhead soccer field.

There were no jobs. No grocery stores. No banks. No recreation centers. No pools. No parks. No police. Just two package stores side by side that sold cheap liquor 24-hours a day.

Life here was a hospice.

A lingering symptomology of circumstances that offered a bleak prognosis for anyone unlucky enough to be trapped here. This was society's Stage Four.

It was hard to believe from a psychiatrist's perspective that more of the residents weren't in a mental hospital. Or at least in the dark federal prison that stood like a castle of the damned at the top of the hill.

CHAPTER FIFTEEN
"Imbecilic and illiterate warlocks, but warlocks nonetheless."

Inside the penitentiary gate, the doctor was a familiar face, both to the guards and to the inmates. In a strange way, he liked it here.

The environment was controlled, with few distractions.

There was a state-of-the-art research and law library. A modern trauma and diagnostic center. A three-hole chip and putt golf course.

There was even a private movie theater for the guards and their families, many of whom actually lived on the sprawling campus. It was one of the federal government's flagship penitentiaries. And problems were not allowed.

The Sins of Angels

Dr. Harris was fond of conducting his sessions in an old piano room one of the wardens had built back in the 1930's. The old timers said it was a gift, paid for with money from celebrity inmate Al Capone.

In exchange, it was rumored, Capone was allowed unofficial "furloughs" to a penthouse fuck chamber at a hotel across from the Majestic Restaurant in Midtown, where he was often seen eating scrambled eggs, fried apples, and pork chops with gravy for breakfast with the guards.

The parlor was opulent with walnut paneling and two marble fireplaces. It was acoustically perfect, encased as it was by granite walls, two feet thick.

An old Mason Hamlin baby grand still stood in the center of the room, though all of its wires had been eviscerated, after an inmate, who was a classically trained pianist, managed to take one out and strangle a guard with it many decades ago before a recital. It was an effective prop, nonetheless.

And Harris' patients seem to feel at ease fingering the muted keys as they spoke. Among them was Ed Lee.

The doctor was by now aware that Ed had passed the VSA polygraph during his initial interrogation, when he spoke of angels and Martian sculptures. He thought it completely out of character.

Geniuses are typically not "believers," people who are easily proselytized, least of all by new age pop fantasy.

Looking through his notes, the doctor had discerned a pattern in Ed's use of grandiose keywords like "epiphany" and "initiates." At first, he thought that Ed was simply building an elaborate fortress of denial.

That was typical of people with personality disorders.

The Sins of Angels

They liked to put distance between themselves and their acts by de-humanizing their victims on the one hand and canonizing themselves on the other. But that never made sense for Ed Lee, given the alacrity with which he described his crimes.

Ultimately, after many months, and without the permission of his scientific training, a small part of Dr. Harris began to believe that maybe Ed Lee, the confessed murderer of more than a thousand children, might be telling the truth about his Pythagorean quest and the bizarre battle he waged with angels.

Privately, the doctor was terrified by the fact that if the tiniest pebbles of his reason could be shaken loose, the avalanche might not be far behind.

"There is a reason angels are always depicted with wings," Ed said, almost thinking aloud.

"It symbolizes their ability to fly."

"Partly. But the real reason is that they have to stay aloft at all times. Interdimensionality is rather like being suspended from a high tension power line. As long as the circuit remains open, you're fine. But the minute you touch the earth holding onto that wire, the circuit closes, and you become grounded. You fry.

"Angels are immortal, but if they touch the earth, the portal closes, and they become trapped here, confined to the physical constraints of mortality, without ever dying. Unless they can find a way out. That is what's properly known as 'purgatory.' They remain supra human, but if they get hurt, they suffer. Break a bone, and it will heal in a day. But lose a limb, it will not grow back. And over millennia, few can survive without physical attrition of some sort. They eventually become ghosts, voices in the wind, the darkness in the shadows."

"So the reason they appear as floating phantasms or apparitions is that they're literally between worlds?"

"Yes. It's like a translucent state. But it's temporary and dangerous. If they close the portal, it's permanent and very often cataclysmic."

"So why do they come here at all."

"Why do people go to Vegas?"

"Sin City."

"Exactly. Many choose to defect here. They are the most terrifying, because they become 'biblical,' as it were, in their malicious avarice. They're the proverbial kids in the candy shop. They do too much too soon to sate their appetite for complete destruction."

"Examples?"

"History, doctor. Wherever the land has run red with blood. Wherever the death toll has reached into the millions. Wherever famine and feud coincide catastrophically. These are the hallmarks of angels. Sometimes many, sometimes a few, sometimes one."

"Everyone of the scenarios you describe has taken place in the past hundred years."

"Yes."

"The World Wars?"

Ed nodded.

"The Rwanda slaughter?"

Again, he nodded.

"Communist Russia? Red China? Ethiopia?"

"Iran-Iraq. Korea. Vietnam. The Congo. Nigeria. Darfur," Ed continued. "Each one, a minimum of a million deaths. And each one marked by unspeakable atrocities,"

"And each one, you believe, choreographed by angels."

"Absolutely."

"Hitler?"

"Not an angel himself. But certainly a consort."

"Spiritually?"

"Sexually too."

"I thought angels were asexual."

"And how would you know that?"

"I could ask you the same about your belief."

Ed smiled.

"In every occult, the highest rite of passage is sexual. More accurately, homosexual. Imparting the secret knowledge is predicated on an act of loyalty, intimacy, and shared vulnerability. As a therapist, you more than most of us know that these are all the virtues of sex, Dr. Harris."

"Good sex at that," Dr. Harris chuckled.

"It is public knowledge that every year the global leaders of the Illuminati meet at their compound in Washington State. A seraglio in the forest where every manner of decadence and perversion can be indulged, and the members can run free as satyrs in the woods. They come to consummate or rededicate their bonds. I've been there, doctor. And I have seen it."

"And they didn't catch you?"

"As you might imagine, in my craft, I have a certain gift for defying detection."

Dr. Harris nodded.

"As I'm sure you know, in all of the Masonic orders, the highest ranking Master of their coven is a 33-degree Mason."

"Coven?"

"Of course. They are all warlocks. Imbecilic and illiterate warlocks, but warlocks nonetheless."

"How do you mean?"

"Look at their patronage of the number 33, the number of enlightenment. In fact, for all of the Illuminati, the Masons, the Rosicrutians, the DeMolays, the Skulls, the Tri-lateralists, the Council on Foreign Relations, 33 is the preamble of the true Satanists' number: 333. And that means that all of those groups are nothing more than minions of the devil."

Dr. Harris thought deeply on that for a moment, studying Ed's face and eyes, looking absently for some flaw in the praxis of his theoretical heresy. "It is said, that Jesus was a Mason, Ed. How do you reconcile *His* being a 'minion of the devil?'

"I don't. He was. There is no unintended irony in the fact that the number 333 is also the symbol of the Holy Trinity; the gestational equation of the Virgin Birth; the age of the Christ at His death plus the three days it took him to rise again."

"There is no deeper end to fall off of here, Ed."

"Bear with me, doctor. Most people think that 666 is the devil's number. And it is. What they fail to realize is that it's not the only one. For both the Christian and the Satanist, 333 means the same thing: Death, Resurrection, and Ascension.

"Any sequence of threes is an obvious clue to their mischief. You'll notice a distinct absence of 666 anywhere in western culture. But you never fail to find something for sale at $9.99, which is simply the beast number inverted.

"Retail conspiracy, Ed?"

"Business conspiracy, doctor. All of the major centers of commerce, not to mention the historic sites of battle, the most important assassinations, all took place along the 33rd parallel. Both Kennedy assassinations. Both World Wars. The founding of New York, a Masonic reference in itself, where…

"…Where Wall Street is based."

"Have you ever been to a Masonic cornerstone ceremony, Doctor?"

"No."

"It is the very embodiment of paganism. They gather with false prayers to bless the rock, their Golden Calf, with offerings of grain and oil. The very same thing the Druids did, just without the human sacrifice. But the modern Masons believe in human sacrifice as well, on a surreptitious yet global scale, with wars that are little more than rapacious bloodlettings.

"Every U.S. president has been either a Mason or some such other member of the Illuminati. Sometimes, they're low-level initiates, who are marionetted by someone in the cabinet, someone with a higher rank in the sect. But sometimes, they themselves are the high haxan.

"Harry Truman was a 33-degree Mason. And during the end of World War Two, even though Nagasaki had no military value for Japan, and Hiroshima had already been annihilated, he had the Air Corps drop an atomic bomb on that city too.

"The only reason is that Nagasaki sits on the 33rd parallel. And that provided Truman with a satiable number of souls for sacrifice, according to the dark tenets of his Masonic faith.

"That's why the Pythagoreans have been trying to exterminate the Masons since the 1600's. But we were not successful, and they've now become the most formidable of the secret oligarchies. We underestimated both the charisma of their leaders and the obsequy of their followers. They are what the Bible alludes too when it is said that 'the lion shall lay down with the lamb.'"

"Ed, you have to know that your stories sound so utterly fantastical."

"I do. And they're not stories. They're accounts."

"I stand corrected."

"Find a map of Washington DC. If you look closely enough, you will see Satanic encoding in the layout. The White House sits at the nadir of the inverted pentacle. The Washington Monument is an obelisk, the residence of Ra, who in our culture is called Lucifer. Logan Circle, Dupont Circle, and Scott Circle, all have six streets intersecting them."

"666," the doctor said slowly.

"Yes. And the Capitol with its contiguous cul de sacs represents a glyph of the head and horns of the devil. These things are not accidental or coincidence. These are the matters of the Masonic Order. The very fact that they are fantastical and seem too absurd to be true is the proper camouflage of intellectual deception. The Masons have learned like the inarticulate children of numbers they are, that sometimes to be invisible, one must be highly visible."

"Here. And not here," the doctor said softly.

"Real. And not real," Ed answered, like a litany. "Remember, doctor, the very motto of the Masons is 'Audacity, always audacity.' They parade in stealth."

CHAPTER SIXTEEN
"Satan is not the devil."

"Ed, if children had not been murdered, on such a production line scale, your words could be taken without so much...."

"Repugnance."

The doctor nodded his head heavily.

"The killing of children is nothing new. Chronos ate his. The Spartans left theirs to die in the wilderness if they were sickly or weak. The Asians and Indians still kill theirs, just because they're female. Remember the Baby Jesus?"

"Of course."

"And the Three Wise Men?"

"Yes. They came bearing gifts."

"But they also came bearing knives. They were Pythagoreans, and like Herod, they knew that Jesus would have to be killed. It was His destiny. They had plotted His birth using an Antikythera, a celestial computer that projected the position of the planets and stars to a specific date in time. The star that was said to point out His location was not a star at all. It was a convergence ripple."

"What's that?"

"It's a phenomenon in theoretical physics. His frequency was so great, that even as a newborn baby, it tore a physical hole in space."

90

"Interdimensionality."

"Doctor, you would have made an excellent candidate for our cause."

Doctor Harris smiled grimly. "I would not have had the stomach for the work, Ed."

"Nor did the Wise Men, who quickly discovered that Jesus was not alone."

"Mary and Joseph."

"And what the devout call the Devil."

"The Devil?"

"It was he who slew the Wise Men."

"That's not what the Bible says."

"Surely you know that the New Testament is not the Bible. It's not unlike the Apochrypha. Sefarim Hizonim."

"The books of the gospel that fall outside the canons of accepted religious belief."

"Yes. You must have minored as well in Theology, doctor."

"No, just an altar boy. There was a time, you know, that you could have been stoned for doubting the veracity of the New Testament."

"Then I'd be drawn and quartered for saying this: Satan is not the Devil. Not exactly."

"You've lost me now, Ed."

"The Hebrews believed that Satan was sent to earth to test mankind, a prosecutor of sorts, whose job was to vet out the true nature of man on behalf of God. Thusly, he plays many roles, which is why he is called by many names. He is, with no small irony, his own devil's advocate."

"Explain that to me."

"Part of his trickery is his ability to cull forth the worst in men, an instinct so profound and prolific within us, that over time he became, rather unfairly and by default, the patron of evil. The truth is he has no allegiance one way or another to evil or to good. He's merely the arbiter of the two extremes, the middleman who renders the thumb up or down. Earth is his court.

"As a former altar boy you know that in the Christian faith, Satan was the best loved by God. He is the purest of all the angels. The others were infected and pariah with jealousy, lust, greed, pride, gluttony, sloth, and wrath."

"The seven deadly sins."

"And those sins offend God more in angels than man."

"Why?"

"Because angels, as the first born, are supposed to be governed by the grace of primogeniture. But in the end, the spiritual incest of their conceit polluted their birth-right, and God cast all but a few out of Heaven."

"Wasn't it Satan who led the rebellion?"

"There was no rebellion. Just eviction. And defection. Satan was not among those excommunicated. He was given dominion over the earth as God's personal emissary. His most important task is to prevent the corruption of mankind by the angels who trespass here. That's why the earth is full of traps to catch them. And prisons to hold them."

"Prisons?"

"Prisons like the pyramids."

"In Egypt?"

"Everywhere. Mexico. Japan. China. Peru. Germany. Australia. Greece. Tibet. Turkey. Spain. Everywhere."

CHAPTER SEVENTEEN

"A terrestrial computer chip."

"It's best to start at the beginning. Pyramids serve a multitude of functions. They have different designs cosmetically, but the principles are generally the same."

"Then let's talk about the big pyramid in Egypt."

"The Great Pyramid," Ed corrected.

"Yes."

"Did you know that the pyramids in Egypt were originally all white?"

"I remember reading that the outside was coated with limestone, and that the people of Cairo removed it to build their mosques."

"Do you know what the capstone was?"

"No."

"Gold. A thousand pounds of solid gold, with a diamond benben stone embedded at the pinnacle."

"Really?"

"All of these fixtures worked in concert with one another."

"How do you mean 'worked'? Like a machine?"

"Like a machine we couldn't dream of making even today."

"We're listening," Dr. Harris said, positioning his tape recorder closer to Ed.

"It is true that the siding on the pyramid was made of limestone. But it was far more than that. It was a colloidal slag enriched with calcium oxide and molecules of hydrogen-60. The natural graphite and organic Fullerides imbedded in the compound would act like a photovoltaic conductor. The silicon from the mortar beneath it would use the sunlight to initiate some type of spark plasma sintering, and that would energize the chip like a ceramic super lattice semiconductor."

"Do I understand you correctly? Are you saying the pyramid is a computer chip?"

"If you render it in a schematic, doctor, that's precisely what a pyramid is: a terrestrial computer chip. As I said, the cap is made of gold and diamond, both of which are super conductors of light wave energy. These two things could be manipulated to act as a transducer to help refocus the flow of electrons directly into the walls of the chamber like a Faraday cage.

"You've heard of the theatrical cliché 'in the limelight?'"

"Mmm hmm," the doctor replied, intrigued.

"That's a reference to the calcium oxide synthesized from the limestone. It burns incandescently, so white that it hurts the eyes to look upon it. But here that light would have turned you into vapor before it could blind you."

"Like the flash from a nuclear explosion?"

"Like the flash from ten thousand nuclear explosions. Let me give you a comparison. The light from a water-cooled xenon bulb in an IMAX projector can be seen from the moon, a quarter-million miles away. It's 15-thousand watts. Not terribly much considering the brilliance and clarity of the beam.

"Now imagine a light so bright and focused that it can be seen from 50 million miles away. The steradian of that light source would have a magnitude of minus-13.6, fully half the luminosity of the sun itself. And much more than the moon. That light hasn't been seen in over twelve thousand years."

"At the Great Pyramid."

"What we see at Giza today are the pitiful ruins of an utterly fantastic creation, whose full potential we can hardly fathom."

"You called it a computer chip."

"It is at least that. A terrestrial computer chip, which responded to specific commands, alone and in concert with other chips."

"Respond?"

"The architects may have used this technology to regulate heat waves or seismic activity emanating from the earth's core, rather like the paddles of a defibrillator. They could literally shock the planet's electromagnetic field to correct tectonic instability or decelerate precession. They most certainly were able to influence or even control weather with them.

"There may also be gravitic applications, used to slow or quicken the earth's orbit or to correct its polar orientation. Perhaps they used it to bend light around the pyramid itself, to either render it invisible, or to transport it."

"Transport it?"

"Maybe."

"Where?"

"Other planets. The Cydonia Plateau has many pyramids."

"Cydonia Plateau? The face on Mars?"

"A face with leonine symbolism, not unlike the Sphinx, or the crests of nobility in royal families and churches and secret societies. Before NASA scrambled the telemetry, the face could be seen very clearly from the Mars Orbiter."

"So now we're talking about aliens?"

"Why not? After all, they and we are one in the same."

"That one's been around for awhile."

"And rightly so, doctor. That's because *they* have been around for awhile. When Neil Armstrong landed on the moon, there was a transmission in which he said very audibly in a fearful voice that *they* were watching the Lunar Lander from the far side of the crater at Tranquility Bay. Mission Control immediately shut off the audio.

"But what they failed to realize in the infancy of the program was that every country on Earth, as well as thousands of civilians with ham radios, continued to listen in on the classified exchange. Without being specific, Armstrong said that *they* made it clear that the Lander was not welcome. It appeared to him that we had interrupted some sort of mining operation. My guess is they were excavating helium-3. A fusion fuel not found in abundance on earth. Either way, we did not stay on the moon very long after planting the flag."

"But we went back several times, Ed."

"Nothing more than the occasional brief sortie, like we were sneaking into somebody's backyard to steal apples. And each time we went, there was a similar communication from the astronauts on the moon's surface. Both Alan Shepard and Edgar Mitchell on Apollo 14 talked freely about the 'visitors' watching them. Ask yourself, why is it now that we have better vehicles, computers, and rocket technology, we haven't gone back to the moon in decades. And don't plan to anytime soon."

"I honestly don't know."

"NASA knows," Ed grinned. "There are many who believe that NASA is the government's penultimate Masonic temple. The place where the secrets are kept and the bodies are literally buried."

"Alien autopsy."

"It does sound funny. But remember what I said about 'audacity.' Things sounding too fantastical to be real."

"The golden rule of deception. I remember."

"There was a time when NASA used to freely stream the images from the Hubble telescope. That was before they put their hubris in check. They failed to acknowledge that the world was full of people smart enough to analyze NASA's data without NASA's help. People who could do it better, faster, and cheaper.

"The geeks had caught them pasting up computer generated mappings of the alleged surface of Mars when the first Rover landed. The pixels didn't line up. Shadows didn't match. Known geological landmarks reoriented themselves. And, of course, the face turned into a pile of rocks 'reflecting' light."

"I think I remember that."

"But one thing NASA could never explain, were the 'naturally occurring' tetrahedrons around Cydonia."

"Pyramids."

"If you wouldn't mind, doctor, I'd much prefer to write down my ideas on the pyramids. That way, I can fine-tune them, and you can better review them. And feel free to present them to any expert you think would be appropriate for any further assessment."

Dr. Harris was hesitant to agree. Prosecutors had recommended that as part of his punishment, Ed not be given any access to computers. However, at the urging of the military and the CIA, the judge had left that issue unresolved.

Jerry had to admit that he was curious about this so-called pyramid "technology." And given the fact that Ed Lee was not a run-of-the-mill new-age nutcase, the doctor was fascinated by what theories he might come up with.

"The best I can do is to get you one of the prison's older decommissioned laptops, like one of those early Toshibas that looks like an accordion case. No bells or whistles."

"As long as it has a disc-writer or even a floppy port that should work just fine."

"All it's going to have is a word processing program."

"Fair enough."

"Probably something ancient like Write or WordPad."

Ed laughed. "That's what I grew up with. It'll be fine, Jerry."

"All right, then. You'll have it tomorrow."

The next day, Dr. Harris was in the prison computer lab looking for a relic that could accept a floppy disc.

Later that week, he took Ed's data-disc home to copy it into an ancient disc-drive connected to his own personal computer. It had not been easy to find. He had to salvage one in a pile of computer scrap at the Goodwill.

The Sins of Angels

At first an error message came up, freezing the screen, saying it could not read the text. But after re-booting the system, the file unfolded like it was supposed to.

He printed it out and spent the rest of the night reading Ed Lee's notes.

Excerpts from Ed Lee's notes:

Truly the pyramids are the wonders of both worlds. Their ability to harness energy cannot be measured. The design would have had the capacity to generate and store a reserve equal to an astonishing third of a google-joule. And once activated, the energy wouldn't need to be replenished much, as it would be in a perpetual state of near zero point availability.

Electropheresis would have been used to bleed the power through the limestone silicate and the granite, which as I said before were really ceramic semiconductors, very possibly doped up with Fullerenes of enhanced hydrogen. The shell of the pyramids would likely have been coated with an electrochromic sheath to calibrate the amount of sunlight allowed to filter through.

Given these parameters, an active pyramid could have had a shelf life of thousands of years, enough to survive the absence of sunlight that would come with the eventual Ice Age.

Yet another function was as a hyperdimensional transporter.

The sarcophagus inside the King's chamber is not a tomb at all. It's a portal of acoustic energy. With more than a hundred million tons of granite pressing in on itself, the chamber is literally ringing with ultrasound. It's well known that Napoleon supposedly went mad after spending an entire night there.

The piezoelectric frequencies from the quartz in the granite resonate naturally at F-minor. They are not unlike the crystals in a radio or police scanner.

In fact, with the thick granite walls surrounding us when we sit in the piano room, if you sit quietly,, you can feel the harmonic energy moving as a low hum in your head.

In the pyramid, with the absorption of energy through the semiconductors, the ultrasonic vibrations amplify and converge on the sarcophagus, much the way light is focused through a concave Fresnel lens.

Anyone inside is transported hyperdimensionally.

For the last two or three thousand years, the power has only been residual, serving merely to interfere with normal brainwave patterns.

If you were to take an electro encephalograph of your temporal lobes while inside the pyramid, the read-out would show the same aberrant neural activity associated with schizophrenia.

To the primitive, that mental distortion was the phenomenon.

Neither they, nor science today, understood the profound implications of hyperdimensionality that exist within those granite walls. The ancient Egyptians were the last to exploit the technology. They called it "Eckankar.'"

"Spirit travel."

CHAPTER EIGHTTEEN
"They may actually be leaking future, the way a dam leaks water."

Excerpts continued:

Possibly the most important function of the pyramid was as a prison.

There is a chamber deep within its center that the Pythagoreans suspect is a still-functioning Faraday Cage, a charged vacuum designed to trap an immensely powerful angel.

The particles of his spirit may even remain there today.

If so, and if his pestilence can ever be freed, mankind will sink into the bubbling tar of his sin. As an angel, his vengeance will be divine, meaning above the ability of humans to comprehend.

Only the enlightened will survive. But not on this plane. Many of the Pythagoreans have seen it coming. Let me explain now how this is possible.

For years, researchers at the Duke University Institute for Parapsychology proved time and time again that ESP was real, if only on an infinitesimal scale.

Test subjects were able to predict random numbers sealed in envelopes, as well as the direction of metal balls falling through a grid. Weak stuff, admittedly.

But even thin gruel cannot be discounted as food.

Of course, they never got any respect from the other professors and were widely lampooned, but that does not diminish the volume of evidence, however 'minor,' that they accumulated through their experiments.

The bottom line is that ESP, or 'psi,' as it's called in the discipline, is real. And it is my belief that the pyramids may play a role.

First of all, there are so many of them all over the world. And each of one potentially has the ability to bend space-time. And depleted as they are, the energy fields are still so powerful and overlapping that they may actually be leaking future, the way a dam leaks water.

When the Navy conducted the Philadelphia Experiment in 1943, they put the theories of Nikola Tesla to work. He knew that with enough electricity resonating at specific frequencies, objects can and will disappear, moving in and out of time.

To many the Philadelphia Experiment is a myth. The story goes that the ship was actually in the Mediterranean at the time of the "alleged" experiment.

Despite its best efforts to classify this astonishing event, the government didn't realize that there are always free radicals it cannot contain. There were hundreds of civilians who witnessed the USS Eldridge as it vanished for more than four hours.

The paramedics who transported the dead and horribly mangled survivors when they returned. The doctors and nurses who treated them. Not to mention the seamen who were there.

As in a court of law, common sense sometimes has to be the arbiter of reason in real life.

The Navy was ostensibly trying to find a way to make its ships invisible to radar, not to the human eye. That was an accidental side effect. So was the time travel component.

But Tesla's work bordered on black magic to many in the scientific community during World War Two, and few dared to pursue it. But we, like the Germans, were desperate. It was rumored as far back as the late 1800's that Tesla had traveled outside time, after he was hit by an electromagnetic arc in his laboratory. To use his theories as a basis for the Philadelphia Experiment, the scientists had to know that time distortion would occur. After all, that's what invisibility is.

Here and not here.

There were reports in 1983 that the Eldridge was seen in the harbor at Montauk, New York. Then it was gone. It had traveled forty years into the future.

I use the Philadelphia Experiment as an illustration of what the builders of the pyramids knew millennia ago. The seeping energy fields that remain around them continue to drift all over the planet today, like electromagnetic clouds in the atmosphere, crackling with nano-voltage. If left unimpeded, they can be received by people who have psychic abilities.

Many researchers will tell you that in all their years they have never seen any hard evidence that electromagnetism has any influence on people's brains.

What is far more commonplace is the knowledge that EM can interfere with the development of embryos in women who live near high power lines. But outside of that, it's true that there's very little evidence of anything else.

That is, of course, intentional. Most of that research is classified. For example, the Navy developed an EM pulsing device called the HAARP that could stop a heartbeat. It was also used to generate synthetic telepathy, images and voices beamed directly into the minds of its targets.

Migratory birds and animals use the earth's EM field to navigate. They can only do that because of the magnetite in their pineal glands.

Descartes considered the pineal gland the bridge between the brain and the mind. The third eye. Literally.

The problem is most people don't have magnetite in their bodies. But the true psychics do. And that would be in addition to the abundance of hemoglobin in our blood. Iron.

Magnetically reactive iron.

I suspect that some of us have an enriched type of iron in the blood that turns the pineal gland into a diapason for EM waves. Those who are sensitive to that radiation may also be able to 'see' the invisible images with their vestigial third eye, much in the manner a television can 'see' microwaves.

My pet theory is that certain humans may have had their DNA implanted with liquid nano crystals made of magnetite. This would have allowed the alien observers to keep track of them anywhere on the planet, rather like an RFID chip, using radio waves to create magnetic resonance. But all of this would have also made them far more sensitive to EMF.

Additionally, these specimens would have benefited from accelerated evolution, especially if the nano-crystals had the ability to repair cellular damage from disease or poor genetic predisposition. And of course, they would have passed these traits on to their descendants.

It sounds crazy. But the same thing is being done by human scientists today. They're already working on prosthetic DNA that can weave itself into a cell's genetic structure. Loading it with behavioral instructions much like computer software or malicious virus. If we can do it, imagine what a civilization thousands of years ahead of us can do.

As for clairvoyance it would appear that it's a random phenomenon based on which waves get through to whom. That's why psychics don't pick lottery numbers.

When I was young and a new member of my sect, I was given a drink called ayahuasca. Tribes in the Amazon used it for shamanic rites. It contained DMT. Dimethyltryptamine. The body's version of LSD.

In large doses it's a hallucinogen. But in the right mixture it's a contact lens for your third eye. It stimulates the pineal, and the visions you have are real. You can see the future. Or at least fragments of it. Some of us could see better than the rest of us. And that became what they do for the sect. See the future.

Sometimes, in order to change it.

One of the elders in the tribe we visited used a resting bell, what is commonly called a singing bowl. I know this may be difficult to believe, but he used it to open a small hole between dimensions. The bowl was made of an alloy of what they considered sacred metals. Silver, gold, iron, and something he said was given to his grandfather's grandfathers by the irmao estrelas, the 'star brothers.'

He would hit the bowl with a small wooden mallet to generate a sound; then he would drag the mallet along the rim of the bowl to sustain the ringing in a frequency that can only be created by the exact mixture of the metals.

The sonic waves, coupled of course with our altered state of awareness, produced images from the other side of the mirror, if you will.

The things I saw were real. Some of them were from the past. Some from the future. But they were definitely real.

Many people make the mistake of thinking of time as an ocean. But it's really more like the tide. It comes and it goes. Over and over, without end.

It's similar to Nietzsche's theory of the Eternal Return. It's close. But it's not a perfect paradigm.

The present is the cresting of an infinite number of infinite waves. How each one breaks is the future for that reality. And they break differently every time. We can influence the waves. We can't stop them. But we can definitely change them.

Using the earth's electromagnetic field, people from the beginning of mankind could always see the future. Few could understand it. But those, who could, helped their tribes to survive by finding water, food, and shelter. Remember, the pyramids were not built to generate psychic powers. That's just one of the beneficial side effects.

Another is the fact that more and more Egyptologists are beginning to realize that math is the true Rosetta Stone.

The facts lie in the empiricism. The Great Pyramid sits at the highest protrusion of the earth's crust. All sides face the cardinal points of the compass. Its circumference divided by its diameter equals, not surprisingly, pi, the numerical nomenclature for enlightened thought.

Godhead.

Pythagorus himself would not be born for many millennia from the time the pyramid was built. Therefore, the foundational ratios of pi and phi, the Golden Mean, found throughout the structure, far precede his authorship.

At the time of the pyramids' construction there were no Egyptians. All of the modern hypotheses about them building the structure are incorrect. No known primitive humans had migrated to the area at the time of its genesis. Frankly, it would have been far too dangerous.

The radiation generated from the light emission would have been lethal for miles around. If you believe Plato, as I do, the only people on earth who could have built the pyramids were the people of Atlantis.

Critics often point out that conveniently there would be no evidence of these beings since they vanished into the ocean.

But they didn't. First of all, the name of their civilization is a misnomer. The origins of Atlantis are in the Mediterranean, more precisely, in the region of Crete. Not in the Atlantic. Northern Africa would have been the likeliest place for them to build the pyramids. And with only a handful of wandering Berbers to contend with once or twice a year, the Atlantians could tend to their work without interference. They were the gods that many of the ancient cultures referred to.

The nomads would have exported the stories all over Africa, the Middle East, and across the Mediterranean.

Except they weren't stories. They were 'accounts.'

Of real events.

CHAPTER NINETEEN
"She was gifted with brute-strength intelligence."

"The salesgirl says these stones have healing powers," Jackie Harris marveled playfully, as she modeled an ancient silver bracelet, anchored with a heavy piece of green turquoise.

"Maybe we had better get the whole set," her husband smiled back absently.

"Ooh," she giggled, eyeing the other pieces. "Yesss."

But as she was about to pick up the earrings, she paused.

Her husband's words were just now beginning to sink in. She looked at him discerningly, the way an art expert studies a favorite portrait for the millionth time.

"What is it, Jerry? What's the matter?"

Gerald Harris had the psychiatry degree. But his wife had the edge. She was gifted with brute-strength intelligence, infallible intuition, and sheer beauty. She also had a stare that could crack stone. It was this that she now directed at her husband.

Jackie Ellis had been the smart one in medical school. The one who shared her notes. Her wit. And her smile.

It was back then that Jerry Harris needed all of these things.

He was struggling on every level of his life with an addiction to amphetamines.

CHAPTER TWENTY
"Cold pills. Batteries. Lye. Ether. Ammonia. Drain cleaner."

At first, he used them sparingly to help him study.

But soon he found that his tolerance far exceeded the doses he could score from the residents who supplied him.

He got into fights. Fell asleep in class. And was on the verge of being expelled. And absolutely none of that mattered.

All he cared about was getting more speed.

Over time, he began to look like a cadaver; a cadaver who could scarf down five Big Macs in a sitting. Dark circles began to form permanently under his eyes, and his complexion broke out into tiny sores, a result of his constant picking.

His apartment was ransacked; his nails were black; and his white lab coat was filthy with stains.

After a while, the residents refused to supply him, for fear of being narc'd out by the obvious symptoms of his dependency.

So in between night classes, Jerry would hit the public housing projects and alleys of the mean West Philly ghettos, trying to score street crank.

But that was a problem in more ways than one.

Back then, black drug dealers in the area weren't dealing much in crystal meth.

But the street names for many drugs were close enough to confuse the average corner boy, who was quick to sell whatever he thought you meant.

Crippie. Cripple. Crimmie. Crib. Crystal Tea. Crash. Crazy. Cris. Crisscross. Cristy. Crissy. Croak. Cross Tops. Crow. Crypto. Crunch. Cupcakes. Cruz.

It all sounded the same to the whistlers who swore they had the hook-up. Just as long as you had the money.

Because finding real crank was hit or miss, when Jerry did score, he bought the entire stash for cash.

Word quickly got around that he carried a lot of money.

And many nights when he went looking for drugs, the robbing crews went looking for him.

Often, he would leave the seedy neighborhoods beaten and ripped off. He had even been stabbed once.

But he had learned enough by his third year at Jefferson Medical School to stitch himself up by flashlight in the basement of the Pharmacy building.

As it turned out, though, there was one drug dealer in the neighborhood named Kilo who was intrigued by the dirty, strung-out, babbling medical student.

And like the savvy businessman he was, he wanted to know more about this drug that could bring a skinny white boy into the heart of the hood all by himself.

In the middle of the night, no less.

So Kilo, who was fifteen at the time, lured Jerry into the "trap" where his people cut the cocaine. He sat him down politely, turned down the loud rap music, and put a gun to Jerry's head.

"What the fuck is this shit you be lookin' fo, white boy?" he barked, circling him like a starving hyena. "You stupid fiendin', mutherfucker. You like one of my bitches, out there trickin' dat ass."

"Huh? What?"

"You a crumbsnatcher, aint you?"

"What?"

"You suck dick? You a fag, right?"

"N-n-no," Harris stammered.

"You'd do it if I told you to!"

Jerry couldn't look the boy in the eyes. He simply nodded his head. "I just wanted to score some meth, man?"

"What dat is? Like pancake and syzurp, or some shit?"

"What?" he said, genuinely confused.

"Pancake and syzurp, fool! Perckies and Tussin."

"Percocets and cough syrup?"

"Yeah. You want dat?"

"No. Just the opposite. Crystal meth. Cris."

One of the trap boys interrupted. "He talkin' about that criddy, man. That shit they be selling down on the southside."

"Aight, aight," Kilo said, stroking his hairless chin. "Criddy. Yeah, yeah. I heard of dat. Them Italian niggas sell it. Here da deal is, white boy. You write down all the shit dat be in dat shit. My boy's go get it. And you stays up in here and make it."

"I-I-I can't do th…"

Before Jerry Harris could finish his sentence, Kilo had hit him hard across the head with his Glock. When he came to, Kilo was standing over him, wiping Harris' blood off his gun. The boy put his hand to his ear like he couldn't hear.

"Whatchu say, white boy? Huh? What wazzat?"

"All right, all right," Jerry said groggily, instinctively raising his hands to fend off another hit to the head. "You wouldn't happen to have a computer would you?" he asked, thinking he could stall his attackers while he came up with a plan.

But in the time it took to walk from one room to another, one of Kilo's boys brought out a brand new laptop, along with the fastest air-card on the market.

He carried it like a waiter bringing out the dessert platter at the Four Seasons.

Jerry shook his head in disbelief then proceeded to call up the Physician's Desk Reference on-line and the Essential Pharmacy Review. After distilling the science out of the chemicals, he wrote down a simple list of ingredients that anyone could understand and handed it to Kilo.

Cold pills. Batteries. Lye. Ether. Ammonia. Drain cleaner. Acetone. Matches. Lots of matches.

Three hours later, everything on the list was in the trap.

"Hey man," he asked Kilo as he set up a lab at the bathtub. "You got anything to eat?"

Jerry was astonished at how smart Kilo was. He had worked around drugs and chemicals since he was six years old, and he knew well how dangerous mixing them could be.

As an extra precaution, he insisted that Jerry mix the chemicals on videotape. Then sample the end product as well to make sure that he wasn't making poison. A thought that had run across his mind. Briefly.

He knew that real dealers were the only ones who just said "no" to drugs. "No" to using them, that is.

When he protested that it would ruin his medical career to be caught on tape making meth, Kilo put the Glock back to Jerry's head and insisted that he reconsider.

He did.

Two days later, Jerry Harris tried the crystals hot out of the microwave. And as his eyes rolled back in his head, the cameras rolled like MTV Cribs on a tour of his own personal hell.

And that included the close-ups of one of the trap boys peeing on him as he lay prostrate on the couch stoned to oblivion.

When he woke up, Kilo was smiling at him. "Dat shit da bomb, mutherfucker! Dat shit da bizzomb! Check dis out here," he said excitedly. "Take some witchu. See if you can move a little weight. Dat might lighten yo' sentence."

"My sentence?"

"Dat's right, fool. You in my jail now, bitch. I'm puttin' you on work-release."

"Huh?"

"You better act like you know, mutherfucker. You comin' back here everyday, till I say. You gonna make dis here meth shit till my crew learn how to do it. Then, you gonna be my mule. Sell dis shit to the rich-ass white boys where you live."

With a limbic reflex, he raised his arms weakly to protect his head. "How am I supposed to go to school?"

"Fuck school, bitch! You fixin' to make me rich!"

Kilo laughed and high-fived the boys in the trap, who celebrated by turning the music up and rapping with the lyrics, dancing hysterically till they were out of breath and panting like they had all just broken a four-minute mile.

By now, Jerry was starting to jones for more crank. He was still high. But he wanted more. Just like those lab monkeys in the cocaine experiments.

And just like them, if he could, he would have chosen the drugs over food, eventually dosing himself until his heart stopped.

At least that was one way out of this cage, he thought.

With a big bag of crys in his pants pocket, Jerry noticed that his dick was actually getting hard. His saliva glands were engorged, and his mouth was sticky. It was almost as if he were about to orgasm. He knew he was completely and pathetically strung out.

He barely noticed the damp smell of urine coming from his clothes. His mind was a tossed salad of jabbering thoughts that shared one thing in common: getting another hit. And he had hundreds at his fingertips.

His stomach was churning painfully with too much acid, and his heart began to palpitate. He was light-headed and dehydrated, almost too weak to stand up without help.

If these symptoms were on a pop quiz, he thought, he would have prescribed a saline I-V with a 40mg valium drip.

And plenty of bed rest.

He would have made a pretty good doctor, he thought grimly, as he gathered up his coat and shoes and shuffled slowly through this crucible of dancing, murderous children.

They sneered at him through the gold grills on their teeth.

Each one in the crew was decked out in a green Eagle's jersey, with a pistol stuffed ominously into the waist of his jeans.

They had all seen more gunfire than most people in the military, let alone anybody on the police force.

They were just like those kids on CNN in the Middle East.

Indeed, Southwest Philly was a lot like the documentaries he had seen on Palestine. Excruciating poverty. Joblessness. Violence. And just like the kids there, the kids here were ready to die. Eager, it seemed.

But they were much more ready to kill.

He now knew how it must feel to be eaten alive by what you had always thought was a lesser creature than you. A bear. A lion. A shark. Animals with brains the size of tangelos.

But these were the mere cubs of a new species.

They were Super-predators. Fearless. Relentless. Hopeless.

And completely unredeemable.

For the moment, they held him gently in their sharp teeth. The way a fox holds a chicken it has stolen from the coop.

He knew from his undergraduate studies that it was likely their parents were no more than fourteen or fifteen years old at the time these kids were born, destitute dropouts with less of a chance of finding a job than a wetback from Mexico.

It was one thing to read about them like exotic animals in some far away zoo. It was quite another to be surrounded by them in real life.

Graduate-level sociology students sometimes lived with impoverished families to give their doctoral theses "verisimilitude." But there was no practicum for being held hostage, cooking drugs, and fearing for your life.

Watching the group dynamics within the trap was an education that Jerry Harris had not gone to school for. And it fascinated him as much as it terrified him.

As he left, Kilo yelled from the door. "Be back here tomorrow night! And you better have my money, ho!"

Laughter erupted from inside the trap. With the ephedrine amplifying his senses, Jerry could hear it all the way down the street.

The sunlight began dazzling in indigos and violets off the distant skyscrapers, bringing the city to life. The birds sang and sleeping dogs rose and stretched on the porches.

And while the rest of the world craned their faces into the warmth of the day, Jerry Harris shielded his with his hand.

His pupils were still dilated.

And the sunlight burned his eyes like radiation.

CHAPTER TWENTY-ONE
"You're terminal, Jerry."

He had already missed one exam during his captivity. Luckily, it was on the integumentary system. Melanocytes and tyrosine. And little lambs eat ivy.

The course, it seemed, was written for iambic mnemonics. And Jerry had learned to associate every system with a jingle or a kid's song.

This was one of the few classes he could ace with his eyes closed. Literally. He often slept in his corner seat in the 17th row.

Especially on those days he was coming down off a speed jag.

He could afford to fail one or two labs and still get by with a decent grade. The problem would be the other classes.

He was an "A" student in those too. But that hinged on his actually being in class and seeing the way the medical procedures were performed.

Those could not be learned from a book. And that was unfortunate. Because books were exactly the way Jerry Harris learned the best.

Even before he started taking crank, he could read in excess of a thousand words per minute. When he was amped, that number tripled. And if he put his mind to it he could read and re-read entire textbooks in a day.

More astonishingly, he could remember nearly everything verbatim. His concentration was already a vise. But the crank could squeeze it until he screamed.

Many times, his classmates would stare in disbelief in the library as his fingers moved in a blur. At the end of the night, his fingertips would be black from the ink on the paper.

But none of that could help him for the procedures.

From enemas to epidurals, even the simple shit had to be demonstrated hands-on.

He knew it wouldn't be long before he was kicked out of school for his absences alone. But not showing up for procedures meant certain failure. No matter how smart he was.

The deans had indulged him for far too long.

They knew he was a wunderkind. But they also knew he was a fuck-up. And up till now, the fuck-up part could be ignored. As long as he kept pulling good grades.

He had been warned by nearly every instructor that he was on thin ice. And each year, the ice kept getting thinner and thinner.

But it wasn't until now that he could actually hear it starting to crack under the weight of his addiction.

That night, Jackie found him hyperventilating on the roof of the Anatomy Building, a place where the medical students liked to hang out and smoke. He had a tall bottle of beer in his hands and a terribly worried look on his face as he studied the nightscape of the city.

He jumped back when she touched his shoulder to say hello.

"Whoa, Jerry. It's just me. Is everything all right?"

"What? Oh, yeah. Yeah. Everything's fine," he lied. "I'm just really tired."

"I should think so," she murmured softly, touching his neck.

"Your pulse is tachycardic, and you're sweating, even though it's forty degrees out here. Your eyes are sunken, and your skin is sallow," she said, examining his face in the ambience of the halogen lights. "I can see my finger marks on your neck. You need to be in a hospital."

"I'm just a little dehydrated," he smiled weakly.

"Uh, huh. Everybody knows you're a junkie, Jerry," she said with a sad matter-of-factness. "Don't you?"

He looked at her long and hard. She looked at him the exact same way. "Empty your pockets," she ordered politely.

Sheepishly, but without hesitating, he threw down the loose change and the big bag of crystal meth.

She kicked it away like dried dog shit.

"I know you like me, Jerry. And I like you. But it'll never happen," she said, "if you can't leave this part of your life." As she spoke, she gently caressed the outline of his face. "But if I'm not a good enough incentive for you to quit, why don't you just jump and get it over with."

"What?" he said startled.

"I want you to jump," she repeated. "Because you're dead already. It may take a month. Or a day. Or a week. But you're as good as dead. And I would rather watch you die like a man right here, right now. Than watch you crawl on your belly for that shit like a maggot."

119

All he could do was stare at her in disbelief. Spellbound. Stunned to silence. By her beauty. And her candor.

"Your bedside manner needs a little work," he finally mumbled with a smile.

"There's no time for that. You're terminal, Jerry." She paused. "So what are you going to do?"

Jerry Harris studied the lights of the city reflecting in Jackie's ocean green eyes. He could see that they didn't need any help at all to sparkle.

"It's too cold to wait," she said impatiently. "Choose."

"Jackie, these guys, they said they'd…" Jerry looked around for the right words to tell a story that he himself could barely believe.

"What did they say, Jerry?"

He sighed heavily before speaking. "They've got me on tape, Jackie."

The chill of that October Philadelphia night cut through Jerry Harris' soul like a scalpel, as he told Jackie the whole story.

But never once did she wince or grimace in disgust. She was completely without judgment. All she said at the end of it was, "I guess we'd better get that tape."

120

The next morning, while Al Roker gave the weather to no one on a big screen television set in the living room, a small SWAT team burst into Kilo's trap.

He and his crew were asleep on the floors and the couches. The beds were always reserved for the cash and the drugs.

And the guns.

It was over in less than twenty seconds. Eleven dope boys stood in various stages of undress, laser dots on their foreheads, their hands cuffed behind their backs with plastic police ties. The captain ordered everybody out of the apartment.

Except for Kilo.

Five minutes later, Captain Paul Billings left the trap with a videotape concealed beneath his body armor. And a hundred and twelve thousand dollars in a duffel bag that he handed to his team leader.

He ordered his men to cut the drug dealers loose.

After that, the SWAT team piled into the back of their van and went to breakfast at Tony's.

The hole-in-the-wall restaurant was a long-time police hangout where nobody asked any questions about the pile of money being split on a buffet table in the back room, next to the eggs and sausages.

In any police department, a captain was like God.

But a captain in SWAT was like God in the Old Testament. Vengeful. Furious. Almighty.

And not above propitiation.

Later that evening, Jerry Harris admitted himself to the Jefferson Hospital drug treatment program. In a week, he was allowed to leave the wing during the day so he could continue his studies.

A year later, he graduated third in his class.

A day after that, he married the beautiful doctor who had graduated number one.

Millions of people recited the Harris' wedding vow everyday. Including them.

"God grant me the serenity to accept the things I cannot change. The courage to change the things I can. And the wisdom to know the difference."

CHAPTER TWENTY-TWO
"There were geese walking in a fuss along the edge of the water."

"Something's wrong," Jackie whispered to her husband.

"What?" he asked, half hearing her in the heavy breathing of Lamaz.

"Something's wrong!" she shouted.

Her obstetrician looked up over the hump in her belly. "What is it, Jackie? The baby's just starting to crown, a couple more pushes, and it's over."

"No! Cut me," she said, grimacing with the contractions.

122

"What?"

"Do it now!" she panted.

"We'd have to bring in the knock out doc, Jackie. We won't have enough time to do a spinal block." As he spoke, he palpated her abdomen, his fingers moving adroitly as though he were playing a sonata on a piano.

Jackie looked up at her husband, who was still holding one of her legs to her chest. She squeezed his hand hard.

"Do it, doc," he seconded.

"The epidural is enough, just squeeze the drip," she insisted, shaking the sweat from her face. "Cut me!"

"All right, Jackie. All right. Nurse, bring me a scalpel."

The doctor made a horizontal incision just below the bikini line. Jackie groaned deeply and passed out. A nurse monitored her vital signs as the doctor maneuvered his fingers inside the cut, where he could gently palpate her swollen uterus. Then, he made a second cut.

It was at that point that he understood the crisis.

The umbilical cord had wrapped itself around the baby's neck and was slowly strangling him as he tried to make his way down the birth canal.

He clamped and cut the cord and gently eased the baby's head out of the opening.

For a second, he was unsure if the baby was alive. He was blue and obviously cyanotic. The doctor cleared the mucous out of the boy's nose and mouth and said a silent prayer.

He tapped the baby's feet. Nothing. He tapped them again.

Suddenly the room filled with the joyful noise of the newborn's wailing. Jackie opened her eyes groggily and looked at her husband and clutched his arm as she wept with happiness. He too was crying and kissed her repeatedly as they slowly began to laugh with relief.

The nurse wrapped the baby in a blanket and an absurd looking cotton skullcap to keep him warm. Then she weighed and measured him before handing him over to his mother.

Jackie counted his fingers and toes, kissing him twenty times, one for each.

Jerry held him above his head, as he admired his beauty.

The baby scowled like a sleepy curmudgeon, shifting his eyes about the room, no doubt wondering where he was.

But a moment later he smiled.

A wonderful, knowing smile that welcomed his parents to the new world they had all entered together.

Every emotion they had known before was completely obviated by the look of wonder in their little boy's eyes. Every cynical thought now seemed so very trite and irrelevant.

Jonathan was already working his profound magic on their souls.

And he was barely five minutes old.

The doctor tossed his scrubs in a basket and walked over to the new family. "You may very well have saved his life, Jackie."

"Thank you, Robert. But it was you who did save his life. And for that we are eternally grateful."

"God bless you, Jackie," he said, smiling in quiet admiration of both her strength and her skill as a doctor.

"Jerry, I'll drop in on you guys in the morning." He rubbed the baby's wriggling fingers. "And you take care of your parents, you little Who from Whoville."

Before he left the room, the doctor paused at the door.

"Jackie, how did you know?"

"I don't know myself. It must be that woman's intuition thing," she smiled.

"Yeah. Unbelievable. You know, you can be my attending anytime."

"Thank you for trusting me, Robert."

There were many days that Jerry could hardly believe how quickly his son was growing up. Aside from that first moment of near tragedy in the birthing room, Jonathan lived an enviably charmed life.

He barely ever got sick. A cold or two, but that was it.

The boy was inquisitive and well mannered. He was a natural ham and a born athlete who lived everyday at full tilt until he was red in the face with sheer exhaustion.

Jerry absolutely adored him. To anyone who saw the two of them together, it was obvious that Jonathan was truly the joy of his father's life.

At one, he could speak in elementary sentences.

So Jerry sent him to Montessori pre-school.

At two, Jonathan thought he was Spiderman.

So he sent him to gymnastics classes.

At three, he could tap out Jingle Bells on his toy piano.

So his dad hired a private tutor and bought a Steinway.

At four, the boy thought he was a Power Ranger.

So Jerry paid for karate classes.

At five, he thought he was Shaggy from Scooby Doo.

So he bought him a closet full of green shirts and brown pants.

At six, he wanted to play for the Olympic Soccer Team.

So his father signed him up for a youth league.

And that's where they were heading now.

Over the last six years, he had watched Jonathan grow bigger and stronger each day in the rear-view mirror of the family's mini-van.

It seemed that he had gone from the baby car seat to the big boy booster seat in just a matter of months.

And it felt that way too. Not a second was squandered.

He and his wife had adjusted their professional schedules around the boy's after-school activities. They never failed to catch a play or make a teacher conference or game.

Like any other proud father, Jerry could never say no to a trip to the ice cream stand or the arcade whenever his son asked.

And even though Jackie often chastised her husband for spoiling Jonathan, she never vetoed any of their adventures. She enjoyed watching them together.

"My two boys," she called them.

As they were driving to practice, a cell phone in the car went off.

"It's yours, honey," Jackie said, as she thumbed through a magazine.

Jerry grabbed the phone from his pants pocket. As he fumbled with it, it slipped behind his chair to Jonathan's feet.

"Hello," Jonathan said as he retrieved the phone, quickly pressing the talk button. "Dr, Harris here," he said cheerily imitating his father.

"Ahem, Dr. Harris. May I take over?"

"Certainly," the boy said with an exaggerated pomposity.

"Thank you," Jerry said as he grabbed the phone. "Dr. Harris Sr. here. Can I help you?"

Jonathan could see the look on his father's face grow increasingly more concerned as he talked. He shook his head as he played idly with his soccer ball, knowing instinctively that they would be delayed.

"Look everyone, I've got to make a quick stop before we get to practice. It's a bit of an emergency, but it's on the way, so I shouldn't be too long. Okay?"

"A 'bit' of an emergency?" his wife asked playfully.

"It's not too bad. At least I hope it's not. Mickey Eldridge is a new patient, and she's still got a ways to go."

"What's the problem?"

Jerry cut a quick glance to the rear-view mirror.

Jonathan was still preoccupied, spinning the ball on his fingertips.

"She's suffering from episodic delusions. Her daughter died a few years back," he whispered. "She can't let go."

Jackie nodded.

"I think any parent can understand that," she said, looking back at Jonathan. "Take as much time as you need."

"I shouldn't be too long. It may just be an issue with her meds. We'll see."

A few moments later, the doctor and his family pulled up in front of the woman's house.

It was a beautiful, renovated Victorian bungalow, with turreted windows and gingerbread trim all along the wrap-around porch. The house was painted a striking green and yellow, and stood out from all the other homes on the block.

The woman who came to the door had a swarthy, exotic beauty to her, like a gypsy. She wore a colorful sundress, and Jerry could not help but notice the delicious way it fit her body.

Her smile was polite and painfully etched across her face.

"Come in, doctor. Come in."

Dr. Harris entered the home and looked around. It was elegant with an unpretentious collection of very fine American antiques. She had excellent taste, he thought.

"You have a lovely home, Mickey," he said as he walked through the foyer.

"Thank you. I'm so glad you could stop by on such short notice. I'm a little bit embarrassed."

"That's all right. Tell me, what's wrong?"

Mickey's face brightened up suddenly. "Oh, no, Dr. Harris, there's nothing wrong."

Jerry was confused. And concerned.

"No, far from it."

"How do you mean, Mickey?"

"Kia, Dr. Harris."

"What about Kia?"

"She's here."

"What?"

"To stay."

Jerry smiled weakly. He knew that Mickey was clearly having a setback. It hurt him to watch such a beautiful young woman have such a complete nervous breakdown.

"I'll be right back," she said. "We just finished making cookies."

As Mickey walked to the kitchen, the doctor immediately began scrolling through the contacts in his phone, looking for an ambulance service that could discreetly transport the woman to the hospital.

He was afraid she might hurt herself when the delusion wore off. Even now, he could hear her in the kitchen, chattering delightedly as though her daughter were standing right next to her.

He looked momentarily out of the living room window at his van. His son was waving to him. He could see his wife telling the boy something. He checked his watch. They could still get to the park without much of a delay.

Suddenly, the slide door on the van opened. Jerry was surprised to see Jonathan running toward the house excitedly.

As he opened the door to tell the boy to go back, Mickey came out of the kitchen.

With a little girl.

She was the spitting image of Mickey, just smaller with shorter, curlier hair. For a moment he was horrified at the prospect that the woman may have kidnapped a child.

But as he studied her face, he realized that he recognized it from the pictures that Mickey had brought with her during some of her sessions.

Dozens of other pictures on the fireplace mantle and hall tables confirmed that this little girl had to be Kia.

For just a fleeting instant, Dr. Harris had to consider that maybe he was having some kind of contagious delusion.

But then his son said hello to the little girl.

Jonathan saw her as well, he thought, relieved that he wasn't being drawn into the woman's fantasy. But how was this possible. If it was some kind of scam or insurance fraud, it had to have been impeccably carried out.

He had seen the death certificate. And the police report.

Yet here she stood. With a plate of cookies.

The little girl sat it down on the table and introduced herself to Jonathan. He did likewise.

"You want to go upstairs and play?" she asked happily.

"Sure," he said, oblivious now to soccer practice.

Before Dr. Harris could open his mouth, the two went bounding up the stairs to the little girl's room. "I'll be right back, daddy," Jonathan called.

"Mickey, what's going on?" Jerry asked the woman soberly.

"Kia's..."

"Dead. I know."

"I don't understand."

"She's dead, yes. But she's not gone. Just like Jonathan."

"What? What did you say?'

"Just like Jonathan, Dr. Harris,' she repeated calmly.

"Jonathan?" he said curiously. But suddenly, he was terrified. "Jonathan!" he screamed as the door behind the children slammed shut. He could hear them laughing.

He tried to race up the stairs, but the woman grabbed him by the arm with an unyielding firmness.

"Let me go!" he screamed. "Jonathan! Jonathan!" he yelled, fighting to go up the stairs to the room.

"Dr. Harris! Dr. Harris!" the woman yelled in his ear.

But the woman was not Mickey.

He turned toward her and saw that it was a nurse.

He was surrounded by an emergency room crash team. He felt searing pain in his chest, where a doctor was straddling him on the table, massaging his heart.

His gloves and jacket were soaked with Jerry's blood.

The doctor wore a mask, but Jerry recognized his eyes. It was Will Thomas, the police surgeon from Emory Medical School. If Will was in the ER, the victim was usually a cop who had been shot and was near death.

Jerry had been to Grady Hospital under many such circumstances. He often volunteered to counsel grieving officers whose partners had been gunned down.

It began to dawn on him now that it was he who was dying.

He knew from his training that he was in shock, in the Netherworld where things could be seen and heard by the mind.

But not always the brain.

He was alive. And he was aware.

But he was not necessarily aware that he was alive.

As he floated upward, he could see his own face, a sad ashen gray. And his eyes, un-living and locked open in mute agony.

But he was being drawn to the next room. By the sound of a woman wailing.

A terrible dreadful sound that was less human than animal.

It was Jackie.

In her arms she cradled the lifeless form of a child.

Their child.

Jonathan.

His body was a broken vessel of twisted limbs and horrible purple bruises. But his face was untouched by the carnage. It was unsullied and pure in its repose. He wanted to touch it.

At that instant, Jackie gasped and looked wildly around the room through her tear-glazed eyes. It was as though she were searching for something.

Or someone.

"*Jerry?*" she whispered tentatively.

When no answer came, she held her son's body even closer.

And prayed.

"Got him!" one of the nurses shouted, as the heart monitor began to beep.

"Let's go!" Will yelled over the frantic din. He jumped down off of Jerry like a paunchy 50 year-old gymnast doing a dismount on a pommel horse. "Take him to OR-4. I'll be there in three minutes."

Dr. Thomas ran to the next room. He looked through the glass and saw Jackie with Jonathan. His heart sank with one beat, but renewed with the next.

"Jackie, Jerry's alive."

She looked up with the most pitiful smile he had ever seen.

"I know," she sobbed confidently. "I know."

"I'm going up right now. He's stable, and I think his chances are good."

She nodded her head with desperate hope.

"Bring him back to us, Will. Bring him back."

Minutes later, Will Thomas did exactly that.

Jerry had suffered broken ribs, a punctured lung, lacerations of the spleen, a concussion, and a torn carotid artery. He would have died had his wife not been one of the best doctors in Atlanta.

By herself, she had crawled out of the overturned minivan, and triaged her family on the shoulder of Highway 316.

Most of the passing motorists were too busy trying to get home or too liquored up on road rage to even try and pull over to help.

Both Jerry and Jonathan were alive in the moments after the crash, and Jackie had to make a terrible choice.

Which one of them to send to the hospital first.

Only one ambulance had made it through the rush-hour gridlock. And the nearest life-flight helicopter had already been dispatched to another wreck near the South Carolina line.

Of the two, Jerry appeared to be the most grave.

But Jonathan was also extremely critical.

The paramedics only had room for one.

When Atlanta police got the call that Dr. Jerry Harris and his son were on the side of the road dying, they broke off one of their Little Bird surveillance choppers and promised to be there within ten minutes.

Jackie made a calculated decision.

Jerry would go in the ambulance. And Jonathan would go with her in the chopper. He was smaller, and she could better tend to him in the tiny interior.

It would be a race against time. And time was a notorious cheater. But she had no choice.

Police motorcycles cleared the carpool lane, and the ambulance with her husband sailed through at over a hundred miles an hour into downtown Atlanta.

People stuck in traffic thought that maybe the President was in town.

The ambulance made the eleven-mile trip in just over four minutes.

The chopper pilots made good on their promise. They quickly loaded Jackie and Jonathan inside. The boy appeared to be in no pain, but his condition was clearly growing worse by the second. The pilots could see that for a few seconds at least, he had regained consciousness and was whispering softly to his mother, who kept telling him that he would be all right.

And that she loved him.

Over and over. Even after he fell back into unconsciousness.

Two minutes later, they were met at the helipad by a team of surgeons. They could tell by the hardness in Jonathan's belly that he was hemorrhaging internally.

What they did not know until they cracked open his chest wall was that a valve in his heart had ruptured in the crash, and that he would have died no matter what they did.

As she watched them pronounce her little boy dead, Jackie fainted where she stood.

When she awoke, the doctors were trying to tend to her ankle, which had a compound fracture.

But she appeared unaware of them as she stood up and limped to the gurney where Jonathan lay. The doctors and nurses moved one by one out of her way, astounded that she could walk at all, let alone without betraying the slightest indication of pain.

Out of respect, they left her alone to say good-bye to her son.

She cried a torrent of tears, as she gently stroked his brow.

His body was still warm to the touch, though she could see in the monitor that his temperature was dropping steadily in tenths of a degree. She detached each of the electrodes connected to his body.

Now he looked like he was sleeping.

The examination light above them cast a queer luminescent umbra over Jonathan and his mother.

She rested her head lightly against his chest. She could not help but search for a heartbeat despite the fact that she knew there would be none.

So many times she had listened to his breathing as he slept.

But now there was nothing.

Just the deafening absence of life. Her Jonathan, her sweet and precious boy, had become an empty shell. She tried hard not to think the word "cadaver."

Suddenly, Jonathan's right arm twitched subtly with a post-mortem spasm. Soon, even the slightest limbic vestige of life would disappear entirely as the residual fire in his nerves left the synapses. He would be gone.

The thought was just too much to bear.

Jackie could barely breathe. Her agony began roiling deep within her until she couldn't hold it back any longer.

She screamed with feral hysteria, causing everyone in the busy corridor outside to stop what they were doing and listen with sad vicarious grief.

If she had been a wolf, the pack would have howled.

If she had been a lion, the pride would have roared.

But she was a mother. And the sound she made was something only a mother who had lost a child could truly understand. And here she was completely alone.

And it was precisely that sound that had brought Jerry back to the living.

He lay in a coma for two weeks, listening to the splendid Mozart CD's that Jackie had brought from home. He could hear her talking to him at times. Not so much understanding the words, as clinging to the familiar voice of the only woman he had ever really loved.

Like a unborn baby, smiling in the womb with its eyes closed, he could tell when she was there even without seeing her.

At 10:14am on a Friday morning, Jerry woke up.

Jerry Springer was on. Transgender Husbands Who Cheat.

Jerry thought for a moment that he might be in hell.

A week later he was released from the hospital.

Jonathan had already been buried. And the first thing Jerry wanted to do was visit his grave.

It was near a pond on a rolling hill at Westview Cemetary. There were geese walking in a fuss along the edge of the water.

Jonathan would have liked that, he thought, as he wept silently for the next hour in the arms of his wife.

Jerry had no memory of the accident. His wife claimed not to remember either. But he suspected she was not telling the entire truth.

So while she was at physical therapy, he had a friend at APD fax him the police report under the pretense that he needed it for insurance purposes.

The investigating officer wrote that Jerry "had become distracted. He was apparently looking for his cell phone, which was ringing at the time. Subject looked up to see that a car had stalled in the lane ahead of him. He overcompensated in his effort to avoid said car, and the van rolled several times before coming to rest upside down on the shoulder. One dead. Son. No charges."

Jerry got up and went to his gun cabinet. It was unlocked.

And empty.

There was a note inside from one of his friends at the FBI, Hampton Wells.

"Jerry.

"When my daughter died many years back, a friend of mine took all the guns from my house.

"It wasn't that I couldn't get another gun to blow my brains out.

"It was simply that somebody, who had gone through the same thing, cared enough about me to save my life.

"I care about you, Jerry.

"If you're reading this, call me.

-Hamp."

Jerry folded the letter back neatly in the envelope, and returned it to the cabinet.

He sat down on the windowsill in Jonathan's room where he used to read him bedtime stories and talk about the things they had done that day.

He could still hear Jonathan laughing, as he curled up in the boy's tiny bed, just like he used to when his son was scared.

And just like he used to, he nodded off there.

But this time, he wept.

Both in his sleep. And in his dreams.

After weeks of seclusion and months of family counseling and physical therapy, Jerry Harris slowly began to move forward with his life.

Jackie's recovery had gone much more smoothly.

That was not surprising to him. She had always been much tougher than he was. For her, the best therapy was diving back into work and never looking back. It was true that a part of her had died in the accident.

But the rest of her had grown even stronger.

For Jerry, the restoration had been much more difficult.

He could still see Jonathan's face every day in the rear-view mirror of his car. He could hear him laughing in the next room. And he could still feel him like a phantom limb attached to his heart and soul.

But he knew that he had to pull himself out of his depression.

Otherwise, he'd become just another pathetic shrink hooked on Halcyon, trapped in a never-ending group-grope of grief support meetings. His life would become an inelastic collision of regret and penance.

He had been in the abyss before. He was not going back.

So from that moment on, he committed himself to carrying the guilt of the accident box-by-box, step by step, slowly, heavily, assiduously up the stairs to the attic in his head.

There, he stacked them neatly in a special place beneath the windows, where they could never get lost amid the often-frightening clutter of his mind.

CHAPTER TWENTY-THREE
"Sucking the life out of their host like a million tiny serpents."

From a purely analytical perspective, Jackie had always been Jerry's enabler. They were codependents who simply loved each other profoundly.

He needed her; and she nourished his need.

In his practice, he often preached against that kind of relationship paradigm. But at home, he could not practice what he preached.

With his history of addiction, he had sworn never to keep secrets from her. But they shared an understanding that his work should be a locked door in the attic. The things inside had no business at the family dinner table.

Still, she could always tell when he was in there.
He looked like he was watching a horror movie.

"What is it, honey?" she repeated.
"I'm sorry, Jack. There's nothing wrong. Just a little melancholia, that's all."
"That Lee fellow, again?" she asked softly.
"Yeah," he shrugged. "Same old potatoes…"
"Different gravy," she smiled. "I know. I know. I think I'm going to prescribe two Corona's for lunch."
"I concur," he deadpanned.

The Drs. Harris laughed together as they often did. Jerry suddenly felt the inertness of his mood vanish like mist in the sun. He squeezed Jackie's hand and smiled in the one mystery that perpetually defied science. Her love for him.

He had always enjoyed antiquing with his wife. But both had grown weary of fighting the weekend crowds. Especially nowadays, with the road shows on television and Sotheby's online.

The Sins of Angels

Everybody, it seems, had become an expert, or at least another loudmouthed dilettante going out of the way to let you know how much he or she didn't.

But today was Monday. And the shops were very nearly empty. And that meant Jerry and Jackie Harris could hold hands and stroll lazily down the aisles like they used to. Lost in everything. Including each other.

Things had been tough from both sides of their marriage lately. Jerry had the Ed Lee case. And Jackie had her battle with breast cancer.

Her doctor had discovered the cancer during a routine check for fibroadenomas. The biopsy showed *"lobular carcinoma in situ in her left breast."*

As a doctor, Jackie knew that meant there was a high probability that a tumor was hiding somewhere deep within the fatty tissue behind her nipple.

Neither her routine self-exams nor her annual mammograms had caught it. For that reason, she looked at the diagnosis as a cause for celebration. The doctors at least had an early start in finding the cancer and killing it.

A week later, an MRI showed a 5cm tumor vermiculated between several milk ducts. A biopsy done by fine needle aspiration showed that the tumor cells were in fact malignant.

In addition to second and third opinions, both Jerry and his wife had reviewed the charts together at home. They held the transparencies up to the track lights in the kitchen about a hundred times.

There was no denying their accuracy.

Both of them felt violated by these promiscuous bacillary villains. They knew better than most, that, unimpeded, the cells would continue to grow like a demon seed, metastasizing and sucking the life out of their host like a million tiny serpents.

But the cure rate for this type of stage-zero cancer was 100%.

That was the good news.

The bad news was the recommendation by the oncologists to remove both of her breasts entirely, along with the lymph nodes under her left arm.

It was extreme. But given the fact that her mother, an aunt, and her grandmother had all been diagnosed with breast cancer, the doctors believed it was best to take no chances. It was a preemptive strike against any future complication.

For now, Jackie was taking Tamoxifen. But the side effects included a higher risk for uterine cancer, blood clots in the lungs, and stroke.

She was faced with the ruthless irony that the chemo could both cure her and kill her. At the same time.

"C'mon," she said, grabbing her husband by the elbow. "There's a shop I want you to see after lunch. I think you'll like it."

CHAPTER TWENTY-FOUR

"He was passionate about killing. But not wanton."

After Ed Lee's execution, Dr. Harris had decided it was best to take a few days off from work. He did not believe in ghosts but found himself haunted just the same by his subject's death.

It had been unsettling.

Not the execution. He had seen many of those.

Neither was it the CIA's efforts to resuscitate Lee's corpse, ostensibly for organ transplant. Though that was truly a first.

It was the fact, quite simply, that he would miss talking to him.

Dr. Harris knew the growing inner conflict would eventually take a toll on his emotional well-being.

He had thoroughly enjoyed his sessions with Ed, yet found it horrifying that he was comfortable with him, completely disarmed and never afraid. How could that be, he often wondered.

Ed was, by any rational standard, a monster.

Nonetheless, the doctor had admired his genius, yet was quietly frantic that he could not discover the source of Ed Lee's madness.

For a long time, he had thought that Ed was suffering from some sort of dissociative disorder.

In the beginning, Dr. Harris had suspected that he had somehow found a way to purge the RAM in his head. To partition his mind like the computer hard-drives he worked on. It was not all that farfetched.

After all, the new generations were being weaned on computers.

Police had known since the turn of the 21st century that kids who grew up playing violent video games made the best killers.

They were expert at target acquisition, quicker on the draw, and better marksmen than the cops. They killed with shots to the head. Making each bullet count toward a higher "score."

To them, their victims were little more than pixilated targets in a three-dimensional setting.

Surveillance cameras often caught the killers smiling as they moved through the screaming crowds, with an eager alacrity that was typically reserved for an arcade.

In the video games of murder, of which there were many, there was an endless supply of virtual ammo that could easily be replenished. But in real-life, the bullets always ran out, causing a malfunction in the program that was typically resolved with suicide.

The "Fatal Error," it was dubbed.

But Ed Lee wasn't the gamer. He was the programmer.

And he always left himself a backdoor to escape from, what had to be in his mind, the "pseudo-reality" of his crimes.

He had grown up building computers. By the age of five, he had learned three code languages and could format a hard drive in his sleep.

School shooters were typically facile youths with limited social skills and an ironic abhorrence to confrontation. For them, reality and fantasy always merged like two colors that make one.

But Ed Lee was nothing like that.

Though he was an adult now, by his own admission, his murders began as a preadolescent. And that was where one had to look into his morphology.

He was a child killing children. A bona fide serial killer by the age of ten.

Such a thing was previously unheard of. It was anecdotal mythology at best.

It was true that children were completely capable of murder. But rage and lunacy had always played a prominent role. The crimes always came with a long burning fuse of dysfunction and emotional angst.

But not for Ed Lee.

It was quite possible that he had learned to transpose his reality with his fantasy at will.

It was called The Looking Glass Effect.

Ed could very well be a mirror image of himself, inversely lateralized with two sets of diametric identities.

Both Cane and Abel at once.

It sounded good, but there was certainly no physical evidence of this, as his CAT scans were clean. The tomography had detected no lesions, no trauma, and no deterioration. Just redundant x-ray slices of a picture-perfect organ that, if anything, appeared younger than it should.

It was well known that people with multiple personalities were generally brilliant. They had to be. Their brains were constantly "on" like a DSL signal, running dozens or even hundreds of programs simultaneously. They even dreamed in different personalities.

They could adapt. They could adopt.

They were quick studies whose minds could synthesize and collate complex and amorphous data in seconds.

It was as if their brains were the symphony.

And their minds were the music.

Indeed, Dr. Harris had discovered that that metaphor was the best way to ferret them out.

Discordant ranting and raving always betrayed an inept conductor, whose cacophonous music was spiked and distorted on the EEG read-out.

But then, there were the virtuosos like Ed Lee, who could fool even a polygraph.

Dr. Harris was not surprised that Ed Lee was one of the top computer experts in the world. Any shrink knows that genius is to deception what karats are to gold. The more the better.

It was Spock who put it best.

Not the doctor, but the Vulcan.

"It is easy for the wise man to play the fool. But impossible for the fool to play the wise man."

In that context, Ed Lee had to be the wisest man Jerry Harris had ever met.

Every conventional test designed to unmask him had failed.

The Myers-Briggs-Jung. The Enneagram. The Eysenck-3. The Cattell-16.

Word-association and handwriting analysis had been an embarrassing joke. So much so, the doctor had felt compelled to apologize for trying them.

Drug therapy was a psychiatrist's best friend. But with Ed Lee, the usual arsenal of psychotropics showed no promise, so the doctor suspended treatment, choosing not to blur Ed's judgment or recollection of events.

Most of the tests were done in the early days of his incarceration.

The one thing that was evident even before they were administered was the fact that he was a classic narcissist.

Not a malignant one, like so many others who shared that trait. But a supercilious one. From the Dizzy Dean school of "it aint braggin' if you can do it."

In the waning days of his treatment of Ed Lee, time was not on Dr. Harris' side.

Or Ed's.

The dueling chess clocks between him and the prosecutors were winding down faster with every passing day. And the doctor knew all too well that if Ed could not be diagnosed with something tangible, his life could not and would not be spared.

Either way, Dr. Harris was conflicted as to whether it should be.

After all his work, all he had were questions.

For one, what exactly were the origins of his violence?

To be sure, the murders indicated a frightening, insatiate brutality on the surface. But upon listening to the murderer, the actual act of killing appeared to be distilled of animus.

How could such a thing be reconciled?

For Ed Lee, murder was like a dead-end job. The awful pun notwithstanding, it was no different than working at a mill or on an assembly line.

It was a merely a dutiful ritual. Complete with the same shallow hypnosis and the same moribund morality of anybody who has a decent work ethic. That alone ruled out his being a sociopath.

It was true that he was passionate about killing. But not wanton. And to Dr. Harris the nuance was not semantic. In fact, the more he listened to Ed Lee, the more rational he seemed to be. Even the different methods he used to kill were not for his gratification, but rather a way to keep police off balance and for him to stay invisible.

As a forensic psychiatrist, Dr. Harris had seen every type of human predator.

But no matter how different their particular stories may have been their lives were invariably composed of three acts.

Like a redundant Shakespearean tragedy.

Act I:

"Aberration."

Enter authority figure with corrupting influence.

Scenes (various) of abuse, both mental and physical.

Act II:

"Liberation."

Enter self-medicating drugs.

Scenes (various) of cathartic violence.

Act III:

"Incarceration."

Enter new authority figure.

Exuent to scenes (various) of resistance, punishment, and compliance.

The predictable declensions of rage and power and penance never changed. Ever.

Behind bars, serial killers always went from bully to bitch.

Never the reverse.

But Ed Lee did not read from this script either.

His resolve remained as unassailable as it was unbreakable. He showed absolutely no remorse, perceiving himself as both not guilty and not innocent simultaneously.

In his mind, he justified the murders using the Necessity Defense. He had committed an evil act to prevent an even greater evil act.

Dr. Harris had conducted several experiments with pictures of children to test Ed's physical responses. There were none. At least none that were empirically negative.

His facial expressions were the only insights that could be seen outwardly.

He smiled at the photographs that showed children in happy and loving scenarios. And he soured at the graphic depictions of violence. Including the pictures of his own victims.

Eventually, after many months, Jerry Harris found himself at the unmarked intersection of his logic and his intuition.

And he had no idea which way to turn.

CHAPTER TWENTY-FIVE

"His heart was beating so hard he could feel it through his chest."

But strangely, the sessions were becoming more and more therapeutic for him than the patient. They had become friendly. A comfortable stasis that gave him time to evaluate both Ed and himself.

But now, in the wake of his execution, there was no Ed Lee.

And more importantly, there would be no Ed Lee.

The alphabet spooks with the NSA, the FBI, and the CIA were already seeing to that, expunging his life from the mainframe. When that was done, they would come for Harris' personal notes.

They claimed they had the public interest at heart.

But for Dr. Harris personally, the void would be visceral.

Ed Lee had said from the beginning of his arrest that the Masons and the other Illuminati would see to it that he never existed. It was a tactic used from Caesar to Stalin. The message was always the same.

Annihilate your enemies' history. They will go from legend to myth to apparition. Whispered words and deeds. Never corroborated and soon to be forgotten.

151

Forever.

To that end, he considered his erasure from the grid a dual death sentence handed down not by the court of law.

But by the law of the Illuminati.

It was the ultimate double jeopardy.

He laughed about it, calling himself a ghost in the machine. But Dr. Harris suspected that on the inside, the thought of eternal anonymity was working on Ed like a spiritual poison.

He would die with neither epitaph nor headstone.

Outwardly, Ed shrugged the idea off. He said that in an ocean of lies, the truth was often invisible, lying just beneath the surface, waiting to grab you like a riptide.

"Life is nothing more than the mirage of death," he had said.

"It's very much like the light that comes from the far side of the universe. Those stars are long dead. But the light remains. For eternity.

"In many ways, life and light are the same things. The two energies simply take on variant forms.

"You've heard all those people with near-death experiences. They all say one thing."

"Don't go into the light," the doctor said.

"Right. There's a reason for that. Light is the release of energy. And so is…"

"Death," Dr. Harris finished.

"We've all been here before. And we'll be back. Just like your son, Jerry."

"What?"

"Just like Jonathan."

Dr. Harris was caught completely off guard during the exchange. It was one of the things a psychiatrist could never afford to do. Shift the balance of power to the patient.

Asymmetrical epistemology they called it. The sin of sins.

Correcting it during a session was like trying to pull an airplane out of a flat spin. Chances were slim to none.

"I heard about Jonathan from one of the other inmates," Ed continued. "I'm very sorry for your loss."

Dr. Harris adjusted his papers, trying to appear nonplussed and preoccupied. But inside, his heart was beating so hard he could feel it through his chest.

As much as he was intrigued by Ed Lee, he could not bear to hear him say his son's name. It was profane.

"Dr. Harris?" Ed whispered after a moment of silence.

The doctor simply could not bring himself to respond and pretended not to hear.

"I've known about Jonathan for quite some time, Jerry," he said apologetically. "I'm sorry if I've made you feel bad by mentioning it. That was not my intention."

Still looking down at the table, the doctor stood up and quietly gathered his notes and tapes. Then he walked out of the room, without looking at Ed. He was embarrassed for the tears in his eyes.

They betrayed the inviolate memory of Jonathan.

Which, by necessity, still remained behind the locked door in the attic of his sanity.

Jerry Harris reflected on all of this as he now ate lunch with his wife. As she spoke idly about the antiques they had seen that morning, he smiled wanly, pretending to people-watch from their table at the sidewalk café.

He was not obsessed with the Ed Lee case. It was worse than that.

It was festering in his head like a bad tooth in the mouth. But it was his mind that would need the root canal. Something to plunge out the rot and fill the void that was growing daily.

The crime scene videos played constantly in his thoughts like a television set left on in the wee hours of the morning.

The still shots of the victims' faces had all but replaced the mental introjections of his mind's family photo album. It was unnerving to know that if he died today, the images that would flash before his eyes would be those of the murdered children.

It was as if his soul were now being carved with their numbers.

As if their pain were becoming his.

Transference was not at all uncommon among shrinks. At least not among those who needed therapy themselves. It was often the harbinger of forced retirement.

Everyday Dr. Harris found himself painted further and further into an illogical corner of compassion for both the killer and his victims. He could not go on like this for long.

There had to be something more tangible behind the slaughter than Ed Lee's far-flung tales of Pythagoreans and angels. Atlanteans and Martians.

It was all so very absurd. Yet, every time Dr. Harris felt he could jettison parts of Ed Lee's "accounts," he would invariably find some nugget of truth or rationality to renew their credibility.

Even the city where he lived. Atlanta.

Dr. Harris knew that many believed it was named in homage to the legend of Atlantis.

And that idea was not without some common sense, given the fact that the city was nowhere near the Atlantic and therefore could not have been named for the ocean.

As for the secret societies, they were their own worst kept secrets. They were everywhere. Especially the Masons, who built stone temples in every city in the country.

It seemed that no matter where he looked there was some germ of truth to the bizarre things that Ed Lee believed. And Jerry Harris could feel each one pulling at him.

Like a rip tide.

CHAPTER TWENTY-SIX

"Pentacle."

After they had finished eating, Jackie led her husband by the arm around the block to a small alleyway off the main street.

Even as he stood in front of it, it did not immediately dawn on Jerry that the building was a store.

It looked like a garage. A dilapidated garage. With a graffiti-covered steel façade that over the years had bled long trails of liquid rust at the seams and hinges.

Jackie, too, looked confused. She had heard about this place from a flier stuffed in their mailbox. But the picture showed only the interior.

As she moved in closer to get a better look, the façade began to rise abruptly. A padlock that could withstand an artillery shell fell heavily to the ground.

A pair of beat-to-shit steel-toe boots could be seen as a voice spoke through the steel. "I'll have her up in a second folks. It's a bad neighborhood."

Slowly, the front of the store began to materialize as the owner retracted the security wall with a hand crank.

The large windows were dirty, as though they hadn't been washed in a decade. Iron bars across the inside of them were anchored deep into the dark wood frames. The walls were lathe and plaster, with a thin vestige of what had to be the original green buttermilk paint.

The old man inside invited them in, casually covering a holstered pistol with his shirt.

As he entered the building, the doctor noticed the transom above the door. The ancient hand-stenciled sign caused him momentarily to stop in his tracks with his mouth agape.

The letters had completely faded away, and the only thing visible was the vestige of the glue backing. But Jerry could make it out clearly enough to feel a curious shiver creep up in his spine.

"Pentacle."

As he walked inside, the synchronicity of the moment could not be ignored.

His wife had taken him to lunch in a bohemian enclave in East Atlanta that was nestled at the intersection of five streets. It was known appropriately as "Little Five Points."

Now, he was about to enter a store called "Pentacle." He shook his head at the coincidence.

The floors were made of quarter-sawn oak that creaked plaintively with every footstep. The varnish was worn completely through down the center of the aisles, which were dimly lit, despite the sunlight coming through the windows.

The store looked like a library.

In a dungeon.

On all sides were bookcases that loomed to the ceilings. There were tables and shelves full of strange and bizarre items and artifacts.

Giant geodes of quartz and amethyst. Clocks of every size and genre. Sextons and telescopes made of brown brass. Amber and fossils. Tiffany lamps. Gramophones. Radios with glowing tubes. Maps of colonial America. Silver from Siam. Water-color sketches of extinct birds and plants. And, of course, the books. Thousands upon thousands of books.

Old and new. Small and large. Leather-bound and paper-back. Dog-eared and immaculate. Textbooks and one-of-a-kinds.

From what Jerry Harris could tell, they dealt almost exclusively with the occult and the mysteries. Most were first editions. And not a few were hand-written.

Some names he recognized. Others he didn't.

There were no prices on anything. And almost everything was museum-quality. In fact, Jerry was struck by how pristine the collection was. There was no dust. No mildew. No cobwebs in the corners.

And despite its obvious age, the store was as clean as a hospital clinic.

The building itself was an antique. Perhaps antebellum.

There were ornate medallions surrounding the light fixtures. Gas light fixtures.

The ceiling was made of tin pressed with fleur de lis. Atop the concrete columns were chiseled cornices, beneath which stared faces.

Stone faces with horns and gnashing teeth, not unlike gargoyles. They were frightening and looked like something out of Dante's Inferno.

"Mischwesen," the owner said casually, as Jerry studied the sculptures.

"Pardon?"

"Mischwesen. Mixed beings," the owner said. "Like Persian Kherubs."

"What are those?" the doctors asked in unison.

"Avenging angels."

Jerry Harris felt that curious chill rising up his spine again.

"You have a remarkable store here," Jackie said to the owner. "How long have you been collecting?"

"Lifetimes," he said.

Jackie couldn't tell if he was being serious or facetious.

"Oh, be quiet," scolded a female voice from the staircase. She spoke with a strong English accent. "Always trying to scare the coostomers. You're a fine shop-keep, you are."

The old man grinned sheepishly as his wife joined him behind the counter. "Well it feels like lifetimes," he chuckled.

"What do you fancy, hon?" the woman asked Jackie, with a smile as big as her girth.

"There's so much. I wouldn't even know where to begin."

"Sorry the place is such a tip," she said, using her apron to dust an invisible spot off one of the shelves. "One of these days, I'll have to give it a proper cleaning. How about a nice cup of *real* tea? None of this soothern American stoof. I've got a kettle on the boil in the back."

Jackie looked over at her husband, who was by now completely engrossed in the books lining the walls.

The owner's wife gently grabbed Jackie by the elbow, leading her to a sitting area in the rear of the store. "Believe me, honey, I've seen that

159

look in a hoosband's eye many times before. Once the men get hooked, they're here for hours.

"You might as well join me. I'll give you the ten pence tour."

"Why not?" Jackie smiled. "I'll be in the back, Jerry," she said lightly, knowing that he was not paying attention.

"Mmm hmm," he responded from a thousand miles away.

"What is it I can do you for?" the owner asked Jerry.

"I'm not sure," he smiled. "Really, I'm just looking."

"Aint we all," the old man chuckled as he walked away. "Aint we all. If you need me, just holler."

"Thanks."

In the back, as Jerry browsed, the women chatted over tea and scones.

"My name's Lilly," the owner's wife said, as she poured the boiling water into the cups.

"I'm Jackie. It's a pleasure."

"Now this is a real tea spoon, honey," Lilly said, as she dipped a sterling silver strainer into Jackie's cup.

"It's lovely."

"Thank you dear. You know, when we're finished, I'll show you some joost like it that we've got for sale up froont. They're from France. Ooh, me da' would slap me giddy if he knew we sold anything from the Frogs. But they're joost so pretty, don't you think?"

Jackie laughed as she took a sip of her tea. A sour look immediately crossed her face, though she tried hard to squelch it.

160

"That's all right, dear. English tea is an acquired taste. Like me mum, I always put a wee pinch of the bitters in mine."

Jackie nodded politely, her face frozen in the same sour look.

"These cakes will more than attend to that, though," Lilly said, as she pushed the plate of scones toward her guest.

Jackie took a bite and agreed that they were very good. She dipped them instinctively to cut the harsh taste of her tea.

"They're absolutely delicious," she said.

"Anoother old family recipe," Lilly smiled.

As she listened politely to the old woman chattering on across from her, Jackie noticed something odd. The tea actually seemed to lighten in color each time she dipped the scones.

It would have been imperceptible to anyone without the trained eye of a clinician. But she swore she could see it. It was almost like some kind of chemical reaction, she thought, just before she slumped forward in her chair, unconscious.

Jerry Harris was too deeply absorbed in the books to notice anything awry. He had an arm full of them as he walked up and down the aisles.

But he had to put them down to reach for one in particular on the top shelf.

"The Book of Signs."

Thumbing through the yellowed pages of illustrations, he suddenly lost his breath in amazement. There before him was the very same hand gesture that Ed Lee had used that first night in the interrogation.

The five-pointed star.

He added the book to the pile he had been carrying. But before picking them up, he began to fidget his fingers in the way of the pentagram, trying to remember precisely how it was done.

At that instant, the owner of the store walked up silently next to him.

"I bid thee, brother, come with me," he whispered with a queer iambic formality.

CHAPTER TWENTY-SEVEN
"Kitte in smale gobets, bleynte bibledde."

Dr. Harris was momentarily taken aback by the strange tone.

At the time, he did not connect the hand sign with the owner's appearance.

Thinking it to be some sort of homespun sales theatrics, he followed the owner up the stairs to another wall of books in a back corner. As he was about to peer closer to the titles, the owner gently extended his hand to stop him.

With his foot, he lifted a kick plate at the bottom of the bookcase and slid to the side a heavy metal latch. Suddenly, the entire wall sprang open.

It was a secret door. A hidden passage way at the back of the building.

The old man grabbed a flashlight from behind the shelf, turning it on as he stepped into the tactile darkness. "Come," he whispered, as he lit the way down a long circular flight of stairs.

"What's down here?" the doctor asked tentatively.

"The good stuff," the owner smiled slyly.

They went well below the first floor of the store. Perhaps fifty feet below street level. Above them, there was a heavy concussion that rode down the banister as the wall-door slammed shut.

The stairs led to a long corridor that seemed to stretch for hundreds of feet in the darkness. As they walked, the owner of the store stopped occasionally to light oil lamps placed along the way.

In the soft orange hue of the lanterns, Dr. Harris could see that the walls appeared to be cut from a translucent vein of white granite.

They were smooth to the touch.

And that had to be impossible, he thought.

He was no architect or civil engineer, but Jerry knew that there should be seams from where the slabs had been butt together. Or at least vertical scarring from blasting.

How else could a shaft like this have been carved out of solid stone?

In the light, it felt like he was walking though a giant emerald. This was no abandoned sewer trunk or old forgotten mine. There was no water on the floor or even dampness in the air. And it didn't smell of any kind of gas, which was a good thing he thought, given the abundance of burning oil lamps.

"We own the entire block," the owner said, his voice echoing down the tunnel. "Got the original deed from King George in the safe upstairs."

"From before the Revolution?" Jerry asked.

"From the 1600's," the owner answered, as he continued to lead the way. "We pre-date the city itself by more than a century."

"Extraordinary," Dr. Harris said slowly. His voice was tinged with the thick adrenaline of curiosity. "What is this place?"

"It is the gate, brother."

"The gate?"

"Yes," he said with an avuncular smile. "Welcome."

The doctor was perplexed. And could do nothing about it.

Most of the time it was easy to carry on a one-sided conversation if you were the listener.

All you had to do was wait like the space between musical notes for the speaker to continue on their own, prodding them with solicitous nods and gestures and murmurs.

But the owner of the store was cryptic. He obviously assumed that Jerry knew what he was talking about. And as they walked deeper and deeper into the underground shaft, Jerry began to feel claustrophobic.

The walls of his tacit deception were beginning to close in on him like the granite around him.

It was too late now to admit that he was clueless about why he was here. And it might be dangerous, he thought, recalling the pistol beneath the owner's shirt.

The tunnel suddenly began to feel like a catacomb.

Indeed, as they continued, Jerry noticed that occasionally there were recesses cut into the walls.

They were dark, and he could not see much past the openings. But he could faintly discern what appeared to be bodies wrapped in cerements. They were crypts.

Most of the openings were small. But some were quite large.

One of them was opposite an oil lantern, and its contents were fully illuminated.

He stopped in his tracks at the sight. It was a veritable avalanche of relics.

Masonic relics. Thousands of them.

Many made of gold and silver.

There were rings and medallions. Swords and sabers. Shields and spears. Boxes and ornaments. Goblets and journals.

There was a bronze plaque affixed to the inside wall of the opening that was hammered with an archaic and foreign script.

"La Mort a Massons."

"Death to the Masons."

The two men reached what appeared to be the end of the corridor. But as it turned out, it was a door. A heavy leaden door that opened with a large double-pronged key and a spinning handle like a bank vault.

It was ornately painted with pastel filigrees and acanthus vines. And at the top, there were several verses of what appeared to be poetry.

It was hard to make out. The writing was small, but the words were in English. Middle English.

"Herkne Palmere, abood ye ne.
"Leef ye her,
"But chees ye tweye.
"And namo eft dresse this way.

"Ave Marie, ful of gras.
"Deus hic, gooth in pees.
"Bileve ye her, abood in drede.
"Kitte in smale gobets, bleynte bibledde."

"Whatever you do, heed those words," the owner said gravely as he pushed open the heavy door.

Dr. Harris nodded, astonished that he was *expected* to understand what the words said. But he did. Always a voracious reader, he had taken an English Literature course translating Chaucer as an undergraduate.

That, plus the Latin he took in Rev. Hamm's eighth grade class had stayed with him all these years, like a stubborn ketchup stain in an old shirt.

He squinted as he translated the lyrics to himself.

"Listen, traveler, do not dwell.
"Leave here.

166

"Choose between two.
"And never come this way again.

"Hail Mary, full of grace.
"God is here. Go in peace.
"If you remain, stay in fear.
"Cut in small pieces and covered in blood."

The message was simple. And horrific.

Go in peace. Or stay in pieces.

By now, the doctor's curiosity had turned to dread.

His eyes instinctively began to dart about, as he looked for some way out of the tunnel. He could feel his reptilian brain beginning to squeeze his reason into submission.

He was fighting hard to stay in control, so as not to make any mistakes in desperation. But try as he might, the reigns were beginning to slip.

His palms were sweating. He could feel the blood leave his stomach involuntarily, and he could taste the bile rising into his throat. Ever the wunderkind doctor, he couldn't help but anticipate the symptoms before they presented.

Cottonmouth was making it easier to breathe, and his lungs began to heave on cue, deeply and quickly.

But the infusion of oxygen made him light-headed and mildly euphoric, and his mind began to swim in the narcosis of self-preservation.

He could feel his legs and arms grow warm as the muscles engorged with blood and epinephrine. His fingers twitched. And his heart was bubbling like a moon-shiner's still, trying to purify every chemical his body could manufacture from the ancient recipe of fear.

The only thought that he could not decipher from the chaos was how to get hold of the owner's gun.

CHAPTER TWENTY-EIGHT

"There was no museum on earth like this."

But as they walked through the entrance of the vault, Jerry Harris abruptly shook off the blur building in his brain. His pupils dilated, and his breathing slowed.

But his heart continued to beat excitedly.

The room was full of untold riches.

Portraits and paintings in the unmistakable hand of Renaissance and modern masters. Golden statues and funerary from the tombs of royalty. Ossuaries. Medieval armor. Signed schematics by Edison. Prototypes by Da Vinci himself.

There were casts from Pompeii. Entire families turned to stone, clutching one another. There were ornate sarcophagi made of marble. Cascades of jewelry from every epoch. Colored diamonds the size of walnuts. Carvings in ivory. Death masks in porcelain. Piles of rare coins. Palettes of bricks of paper currency, past and present, foreign and domestic.

168

There were thousands of artifacts of war, with flags and battle emblems of every culture dating back from Sparta to the Nazis.

And in the distance, in an area that was still unlighted, Jerry could make out what had to be thousands of gleaming stacks of gold bars.

The inventory was endless, like the chamber itself. The room stretched out for hundreds of feet like an airplane hangar. And it was tall enough to float a blimp inside.

There was a section dedicated to just books.

And another for a glassed-in wall of neatly stacked copper cylinders, chiseled with rows of characters.

Dr. Harris held his breath as he beheld these. He had seen only one thing similar to them in his lifetime. And that was on the History Channel. A show on the Dead Sea Scrolls.

But these had markings that appeared to be Greek. And on the front of each case was a royal stamp bearing the image of a man with a halo formed by rays of light. The crown of enlightenment.

Worn by Alexander the Great.

"They are from the Hall of Records in Alexandria," the old man said softly.

"The School of the Mysteries?"

The owner of the shop nodded.

"You're kidding."

"Not at all."

169

Jerry was now giddy with wonderment. His eyes could not drink in fast enough the vast spectacle stretching out before him.

There was no museum on earth like this. Not the Louvre. Not the MOMA. Not the Smithsonian.

Nothing could compare to the treasures hidden here beneath the street at a battered antiques shop called Pentacle.

Nothing.

A strange sweet smell filled this part of the room. It was both heavy and light at the same time, very much like the perfume of a magnolia blossom.

In the low light he could not tell where it was coming from, though it was strong enough almost to taste. He followed the smell to a section of the chamber that made him stop in his tracks.

The statues of hundreds of golden sphinxes stood draped in armor, pikes at the ready. They were matched up according to style and size, culture and region, grimly facing one another down a long line to the center of the chamber, which betrayed a peculiar concentric emptiness.

There in the middle, Jerry could see something glowing, pulsating a cold purplish-blue.

The light was bright enough to cast flickering shadows across this part of the room, making it appear as though the metallic eyes of the statues were following him as he made his way down the line toward the object.

"What is that?" he asked.

There was no answer.

Jerry looked around and realized the shopkeeper was nowhere to be found. Nevertheless, he was still being drawn to the middle of the room, ineluctably, as though his legs had hijacked his reason.

The closer he got to the glowing object, the more the down hairs on his neck began to rise. He attributed that to fear at first, until a queasy sensation began to rise from the pit of his stomach.

It was almost like seasickness.

As he got to within a few steps of the object, a tingling sensation began to traverse the dorsal root ganglia along his spine.

The fluid in his inner ear began to gently depressurize.

The fluctuation momentarily caused him to lose his balance.

He steadied himself by putting his hand on one of the sphinxes and fell backwards when it turned its head and hissed at him.

The sphinx had the body of a lion and the head of a hawk, which was now turned menacingly in the direction of Dr. Harris as he thrashed his legs about wildly, trying to get back on his feet.

The creature slammed the butt of its pike hard against the granite floor. In rapid succession, each of the others followed suit in a machine gun-like staccato. The doctor stopped moving and held his breath.

"They won't hurt you, as long as you stay within their ranks."

It was the voice of the storeowner. Jerry squinted into the darkness looking for him but could not see him anywhere.

"But if you try to go outside the aisle or turn back, they'll rip you to shreds. Remember the sign over the door."

"H-h-how can this be?" Jerry yelled. "They're statues!"

"Mischwesen!" the old man corrected, laughing loudly.

171

Mixed beings, the doctor reminded himself, shaking his head. "But they're made of gold!" he yelled out.

"They are chimera, Dr. Harris. Protean creatures of genetic alchemy. They can change their very make-up, the way a chameleon can change its colors. Remember that stuff you doctors call 'junk DNA?' Just keep on going," the old man encouraged. "There are wonders still to behold."

The doctor sat there for a moment, stunned like a clubbed seal. The old man knew his name. Suddenly things became clear.

The owner had seen him make the sign of the pentacle with his hands. That was certain. But the serendipity of their meeting had to have been contrived.

Jackie said she had heard about the store through a flier. Had they been singled out? If so, then by whom? And why?

That's when Jerry remembered the data disc he had given Ed Lee to write down his theories on the pyramids.

Like an idiot, he had underestimated Ed's hacking abilities even with a gutted dinosaur of a computer.

He had obviously loaded the disc with encrypted language.

When Jerry put it into his office computer, the disc must have activated his internet server and sent out a hidden message to members of Ed's cabal, arranging this visit to their underground repository.

The question now was why?

The doctor scrambled to his feet, taking great care not to touch any of the sphinxes or go outside of their phalanx. He wiped the sweat off his brow and continued walking forward to the glowing object.

It was clear to him now that his motion sickness was something more. The symptoms were very much like those in an article he had read in a science journal.

Symptoms described by astronauts on the International Space Station.

But how could it be low gravity that he was feeling? After all, his feet were still on the ground and neither his clothes nor his hair were floating upward.

But every drop of his blood seemed to be accelerating in his veins. Fear can do that, he thought.

And so can a strong electromagnetic field.

"It's both, Dr. Harris."

Jerry wasn't quite sure if he had actually heard the old man's voice or simply thought it.

"Both again."

"Wait a minute!" he yelled, wildly looking around the room. "Are you talking to me *telepathically*?"

"Yes, I am."

Jerry was dubious, and searched his mind for some other rational answer. This had to be some sort of a trick.

"As of course you know, doctor, it is impossible to speak as fast as one thinks. Most of the time, we don't even know where the words are coming from. Let alone the thoughts. It is a mundane mystery that we take for granted. Telepathy comes from the same place as our thoughts. It just takes a little longer to learn to speak without a tongue. The animals do it far more easily than we. It is no accident that our DNA is shaped in a double helix."

"Like an antenna," Jerry thought.

"Exactly, Doctor. Dielectric conductivity. Tapping into the Wi-Fi of the universe itself. That *Zeitgeist* people talk so much about."

"The thought pool," Jerry said as he continued to search for the owner.

"You can stop looking for me, Dr, Harris. I had to go back upstairs. I'll be back presently. It's best you attend to this on your own."

Jerry looked up and gasped.

"Your wife is fine.... "

He looked at his watch.

"She's sleeping....""

His gaze tightened.

"Benzodiazepine. Completely harmless. You, or more precisely, your failure to complete your journey, are what poses the greatest danger to her. Now please, doctor, you must finish your task. All will be made clear in a few moments."

Dr. Harris walked slowly, as though in a deep somnambulant trance.

The object before him seemed to respond to his presence.

The closer he got, the brighter it glowed.

CHAPTER TWENTY-NINE

"The belt of Orion is on fire."

It was made up of two distinct parts. The outside was dark and smooth, like a metallic stone, scarred with deep vertical striations. And it was as big as a Volkswagen bus.

It may have been a meteorite. But the inside of it was hollow, and the edges around the opening appeared to have been sculpted with designs like fancy cornices.

From deep within it emanated the strange light, which actually seemed to pour slowly over the brim of the opening like a heavy liquid.

He extended his hand cautiously to touch it. And like an electric charge, the light shot incandescently into his fingertips.

There was no pain. Just illumination.

All around him. And within him.

His watch stopped. And time stood still.

His eyes filled with images. His mind with answers.

He could see the ocean. The waves were crystal blue, and over the millennia they had carved long channels into the emerald landscape. It looked like Ireland.

The rocks were the color of merlot. So was the soil. Cliffs towered over the water. There were trees and flowers everywhere. The smell of them filled his lungs, and he swore he could feel the ocean spray against his face.

In an instant, the scene had changed.

There were now cities visible. Gleaming, brightly clad in metal and stone. There were vehicles moving in absolute silence. There were also crowds of people.

Their features were hard to make out. But they were obviously of many colors and appeared to speak with one tongue.

They make a joyful din. And children could be heard laughing.

A new scene now.

All faces are raised to the sky. It is night. And the belt of Orion is on fire. It is the day astronomers have been dreading for fifty thousand years.

The tenth planet, Sekhmet, has broken free of his orbit. Again. His very name means destruction. And in 56 years he will rain infinite tons of magma onto the pacific face of the world.

The first of many fleets of spacecraft prepares immediately to launch. They will establish a colony on a planet they have visited before, where the atmosphere is suitable to sustain life.

Doctors. Teachers. Engineers. Artists. Musicians. Writers. Soldiers. Historians. The best of these will be the first to go. Along with the finest instruments of their crafts.

Thousands of ships will depart before no more can be built.

Fifty-two years forward now.

Sekhmet rages and burns terribly like a second sun. It is daylight at night.

The polar axis of the planet has shifted.

The ground quakes almost hourly. A subterranean rip in the ocean is slowly boiling the sea to vapor.

Super-storms tear across every corner of the world. Tornadoes last for weeks. Hurricanes for years. The land grows desolate. There are deserts and glaciers and very little in between.

Food is in short supply.

There is voluntary starvation and suicide. Millions are sacrificing themselves so that the engineers have enough to eat to continue their labor. Thousands offer their own bodies as food.

The many will die for the few. Willingly.

Year 53 of Sekhmet.

There is no one younger than twenty now. And few older than forty. By global consent, no more children were born after the 34th year of Sekhmet. Only the fittest can expect to survive life on the new world. And no one wants to perish miserably on the old.

Females will outnumber the men three to one to assure the genetic stability of the race. Stores of fertilized female eggs in cryonic suspension will also be transported for future implantation.

The cataclysmic upheaval has already killed 95% of the world's population. Only the remarkable topography of this plateau has allowed the work here to continue unabated. All other efforts elsewhere have now been utterly destroyed.

A paucity of workable technologies remains.

Heavy magnetic disturbances have rendered most of the advanced tools useless. Satellite power plants have become unstable in the ionic surges. Most have exploded.

It is only due to the genius of the project architects that the work can continue at all. They are somehow chemically bleeding synthetic electricity from mineral deposits deep below the ground.

Solar power is also being used, though it has become an unreliable source of energy given the changing atmospherics.

Year 54 of Sekhmet.

Giant pyramids now stretch across the outskirts of the city.

The frenzy of activity around them is unending. Crews work around the clock to complete the project. They grow weak and weary but are undeterred by their own frailty.

Many die where they work.

An identical race against time is underway on the sister planet. Their work will be the hardest to complete before the deadline.

Year 55 of Sekhmet.

The crews dispatched to the sister planet were forced to improvise from indigenous materials.

With the remaining population at home being slowly annihilated, cargo space on the later ships has been reserved more for people than equipment.

The orbiting space stations have also departed. It is too dangerous to stay. They will bring additional technology, but will arrive too late for the exodus.

Nevertheless, the work on the sister planet is now nearly complete.

A handful of aborigines have been enlisted to care for the babies who are born here. Thankfully, the children are many. The aborigines have been allowed to live on the spacecraft, both those in orbit and those on the ground. These people have proven to be as brave as they are curious.

The two species are not unalike in that regard. And thousands of their aboriginal women have been impregnated by the fertilized eggs that were transported in the ships.

Soon, full-power testing on the pyramids will begin. They are exact duplicates of the ones on the home planet, down to the millimeter.

Meanwhile, back home, an army of artisans has carved a colossal face out of a ridge of phosphorescent stone. The colonists can see it through their orbiting telescopes.

It is the headstone of their dying planet.

Year 56 of Sekhmet.

The survivors now number in the tens of thousands. The weakest of them will stay behind and operate the controls.

Decades of work and billions of lives have been given for this moment.

With the dawn will come the final catastrophe.

The destiny of the planet is now in the hands of a chosen few.

Two hours before dawn.

The heat of Sekhmet is unbearable. The evacuees have retreated underground and will be transported in waves. The first of them fill the interior chambers of the pyramids. All around them, the walls turn luminescent as they line up and walk through the portal that has opened up to the new world.

The project is working.

The evacuees pray as they wait their turn in a subterranean cavern that opens into the chambers. A similar cavern sits beneath the chambers on the sister planet.

The flashing light from the pyramids on both worlds can be seen across the solar system, like mirrors shining in the sun. But the light is lethal. And no one can be above ground within a radius of two miles without being incinerated. It is a wormhole, lit up on both ends like an invisible fiber optic cable connecting the two worlds.

Dawn.

Only three waves of the thirteen make it through.

A total of 127,036 people.

Before the others have had a chance to escape, an unceasing fusillade of asteroids and molten rock slams into the face of Mars.

Even though the pyramids remain active for several more hours, no others have come through the portal. Rescuers bravely go back and find that the evacuees are trapped in the subterranean caverns. They can hear them singing.

They are rejoicing that at least some of them have escaped.

They know there is no way to free them. And no time.

The rescuers weep. They have traveled fifty million miles with a few steps. But cannot move the fifteen feet of stone that blocks the passage to the chambers. Electrical devices cannot be used without closing the portals. Explosively.

Prayers are said. And more tears are shed, as the rescuers leave behind the last of their kind.

On Mars.

On Earth.

It is 12,902 BCE. The chambers beneath the pyramids will be sealed like a tomb.

180

Equipment and records will remain here along with the corpses of the many who died in the weeks and months following the evacuation. Most of those were accidental victims of residual radiation poisoning.

A massive androsphinx has been placed nearby to ceremonially watch over the site. A sentry for the dead. Such is the custom of their people.

Grief and depression sweep over the survivors like a plague.

At night, they can see Mars burning.

The land is lava. And the sea has dissipated many miles into the atmosphere, spinning in iridescent granules of ice like the rings of Saturn.

If it weren't for the apocalypse that it represented and the complete annihilation of their home and their people, the spectacle might actually be beautiful.

10,333 BC.

Sehkmet returns.

A large remnant of the prodigal molten planet has attained a radical and perilous orbit within the solar system. And now it careens on a path between the Earth and her moon.

Astronomers predicted centuries ago that this day would come. The remnant will miss, but already it has created a gravitational distortion that nudges the Equator out of torque.

The global climate will soon change.

Devastation will follow.

10,274 BC.

The pyramids will be used to correct at least part of the planet's wobble. Many of them have now been built at locations corresponding to the Earth's normal gravitational geometry.

They can slow down the precession. But they cannot stop it outright. A meteorological catastrophe will occur.

Once again, the people prepare for survival.

But this time they cannot flee to the heavens. So they go below.

Some establish colonies deep within the Charybdis abyssal of the Mediterranean Sea. Others find similar trenches beneath the ice of the Antarctic or in the warm waters of the Caribbean.

Missionaries will remain for a time on the island of Crete. They will observe the aborigines to ensure that they can weather the coming Ice Age.

The indigenous peoples are smart and resourceful.

Remarkably, some already seem to sense intuitively that a terrible event is about to take place. This is of great interest to the scientists. And will merit further study.

Some of these intuitives will be selected for genetic evaluation. And possible enhancement.

10,125 BC

Darkness falls over the Earth. The sky scintillates in the artificial night with lightning storms that rage for a decade.

The aborigines migrate. But the physical toll of the event has been great and terrible. Less than ten thousand of them remain on the planet. They find livable climates in the areas around the global pyramids. Their positions have been synchronized with the orbiting space stations, which have mapped the Earth's electro-magnetic field.

The pyramids have been adapted to pull heat from the planet's core. They give light and warmth and punch great holes in the turbid atmosphere, opening their respective regions to the sun.

Even as the rest of the planet sleeps in a glacial blanket of ice and snow a quarter mile thick, the aborigines around the pyramids thrive. Their crops grow, while they and their livestock multiply.

846 BC.

Much of the ice has long ago melted.

The Earth has returned to balance.

Designated plants and animals have been genetically modified to resist disease and environmental changes.

The aborigine cultures advance at an exceptional rate, but something is not quite right.

There has been an unquantifiable, non-specific intrusion on the planet. It is not the scientists who detect the breach. But the empaths.

They call it a "polarized rip" in the planet's spiritual balance.

804 BC.

In less than a generation, the aborigines have changed.

At first, a virus is suspected. But that has proven not to be the case.

They have become bellicose and ambitious. Cruel and rapacious. Their cunning for mischief far exceeds their former benevolence.

Great wars break out as the tribes develop a sudden and irrational desire to conquer lands. A fearsome warrior has emerged and sweeps through the East with a dreadnought army.

His reign is terrible. And growing.

The Sins of Angels

The descendents of the Mars survivors vote to leave this world. And return to their still-smoldering ancestral home.

Such is the breadth of their fear.

Foundries and mines, both on the Earth and the moon, churn out the materials needed to withstand the heat and pressure they will encounter on Mars.

Orbiting hydrogen generators will produce the fuel for the trip, which with new technology will take less than seven hours even though Mars is now at the apogee of its elliptical orbit some 400-million miles away.

An armada of giant transport ships now rings the Earth, ready to ferry home four and a half million people.

An expeditionary force has already been to the planet and has determined that the best place to return is the same place as the departure. The Cydonia Plateau.

The people of Mars will monitor the evolution of the aborigines. From a safe distance.

800 BC.

The world pauses to watch as thousands of lights rise from the oceans and the great cities.

The exodus lasts for six days and nights.

In every tongue of every land, people write of this. Many of their shamans predicted this day would come.

Just before the land runs red with blood.

At that instant, the light released Jerry.

He fell with a hard thud onto the stone floor of the chamber.

184

He could see the shining eyes of every one of the golden sphinxes staring at him, just before he passed out.

CHAPTER THIRTY

"Did you see anything there that caught your eye?"

When he came to, he was lying splayed out awkwardly in the backseat of a Mercedes Maybach limousine. It did not feel like it was moving.

A small magnetic lamp on a table at the far side of the vast compartment softly lit up the interior of the limo.

The windows were darkly tinted and rolled up, making it impossible to see outside.

"Hello?" he said weakly. "Is anybody there?"

A moment later, the limo gently glided forward. As it drove, the partition between him and the driver lowered an inch or two.

"We'll be at the hotel momentarily, Dr. Harris. If you're hungry or thirsty there's a wet bar on your left."

With that, the window slid back up.

Jerry was still woozy and slightly disoriented from the experience in the repository. He was still trying to collect his thoughts when the limo pulled to a stop. A second later, the door opened.

Outside, holding the door handle stood a very tall man, dressed head to toe in black. His eyes literally shone in the darkness like a nocturnal animal's.

"Your room is in your wife's name, doctor."

"My room?"

"Yes."

"Where am I?" Jerry asked as he climbed slowly out of the car.

"You're at the Ritz Carlton Buckhead. The concierge will take care of you. Do you need any further assistance?"

"No, no, I don't think so. Who are you?"

"I am the driver, sir. Are you strong enough to walk on your own?"

"Yes, I'm fine, I think. Where's the old man?"

"He's where he should be, Dr. Harris," the driver said, helping him out of the limousine. "Be well."

With that, he quickly got back into the car and drove off into the night. *Night?* Jerry suddenly realized that he had no idea how long he had been unconscious.

Or for that matter, how long he'd been in the cavern beneath the Pentacle.

As he walked to the lobby, he noticed the long line of cabs parked in front of the hotel. The engines were all idle. In each of them, the driver was reclined in his seat, sound asleep.

He looked at his watch. The second hand was not moving. But according to a giant grandfather clock beside the concierge's table the time was nearly four o'clock AM.

Before Jerry could open his mouth, the concierge had emerged from behind the desk to greet him.

"Good morning, Dr. Harris," he said, cheerfully. "I'll take you to your room."

The "room" turned out to be a palatial suite one floor below the penthouse. It had a chef's kitchen, a marble bathroom, a sauna, a baby grand piano, two sitting rooms and a mezzanine balcony with a million dollar view of the city.

"Jerry?" a voice called groggily from the bedroom down the hall. "Is that you?"

It was his wife, Jackie.

Jerry rushed to the bedroom. His wife was still crawling out of an undulating ocean of imported silk sheets and Egyptian cotton blankets.

"Sweetie," she said with a tired smile. "What happened?"

He wasn't completely sure himself. He just knew two things for certain: that they were both okay and that Ed Lee wasn't crazy after all.

"What a nice surprise, honey." Jackie whispered as Jerry held her in his arms. She looked across the bedroom, craning her head so that she could see the rest of the suite. "My God, this room must have cost a ton. I'm sorry I fell asleep. Must have been those Tylenol-3's I popped before lunch. The limo driver told me you would be late. I think. God, I can barely remember anything after those Coronas."

Out of habit, she sleepily tried to smooth down the bed hair spiking awkwardly from her head. He couldn't help but smile at her.

"By the way, when *did* I fall asleep?" she groaned.

"At the shop," her husband answered. "You were talking to the owner's wife."

"Oh, yeah," she said quietly. "My God, I must have looked like one of those drunk ladies who lunch. I hope you made a good excuse for me."

"Yeah… I just told her you were one of those drunk ladies who lunch."

"Mmmm, good," she grinned dreamily. "From what I can remember it seems like they had a lot of nice stuff at that store. Did you see anything there that caught your eye?"

"A couple things," Jerry said softly. "You get some rest now."

"Mmmm," she purred again as she curled up in the sheets. "I could sleep for a week. You coming to bed?"

"In a minute. I'm really not sleepy."

"Okay. I'll save your place."

"Thanks," he chuckled. "Now, go to sleep."

CHAPTER THIRTY-ONE

"His muscles ached down to the cells."

Jerry Harris poured himself a generous snifter of fifty year-old Cognac and walked upstairs to the mezzanine. He pulled a leather club chair up to the giant picture window and sat down wearily. It was a beautiful morning.

The sun was just beginning to rise in a luminous saffron tide above the horizon.

He could not believe how many trees there were in this city.

Indeed, just beyond the sundial shadows of the skyscrapers, the metro area was a forest.

Deeply green. Like the emerald coast.

Of Mars.

Jerry awoke a few hours later to his wife singing.

He had fallen asleep in the club chair. A good and deep sleep that had let him drift in the dreamless vacuum of exhaustion.

Jackie was wheeling a silver breakfast tray to the sitting area below the balcony. He could smell eggs Benedict and vanilla rum cinnamon toast.

"Honey, you awake?" Jackie called.

"Yeah," Jerry said, rousing himself from the chair. "What time is it?"

"Time to eat!" his wife called laughing. "I'm hungry."

"You're in awfully good spirits this morning," he said as he walked down the circular staircase.

"I know. I can hardly believe it myself."

"You look good. I mean, you always look good, but uh…"

"Uh huh. C'mon, take your foot out of your mouth. Leave some room for your breakfast."

"You know what I mean."

"I feel good, doc," Jackie smiled. "Really good. So good, I'm going to get checked out later today, just to make sure something's not wrong."

"What, are you into contrarian medicine now? Maybe you're just feeling better, dear."

"I know it sounds stupid," she laughed, shaking her head.

"It's possible that your meds are giving you some kind of bi-polar high, Jack. But I sincerely doubt that."

"I know it's not that," she said ladling out the eggs with a Tiffany serving spoon. "But I do feel different. And I do feel better."

189

After eating breakfast, Jerry checked with the concierge and learned that the room was theirs for as long as they wanted it. The bill would be settled by an anonymous third party as a gift, and their tab was unlimited.

He decided they would stay for a few days and enjoy the rest of their vacation here. It would give him a chance to rest and reflect on the bizarre events at the Pentacle.

The whole episode had left him enervated and confused.

And while his wife went up to the roof to do some laps in the VIP pool, he lay down and went to sleep again, completely drained.

Whatever had truly happened in that cavern beneath the store had taken a toll on him physically.

The liquid light had attached to his body and his mind like a giant synapse. He wasn't just watching the events unfold in the disembodied third person. He was feeling them in the first. Experiencing them.

The terror of Sekhmet.

The elation of the escape.

The resolve of the return.

In his sleep, he felt these emotions even more vividly and tangibly than before.

His eyes were actually open as he watched the pictures replay over and over in his dreaming. He was sweating and his heart was beating a furious fugue.

What he could see was uncanny. The scenes were actually starting to meld like transparencies being stacked on top of one another.

Nonetheless, he could discern each one individually.

Simultaneously.

The channels were playing all at once.

He awoke panting and soaked with sweat. His eyes were bloodshot, and his muscles ached down to the cells. He was nearly too weak to stand, almost as though he were suffering from acute anemia.

His vision was slightly blurred, but he noticed two notes on the table next to the bed. One was from his wife, who had gone to a private fashion show and champagne brunch being held at the hotel.

The other was simply one word. It was handwritten on letterhead from the Pentacle.

"Eat."

A plate of scones like the ones his wife had eaten was sitting on a tray on the nightstand. He had no appetite, and he was starting to get profoundly nauseous.

But something in his mind told him to obey the note. He swore it was the old man's voice. But he was growing too faint to care.

He took a bite. And fell back into a deep, comatose sleep.

"Thirty-six more hours, and you would have died."

It was the old man's voice again. But this time, Jerry heard it clearly. He was still asleep, but he followed the voice back to consciousness, the way a disoriented diver follows the bubbles back to the surface of the water.

"You were suffering from radiation sickness. Now, you live as you will."

191

CHAPTER THIRTY-TWO

"They are such things as few men have ever seen."

Jerry awoke with a start, gasping for breath and looking around the room for the old man. But he was alone.

Less than an hour had gone by since he had passed out, but suddenly he found himself full of strength and vigor. He was completely renewed.

"The scones," he thought, as he looked to the nightstand.

But the tray was gone.

He bounded out of the bed, calling for Jackie. But she was still downstairs at the champagne brunch.

Then something on the piano caught his eye. He could read the card in front of it from across the room.

"Thrice gifted."

It was an extraordinary Edison Gramophone with a colorfully painted Morning Glory horn. It appeared to be brand new, but it had to be more than a hundred years old.

Lined up in front of it were nine waxen cylinders.

And a journal.

Jerry opened the card.

"You have crossed the gate into the new world, brother. Welcome. Again. As you now know, the wonders here are many. Read the journal. Then play the discs in order. They are such things as few men have ever seen or heard. And I now give them to you. We shall meet again. When it is time."

Jerry grabbed the journal and sat down on the piano stool. His fingers caressed the embossed lettering on the leather binding. Unlike the gramophone, the book was in terrible condition.

The cover was torn, dirty and water-stained. But when he unbuttoned it, he discovered that the pages were remarkably well preserved. And the writing was legible enough to read, despite its fancy Victorian script.

"The Journal of Sir Edmund Deloit Philips Skyers, MBE. "

CHAPTER THIRTY-THREE
"Their armor dripped as though they had waded through swamps of gore."

The Journal.

March 19th, 1897:

Having taken ill with a sudden and pernicious bout of altitude sickness, I am forced rather against my will to recuperate in the base camp beneath the summit of El'brus. It is a Spartan affair with few amenities and accommodations, mostly a roaring fire, and a few clean beds. But there is an abundance of dilaudid and brandy. And the surgeon, a man called Ali Rhakmir Ali, is exemplar. Battle-forged on the front lines of the Indian skirmishes, he is expert at improvising

193

medicinal recipes that, not surprisingly, rely heavily on an abundance of dilaudid and brandy.

Indeed, the bouts of nausea and bronchial distress have subsided, though my handwriting still withers to a penurious scrawl after only a few moments, a symptom of the palsy that persists on my right side. The surgeon, however, says that I shall make a complete recovery upon returning to the oxygen-rich environs of the sea's level.

Dr. Gilmer Fitzwater of the London Geological Society has promised to take my spikes in his bag for the final assault, so that I too might be able to leave my footprints in the ice, albeit in absentia. It is a touching gesture from a gallant fellow worthy of his place in the company of those ascending the very pinnacle of the world.

They are now in their third day, having weathered a vicious ice storm that sent many of the sherpas hurrying frantically back to camp with dire prognostications as to the viability of the climb. But in my estimation, Admiral Winston Falstaff is certain to be aware of the vicissitudes of the weather. An honorably retired commander of Her Majesty's Navy, he has sailed vessels in every clime imaginable and under every possible condition. He himself told us on the eve of the ascent that braggadocio has no place at the helm of any adventure, let alone one perched three nautical miles heavenward in permafrost as old as the Earth itself.

March 20th:

I continue to hear thunder. At first I thought I might be delirious, as there are no clouds in the sky. But the very ground shakes in the concussion, and once again the sherpas are chattering excitedly. I overheard the surgeon speaking with them in their native tongue, and I am certain I heard him use the words nitrogen and glycerin. It may be that Falstaff's party is using explosives to dislodge impassable ridges of ice and snow. If that is the case, the team may be trying to pick up its pace. Perhaps, they sense that poor weather is imminent, though from where we sit, the sky remains as richly blue as the Queen's good china.

March 21st:

It is the first day of spring, and for the first time since my infirmity that I have seen Falstaff's team! The admiral left his telescope behind on the summit, and today the surgeon and I assembled it on a tripod. After some time, we managed to espy the group amid the rocks and promontories that pock the side of the mountain's face. Extraordinary! Sitting beneath a small pile of wonderfully warm lama hides, I celebrated with the surgeon, sharing a piping hot kettle of tea and sweet cakes that I had secreted deep in the bottom of my back pack.

It was here the surgeon proceeded to tell me the most marvelous story, though he insisted it was not a story at all, but rather an historical account passed on through the ages by the local villagers.

It turns out that he himself is of Armenian parentage and something of an esoteric exegete. A scholarly prodigy as a youth, he grew restless at the age of fourteen and managed to talk himself onto a French whaling ship as an apprentice.

As such, he carved over the years a remarkable scrimshaw of colorful adventures that led him to nearly every major port in the world, many battlefields, and ultimately here to the summit with the rest of us. But, queerly, unlike the rest of us, he was not interested in climbing to the top. It appears to me that he is here doing some sort of personal research.

He profoundly enjoys speaking with the sherpas about the local lore and legend. He takes copious notes and draws fastidious diagrams and maps. Over these, he would occasionally lay a translucent onion paper, adorned with the intersection of every imaginable sort of number and symbol of Mathematica. I asked him to explain this bizarre calculus.

He called it a "perfect cube."

It was then that I suspected that Ali Rhakmir Ali might be more metaphysician than actual physician. If that were indeed the case, he is clearly well beyond the dark matriculations of Aleister Crowley and his lugubrious ilk, they who spend more time smoking opium and conjuring specious apparitions than true occulted empiricism.

All that be as it may, Dr. Ali was nonetheless a fascinating and affable chap, who held me spellbound for the remainder of the afternoon.

I asked him if he would not mind committing his voice to the Edison Dictaphone that the team had brought along to chronicle the various stages of the expedition. Dr. Ali readily agreed and spoke with

his clear and exquisitely robust Gaelic accent. Though the oaken housing cracked in the cold and rarified air, the reproducing machine worked exceedingly well. Dr. Ali's story took eight of the waxen cylinders to complete. However, as I am afraid that some will not survive the journey back down the mountain, I will spend the night faithfully transcribing their contents.

Cylinder One.

(The voice of Dr. Ali)

The elders wore bearskin parkas to protect themselves from the arctic cold that swirled at the base of the Caucasus Mountains. Each of them had slain at least one giant Cossack Bear hand-to-hand in their youth with a blade or maul, and the thick fur coats were the unchallengeable proof of their manhood and bravery.

They used the trophies' heads for hoods, and from a distance in the blizzard they looked like a fearsome pack of actual bears. They moved in a slow lumbering procession, one behind the other, appertaining to their rank. Their footsteps crunched audibly, like peanut husks, in the snow and led to a giant white tent that was only discernable against the landscape by a small tornado of black smoke pouring through an opening in its roof. This was the tent of the High Khan of Northern Abyssinia. Khii Al Muton Achbar. The general of all the Khans.

He sat at the head of the feast wrapped in a white pelt with soft gray stripes, his face completely enshrouded by the hollowed head of a Snow Tiger. The predator's long yellow fangs snugly traced the edge of the Khan's temples and touched the opposing fangs of its lower jaw, the teeth of which rested across the front of his neck like a piece of savage jewelry. Indeed, he often laughed that with one wrong move the animal's spirit would cut his throat in revenge.

To the Khans and Mongolian warlords, gold and gemstones, while important to horde and ransom, were still the trinkets of soft-handed merchants and women. And neither was needed here. But the skins and the teeth and the heads of the beasts made for their own wealth of legends and stories to be told again and again, each time richer in detail than the last.

A giant fire fed the inside of the tent with heat so intense that many of the men took off their clothes and roamed naked through the gathering. The walls were draped with plush and beautiful rugs of silk and wool. And even more of these were piled high on the lama skins and reindeer pelts on the ground. The hides were so thick that the cold of the ice and snow beneath them could not seep through, even as the revelers danced and wrestled atop them. It was here that they ate until their bellies were swollen with flank steaks and cheese and wine. The last of the battle stocks.

The other soldiers, whose camps stretched for as far as the eye could see, were ordered by their sergeants to eat their animals. This was the most saturnine ritual of war. The last supper.

By sunset the next day, there would be only one of two realities. Victory or defeat. Life or death. If they lived, they would ride home on the beasts of their enemies.

The armies of the Khans, whose green and red banners were feared from the Far East through Europe to the tip of Africa, were now decimated and ruined. Perhaps a million of their men lay buried beneath their feet in these oceanic drifts of snow. Another ten million had been slaughtered in different parts of the country in the long generation of war that had ushered in the 314th year of the Rat.

That was the year the oracles had all foreseen the same harbingers and prophesied what they had called the "Dawn of the Deity."

Cylinder Two.

Sanji Rondu was the elder priest at the Hindu Temple of Rats in the city of Kirjath-Baal. He had come to the temple as a small boy, orphaned by plague. The rats adopted him and lay food at his feet, or so he was told by the holy men who had found him. He was small and wiry, with a quick wit, not unlike the rodents that swarmed at his feet. Over the years, his black hair grew long and straight, down to his ankles. And as he slept, it often covered his entire body, giving him the appearance of a very large rat, especially as the others curled against him when the colony slept.

One morning, the monks arrived to find that the boy and the rats had disappeared deep into the labyrinthine maze of the shrine. He was gone for a week, and the priests were preparing to perform the ritual of the dead for him when he suddenly emerged, wet and shaking with fever.

He spoke in a strange tongue that no man understood, but whose words seemed to gather the rats to his feet. From that day forth, he lived only as a visitor among men.

Over the years, his legend grew. Many flocked to see the curious boy who could speak to rats. The faithful began to amass at the temple in huge numbers. And once a day at dusk, Sanji would crawl from the dark stones timidly as the crowd fed him the same way they fed the rats, with pinches of grain and tiny saucers of warm goat's milk.

As he grew older, Sanji would come to have visions.

And on special days, he would ring the ancient iron gong to announce his portents. To the rats. He was completely indifferent to the crowds who would assemble as well. But his accuracy was inerrant, and people of every caste would huddle close together, listening to his every word.

He too had seen the fateful omens. They so distressed him that he would later pluck out his own eyes, believing that it was his sight that had brought the evil forth.

He sat now in the tent of the High Khan, warming his face in the glow of the fire, flaring his nostrils wide at the aroma of the meat cooking on the spit. He licked his dry lips and counted the drops of fat as they hissed in the flame and turned into a delicious, almost edible, smoke. Such was his ravenous hunger. And that of the men around him.

The journey from Kirjath-Baal to the war camp had taken three weeks. The weather changed on the trip as though the very seasons had, from arid heat to monsoon rains to frigid cold. The air here was thin, and the old priest had trouble breathing. His lungs wheezed like a punctured billows, and at night, he was given his own tent, as no one could sleep with him for the noise.

But the High Khan had asked for him by name upon hearing of his many auguries and for his astonishing penance at having seen in advance what had now come to pass. But Sanji Randu also knew in advance that the Khans would summon him. The rats had told him.

Indeed, when the soldiers had arrived to escort him, he was standing in front of the temple waiting for them. In the middle of a dark rippling sea of his brethren.

At the temple, he slept with them, ate with them, bathed with them, and prayed with them. On the trip, he could take only a few, the soldiers warned, and the best of these he kept in the pockets of his robe.

He had chosen Old Kalil first. His wisdom was renowned and he was much revered. The two had journeyed together far in days. They were a strange pair and yet perfectly matched with an enviable fellowship that few married couples could claim.

One was fat. The other was thin. One slept at night. The other by day.

But both labored as they breathed. And Old Kalil's teeth were as bad as the priest's own. The rat's had grown too long to bite with. The priest's too short.

Nevertheless, Old Sanji would chew on stalks of wheat or kernels of corn and rice, so that he could feed the rat through a special straw that he had carved and hollowed from the wither bone of a cat. It was their little joke. The spirit of the cat would no doubt be upset by his karma.

Together they would laugh at this as the priest gently filed down the old rat's teeth to keep him from impaling himself.

In exchange, Old Kalil would lie awake and guard Old Sanji from his breast pocket while he slept, keeping scorpions and enemies at bay, though the latter were far fewer than the former.

For his strength and courage, Tanitkaa also was invited to journey with them. He was a large rat with black and white spots and a thick fleshy tail about a foot long. He weighed at least five pounds, and his teeth were pure white, hard as rock and sharp as broken glass.

He was a cat killer and had often protected the warren from even larger predators, like dogs, or pythons, or owls. He was well loved and had fathered hundreds of pups in his two years at the temple. All of them were big, fierce and spotted as well.

If a warrior were needed on this journey, Sanji wanted Tanitkaa over any of the Khan's battle guard.

Rajiv the Quick had invited himself, apropos of one so very curious and cunning. He too was something of a prophet to his brethren. He had notched the walls inside the temple with teeth-marks, precisely three, one above the other that led to an inner chamber.

The reason for this was not known until the Day of the Deity.

The rats that followed their direction had survived the collapse of the temple.

Of course, several other rats were brought along on the trip as concubines or servants. These Sanji kept in cages by day. But in spite of their humbler station, they too were allowed to roam free in the tent at night.

None of them, however, was permitted into the white tent of the Khans. Lest they become food in the frenzy of the feast.

The Khans were not Hindus and believed in rats only as substitutes for rabbits over the fire.

Cylinder Three.

As he sat face to the warm flames, Sanji could not help but remember that terrible Sunday. It was ironic, that even after blinding himself the memory of that day grew clearer and clearer than the actual vision of it ever was.

In pitiful futility, he had pushed the wooden ram hard, over and over, into the gong to rouse the soldiers for the war that was mere moments away. But it was already far too late.

At first, through the morning fog, all the sentries could see was something shining in the distance, like a meteor on fire. It tricked the eye. It was clearly far away yet appeared close enough to touch. The captain of the guard used an amber lens to shield the glare and could now see that beneath the glinting light, stood a gargantuan African elephant whose tusks scraped the ground as he walked. He wore a mail of gleaming metal. And as the fog lifted, a train of other elephants, a mile long, could be seen. As they marched forward, the ground shook.

There was an awful noise that to all sounded like it came from the sky. And then came the sound of crashing stone, as the elephants lay siege to the wall that surrounded the city. And as the buttresses and turrets collapsed each upon the other, the soldiers of the shining light pulled their bronze weapons and descended upon the people with a sadistic fury.

The smell of them was putrescent, and their armor dripped as though they had waded through swamps of gore. Their swords were pitted and rusted with blood. They were not particularly skillful with their blades. Just ruthless and efficient.

They moved through the crowd, gathering hostages in large wailing hordes to watch as they hacked off the arms, hands, legs and heads of the soldiers they had captured. Then they turned and did the same to the crowd, including the women and children. Thousands of them. In minutes, the entire city was left literally crawling on its belly in endless trails of blood and agony.

The only ones to escape the massacre that day were the messengers dispatched to warn the other Khans of their impending fate. And, of course, Sanji Randu, the seer of doom, who had retreated with his rats deep within the temple. He was the only man seated here in the tent of the High Khan who had actually lived through the Dawn of the Deity.

The deity called Jibril.

Cylinder Four.

Jibril was an angel. And a warlord. A Berserker of many lands. In many ages.

But the Earth was not his domain, and he had to affect the guises of many over the centuries to escape the notice of one. His older brother.

Apollyon. But Jibril always revealed himself. Eventually. By the sheer avarice of his mayhem.

His footsteps could be found in the blood of continents. Wherever he washed his hands, the water ran red with death and churned with the burning fomentation of madness and violence.

He was a Holy Warrior. And to him, man was an unholy abomination.

But Jibril was not without sin. He had many vices that God turned a blind eye to. The biggest of these was his strange and insatiate infatuation with gold. He especially coveted the fine metal crafted by Roman artisans. Its purity reflected the color of his eyes.

For an angel, it is said, gold is easy to find buried in the rock. It revealed itself beneath the stone with a luminosity not unlike patches of marigold in a field of deep green grass. It could also be made slowly with base metals in a complicated alchemy of words. But it was far easier to simply purloin and plunder by the wagonload.

His armor was hammered three inches thick with it. The breastplate took four burly men to heft into place. Heavy pins of polished silver were pushed through its hinges; and in the sunlight, soldiers had to shield their eyes or risk having their retinas permanently bleached by its radiance.

Jibril liked to fight with two bronze swords. One was a broadsword that weighed more than one hundred pounds. The other was smaller and was used with the adroitness of a shield. A shield that could kill quick as a cobra strike. Men, in many languages, and in many times, called the two swords by the same name.

The Father and The Son.

Jibril stood over eleven feet tall, with deep red skin that mimicked the patina of fine rust. His hands were immense and spanned the waist of a regular-sized man. He was the most fearsome and imposing of God's angels.

Except for size, there was no overt difference between the average angel and the average man. At least not in this dimension. Still, the angels possessed gifts that men did not. To them, the earth was a place to wear corporeality the way a whore wears perfume. It was burlesque and bizarre. Few ever came here for more than a tourist's glimpse of this zoo. But others stayed forever. Jibril was the worst of the latter.

He embraced and indulged the easy perquisites of divinity. He especially enjoyed the ability to infect humans with his spirit, to do his bidding with alacrity and without question. But moreover, he preferred to grow them, rather like mushrooms, from the dirt of the grave. These were his loyal progeny, the bellicose children of war.

Jibril saw war as a way to hasten man's journey to the foot of God. In his mind, he was, after all, a minister. A minister of death. An itinerant evangelist, who wielded the will of God in his two hands. To any angel, it would be dirty work. But fortunate was Jibril and, in his mind, much blessed, that he loved his job and was committed to it. Eternally.

However, his prowess of mind was not nearly as impressive as that of his body. He was by no means extraordinarily intelligent. Even as men go. Over the epochs, many human generals had confronted his mighty legions and cornered them into retreat. Indeed, a few had struck what they thought were mortal blows directly upon him.

206

The Sins of Angels

And while it is true, that angels are immortal, they are not impervious to the laws of life and death that govern mankind. That is why God warned them in no uncertain terms to steer far from man, with the admonishment that dishonor, too, is eternal.

Though angels could not die by the hand of a man, they could suffer. Long and pitifully. They could be felled in battle by this creature born of bone and sin. And healing could take centuries or millennia.

During this time, if another ambitious angel were of a mind to, he could send his wounded brother to purgatory. If he could find him.

Jibril, not unlike other angels who consorted in the dimension of man, was known to have hidden in stones or trees or bodies of water during forced quiescence.

But as a wounded angel got stronger, whatever object he had sought asylum in would begin to betray special properties not of this world. Such an object could heal or kill when touched. It could bring luck or disaster. Feast or famine. A shaman with an evolved third eye could discern this. Sometimes they could even trap the spirit with the right talisman. Or the right prayer.

To the right ears.

Cylinder Five.

Apollyon and his minions guarded their world jealously. And they listened for just such a prayer. If it were known that another angel had interloped and then fallen prey to the perils that lie between Heaven and

Earth, that angel would be captured and punished with imprisonment. Forever.

That was the law of Apollyon, who had greater powers over the Earth than any other. God had made him sovereign over this place, and not even Jibril was above Apollyon's law. Indeed, he feared it.

Jibril's horn of legend was real. It was made of a metal that no man had ever seen. Or touched. And before each battle, he would put it to his lips and blow. One note. Made of the music of misery and woe. It sounded like the screaming of worlds.

Whole forests would shake, and brave souls were filled with thoughts of flight and desertion from their comrades in arms. But there was nowhere to run.

His armies never numbered more than a few thousand. His soldierss were more or less human mules, sterile and strong, mindless and cruel. They were his seed. Propagating these divine beasts of burden was not against the law of God. But it was not His will. He looked upon them as hapless orphans and bastards, whose names would be lost to the Book of Life.

Jibril fathered his children in the way of all angels, through the anointing of his blood, not through sex and birth as humans know it.

Indeed, Jibril found the idea of copulating with a human repugnant. Not unlike bestiality, though there were many angels who enjoyed this act. After all, while angels could have congress with people, they could not with each other. That would be incestuous, and God strictly forbade it under penalty of eternal damnation.

208

The Sins of Angels

But for those angels who could quell their initial distaste, humans took on a strangely attractive quality. They were a queer and wanton species who screamed and writhed and laughed and cried during this savage dance-rite. Apollyon loved it. After all, it could be argued, he was the one who had started it.

To the other angels, men and women were disposable vessels in which to pour their salacious dross. They were immune to one another physically.

But spiritually, humans could be damaged by an angel's karma, or his *Icar*, the seeping plasma of his soul.

Humans called this pollution "bad seed." And Apollyon, sadly, was guilty of spreading it first. Thus was he the father of both good and evil, in a world that is, as his prophet Nietzsche correctly wrote, beyond good and evil.

Humans could not bear an angel's child. But they could bear the sins of their carnality. And there were seven of these carried individually, depending on the angel. Jealousy. Greed. Sloth. Gluttony. Lust. Vanity. Adultery.

Each one could be passed down through intercourse like a defective spiritual gene into any child the human might later bear.

In most of these offspring, the germs of good and evil sit within them in a dormant silence. But others are born as monster-children, drunk and insatiate with the karma that may have fermented for centuries in the blood of his or her ancestors. And worse still, sometimes these infected humans mate with one another, permuting new strains of vice and dissolution.

The Sins of Angels

These were the children for whom the seven deadly sins read like the Ten Commandments.

Apollyon spent many ages in celibate contrition before learning how to control his essence. He was careful now, but the damage had already been done and was made worse by the visitation of others like him. This explained his merciless vigilance in his domain.

But to Jibril, sexual consorting dirtied the ego of his divinity. He simply sought out newborn babies, whose mothers did not thank God for their good fortune at the time of their birth. He would then touch and infect the children with sleeping sickness in their cribs. That way, he could trick their souls into leaving, so that he might harvest their bodies later.

There, he would breathe ballast into their beings and rub his *Icar* into their flesh so that they would grow quickly into adult men or women. Their destinies existed only at his pleasure. And his pleasure was brutality and death.

They ate nothing. They dreamed nothing. They simply killed everything in sight.

Apollyon had many times petitioned God to condemn this atrocity, but a parliament of Jibril's defenders had prevailed, manipulating for their benefit God's own great disgust toward man.

Cylinder Six.

Long before the birth of Jesus Christ, Jibril rampaged through the Mountains of Outer Mongolia, far beyond the northern sea of Euxine and

210

the ridges of the far-flung Caucasus. His wars with the Asian battle-lords lasted decades. And the dynasties of the Mongols were now beaten.

Utterly.

But the last of the great Khans rallied them from annihilation. And when Jibril tried to finish them off as well, they in turn managed to push him back into the Urals.

But the price of their courage was great. Only the heaviest of snowstorms could obscure the permanent red ice that stained the summit. Its breadth and width grew with each passing season, and could be seen saliently from the assault camps in the valleys far below. The flags of their descendants would one day pay homage to this with a red circle in the middle of a white banner.

Year upon year, winter upon winter, the symphony of war echoed angrily in these mountains with the brisk terpsichorean of swordplay and the slow moan of dying. Soldiers had to fight past the frozen, mummified corpses of their comrades, men whose faces died screaming in a posthumous pantomime of fear. The soldiers could never beat back Jibril's army any farther than here, this place they called the Valley of Death.

Young boys were brought in to take their fathers' places on the front line, wed to steel and bronze before women and love.

That is why the tribes of the Khans were drying up. Their women were fertile; but they were barren of men. While still many years away, their defeat was nonetheless imminent. Eventually, messengers were sent with orders to prepare the women and children to flee their cities, if no word came soon after to reverse the fiat.

The Sins of Angels

The Khans conscripted a select team of assassins to kill the shining general of their unknown foe. Imams and ayatollahs, Hindus and Buddhist monks, had all prayed together for exactly one day and one night in the bitter cold that the warriors would prevail in this their greatest battle. Then, on the day after the Last Supper, the assassins gathered and stood in a line to be anointed on a stone altar facing the summit.

A giant cauldron of burning oil flared loudly against the wind as it swept in whistling sopranos from the farthest height of the mountain. The thick fur of their shrouds flapped steadily. Pin needle shards of ice pierced through their beards into their faces. But it was too cold to bleed from anything less than a mortal wound. This, all agreed, was a good day to die.

One after the other, the priests, led by Sanji Randu and his pocketsful of rats, moved down the line, taking great care to cover the soldiers with the thick pink smoke that poured out of the incense urns being carried behind them. And as they walked, they prayed in unison, albeit in different languages.

"Oh, One, who sleeps with his head upon the world, hear us. Protect thy brave and humble servants from the Golden King of Devils. Make their eyes even as the moon, seeing lights, in the unholy darkness. Take their hands, Ye Mighty, and silence for all ever The Father and The Son."

A week before this day, fifty scouts were dispatched to find Jibril's camp. Only two had returned, near death.

One had to bury himself in the snow for several hours, while Jibril's guards hunted for him, thrusting their pikes into the deep drifts to try and spear his body. When he finally escaped, his hands, feet, and legs from the knees down were numb and black with frost-bite. Nearly paralyzed, he had to crawl on his belly a half-mile to the camp.

The second scout was returning uninjured when he stumbled upon one of Jibril's soldiers, not a hundred yards from the Khans' tent. In less time than it takes to scream, he had lost an arm to a broadsword, but impaled his attacker through the neck with a dagger. He carried his severed arm back with him, for fear that if he left it behind, the ghouls who fought with the deity would take it. Along with his soul.

Before they died, each man reported that he had espied Jibril going into a cave, half a day's climb into the summit's western face. It was the first time anyone human had ever seen Jibril actually leave the battlefield and go some place without the company of his soldiers.

This is where the assassins were sent, with an escort of twenty thousand soldiers. Many died during the trek, after encountering the army's fiercest warriors, who formed a strong perimeter around the cave. Those who survived spoke of engaging both men and women, who fought naked in the snow, clad only in light armor.

Cylinder Seven.

Jibril's legion fought without words, and they fought without rest. In the cold air, heat rose off their heads in thin plumes of steam, such was the ceaseless fury of their labor; and they foamed in frothy patches of sweat on the skin like horses. Their eyes were glazed and empty as milk glass, and in the torchlight, they shone in strange colors, not unlike the

213

eyes of rogue dogs or wolves at night. But the armies of the Khans were no longer afraid of them.

In their minds, they themselves were already dead and thusly fought as hard and fierce as the dreadnoughts of Jibril. And on this day, the omens were with them. Sanji Randu had heard from Old Kalil that he would die on the first new moon of the year of the Dog, which was more than a decade away. That meant they would all be going home.

The soldiers cheered at this news and ran into battle screaming the names of their wives and mothers, so that they might hear them in their dreams and bear them up with hope. And so the last armies of the Khans and Mongolian warlords beat down the unholy host in bloody waves. They were invigorated with what they believed was God's blessing.

And God did bless them. By not lending a hand to Jibril.

One of the archers sent out to cover the right flank of Jibril's army was a young boy named Hussein. He had been raised to hunt in the Siberian tundra. His parents were boot-makers whose eyes were weak and useless beyond ten or fifteen feet.

He often thought of them in their thatched hut, sitting near the oil-lantern, stitching the skins together with bone needles and tanned leather strips. In better days, he would sit captivated by their toil; the boots would begin to take form in just a matter of hours; a day later they would be ready to wear. Even though they didn't charge much money to make them, the craftsmanship was nonetheless extraordinary, and the boots were known to last years. In fact, they had made the ones he was wearing now, and his feet were warm and dry because of it.

His parents sewed more from feel than sight and would have to hold the boots close to their eyes just to inspect them. Then, they would nod at one another and begin work on another pair of skins, celebrating with a cup of rose hips tea to sip and hold in their hands, warming their ancient, sinewy fingers, which were now as tough as the leather hides they stitched together.

When the boy's father was young, he could see a small fawn hiding in the trees a hundred yards away. But his eyes had grown weak with snow-blindness and cobbling. He and his wife could still plant crops, but over the years he began to rely more and more on his only son to bring back the reindeer and pheasant meat that would get them through the winter.

For many nights, when he had first arrived at the front, the boy cried with homesickness for his parents. But he had been gone two winters now, and he worried not for himself but about whether his mother and father would have enough to eat. Or whether they were even still alive.

Often when he cried, he wasn't even aware of it. But the other soldiers were. In wonderment, they would watch him weep a child's tears, as he fought with a man's rage. The more he cried, the harder he fought. And the harder they fought too. They called him the Baby General. And posting him on Jibril's flank was a supreme honor.

These soldiers were hand-picked by the Khans themselves to form the killing wall. It was their job to trap Jibril and his troops if they tried to escape. And the Baby General was given the rank of First Archer. The men did not question the appointment of a child as their commander. They all knew that there were no children here.

The archers could see the corona of Jibril's mail as he approached the crest of the ridge before them. They looked over in unison at the Baby General, who already stood poised to shoot. They expected to see tears freezing on his still-plump cheeks, but the boy's eyes were clear and focused with purpose.

He blew softly out the side of his mouth on his frozen fingers, and pulled hard on the bowstring. Like a virtuoso violinist, he could feel the catgut stretching in silent octaves to the place of perfect resonance and tension. Unconsciously, his free fingers gently traced the back edge of the arrow as he waited. He had quilled it himself with the prized feathers of a rare blue bird.

The arrow stayed anchored in its place and did not shake in his fingers despite the cold. The bow creaked like a plank on a ship as the tension gently increased. And as the boy released the arrow, he listened to the string vibrate near his ear, as though he had plucked a perfect note on a harp.

He had heard this sound a thousand times before and could tell from the bitter music that the arrow had enough speed to carry it across the white expanse. Right into Jibril's ear.

His scream shook the rocks and sent loose drifts of snow roaring into the Valley of Death. But there were no more men there left to kill. They were all here now. All around Jibril. And closing in.

Cylinder Eight.

The thin air was a boon to the archers. It allowed the arrows to fly longer and faster than they might at sea level, six thousand feet below them.

Soon, the air was whistling with a torrent of arrows freeing themselves from the Khans' killing wall.

The only man left standing in the barrage was no man at all. Jibril was on foot, and arrows protruded from every part of his body left exposed by his armor, including his face.

Men say that he did not flee on foot. They say he rose up on a comet tail of light that shot deep into the cave where the scouts had seen him retreat before.

When the gore was finished and the last of the ghouls lay slaughtered and writhing by decapitation, the Baby General walked to the spot where his arrow had found Jibril's ear. There were holes with steam rising furiously out of them like geysers.

The boy put his hands over the steam and instantly felt them grow strong and warm. He knew there was magic here. He opened his goatskin bag and scraped several handfuls of melting snow into it. He would take it home. To wash away the blindness in the eyes of his mother and father.

Twelve assassins had made it into Jibril's cave, and they crouched in wait. And wonder. The walls were smooth and translucent with polished quartz.

Beautiful gold torchiers shaped in the form of cupped hands illuminated the deep expanse of the cave. Around a corner, a giant forge had been constructed, still hot with cooling rivers of molten gold. The assassins surmised that the smiths had probably not too long ago been forced to take up arms and join the desperate battle being waged outside.

Together they crept silently, like a pride of lions stalking some strange new beast in its own lair.

The Sins of Angels

The assassins were swathed in white cloth that hugged their bodies and clung tight to their muscles. They spoke with hand signals and gestures with the eyes. The leader among them carried no weapon at all, for he was his own weapon.

He could kill with a finger thrust through the eye or four fingers through the chest and heart. He was a tall thin man of dark skin, gristle, and nails thick as a falcon's talons.

He wore a leather mask over his face and a hood over his head, so that only his eyes could be seen. The slow-blinking eyes of a predator. The kind that could lay in wait for days beneath sand or water for the one instant it would take to kill its prey.

He ordered his men to extinguish the flames in the torches, so that only the hot, golden glow of the forge could be seen faintly at the deepest expanse of the cave. The assassins lay in wait in the dimness, like vipers in a grain basket.

Suddenly, a thick fog flooded the cave like a blast of steam. Then it settled, gently undulating with placid waves at its height, like the soft wake of a canoe on still water.

Beneath the surface, it was almost impossible to see what was directly in front of you. Then came the screams. Slowly. One after another. They were not screams of fear, but of alarm and warning, as something in the mist preyed upon the assassins

The leader counted eleven and knew that he was the last man. But that he was not alone. He held his breath in the way his *Sifu* had taught him as a boy. And he listened.

He could hear the embers of the forge crackling from far within the cave, whispering softly as the fog hissed against the fire pulsating in gentle bursts from the glowing wood.

He listened even harder and heard something that did not belong.

The fog itself.

He could not hear it so much as feel it beat almost imperceptibly against his eardrums. The pulse grew closer, but the assassin stayed still as stone, channeling his *chi*, so that his heart beat slow as an elephant's and as soft as a butterfly's. His eyes remained open like a lizard's, and he shifted them slowly to the left and the right. Up and down.

And with infinite suddenness, he watched as a pair of eyes materialized before him. The eyes seemed made of the very mist from which they came, and they searched for just an instant, until they found the assassin's.

But in that instant, the assassin pushed his hands like spears into the eyes. The warm wetness of the aqueous humor spilled over his fingertips as the phantom took form. Screaming.

The assassin would later tell the High Khan that the demon stood as tall as a bull camel and had shoulders like an ox. As he screamed, he turned to blood. Black blood. The kind found in the cadavers of the diseased. It pooled in a perfect circle at his feet then it poured downward through the rock floor of the cave, though there was no hole through which it could possibly flow.

And as the last of it disappeared, the smooth, quartz walls cracked into bits that revealed hidden chambers. In one of these, the assassin found a simple horn shaped of a silvery metal he had never seen. Behind another, he found the mail of gold.

The Journal.

Upon review of the story as told by Dr. Ali, I have begun to wonder whether he believes that the very ice upon which our camp sits is the same as the battlefield in the tale of the Khans versus the angel Jibril, or Gabriel as he is called in the King James Christian Bible.

An absurd conclusion, I am sure. However, just this evening, I espied the doctor setting off with a lantern and his backpack, and what appeared to be his curious map of numbers.

He has yet to return, despite the fact that it is now completely dark outside.

I will soon suspend my writing for the evening, as the thunderous explosions from the high ridge have gotten louder and more frequent, unsettling my concentration.

Also, the sherpas have begun running about again, talking in their frightened gibberish.

Many of them appear ready to leave the plateau, regardless of the fact that it is nightfall. I can see their torches moving about in the darkness outside the tent, like a swarm of scared candle flies.

Another blast.

This one is different and much larger than any of the others preceding it. The ground has begun to shake violently as though the earth itself is quaking. I can hear what seems absurdly to be a distant locomotive.

I shall now activate the Dictaphone to capture the sound on wax.

If I can.

As I write, I am also speaking out loud, actually yelling above the growing din. It is unlike anything I can describe with words. It is getting closer, and I am now afraid that General Falstaff and his team have been consumed by it.

I also am afraid that the base camp is in grave peril and that I too may not survive the catastrophe. My legs are still weak. I cannot run.

And the sherpas are gone.

Time may be dwindling quickly, so I have taken out my pocket watch to chronicle what may be my final moments.

Minute One.

I can actually feel the wind building as the sound in the distance grows, like a storm blowing in from a violent sea.

Minute Four.

I have seated myself next to a small escritoire outside the tent, with a lantern, the Dictaphone, my journal, and a large snifter of the surgeon's finest brandy, laced with a generous dose of dilaudid.

Between the Dictaphone and myself, one of us, I suspect, will capture this mystery for the tomorrows.

I know my death approaches.

Minute Nine.

The lantern has begun to flicker wildly in the gusting wind, and my hair is a dancing lunatic. The snow feels like flying sand, and I can barely see for wincing.

The temperature has dropped twenty degrees or more.

Perhaps it is the hydromorphone vexing my sensibilities, but there is now a strange glow coming from the summit, like the reflection of a blood-red moon.

Minute Thirteen.

The mountain, I fear, is coming to Muhammad.

Jerry Harris lay the journal back down on the piano. He placed the final cylinder on the machine and rewound the crank handle.

As he placed the needle in the grooves, the voice of Sir Edmund Deloit Philips Skyers came to life with a frightening scream. And even though it crackled with age, the integrity of the sound was startling.

Sir Edmund was shrieking at the top of his lungs above the deafening ambient roar. In between his words, was a noise that sounded truly like the end of the world.

And then there was a sound unlike anything he had ever heard. A terrific bellowing that grew in volume until the horn on the gramophone actually began to shake. Violently.

In the din, he could hear a scream. Or was it a thousand?

He could not tell.

Then there was silence. Except for the pounding of his heart.

CHAPTER THIRTY-FOUR

"A prayer with cupped hands floating at her fingertips."

It was the middle of the afternoon. But the room was dark and looted of light.

The black was almost liquid. Like it would stain the walls and pour out in a puddle if you lifted the shade or opened the door.

Emily's pupils were dilated wide like a saucer-eyed tarsier in the deepest tropical jungle at night on a new moon. Here she could immerse her eyesight into an opaque coalescence of shadows and atrophic melancholy. She did not want to see.

In the outside world, without her glasses her vision was blurred and sensitive, and the sunlight made her wince. But here, Emily could soak her eyes in the darkness, like two feet in a footbath.

And everyday when she came home from work, that's exactly what she did. She sat on the floor at the edge of her bed with her arms wrapped tightly around her knees. And her eyes wide open.

Listening to Billie.

Billie was the whore who lived inside her, the one with the eyes of a hawk that could spot a john in the darkness like twin military night scopes. She's the one who nagged at Emily and dragged her out of the room and into the street at all hours. Billie was the boss. And nightfall meant it was time to punch the clock.

And then there was light.

A spark in the ether.

Promethean. And precious. A prayer with cupped hands floating at the tip of her fingers.

Emily felt her eyes burn and well up with tears. She could hear Billie coming from the inside of her head.

Footsteps.

Running up the stairs like a stampede of one. Stumbling and frantic. Drawn to the blue flame of the butane lighter like a moth to a garden zapper.

That delicious light.

It made her mouth water and her pussy wet. That beautiful light at the end of the tunnel where the ancestors lived. That light in the paradise of blinding ecstasy.

Emily was paralyzed by it. But not Billie.

She crashed through the door so hard that she knocked Emily over. And it was Billie who got back up.

It was time for her to go into the light.

Emily had no voice in the matter. Literally.

She lost it when she was twelve. The same day she lost her virginity. To her father.

She could still see him through sleepy eyes standing over her bed in the dim light of her night lamp, casually rubbing Vaseline on the swollen glans of his penis.

The last Emily had heard of herself was the scream that tore open her soul and brought Billie up from the sludge of her lost innocence.

She got along with Billie tepidly. Like the silent partner in a corrupt company.

On the street, they called her Sniffles. The joke was that sniffles are what a hooker gets when she's full. And Billie was always full.

But nobody ever called her Sniffles to her face.

She carried an old barber's razor in the spandex above the crack of her ass. She was good with it. And quick. A lot of hookers carried the keloids to prove it.

The flame hissed as it burned in front of her face. Billie took a piece of shiny scrubbing mesh and gently laid it on the side of a beer can that had a hole punched in it.

She put the rock on top and caressed it with the fire. Then, she put her lips to the open top of the can and slowly sipped the smoke into her mouth.

The jinni was free. At last.

It slid like down her throat like a python and began to squeeze the oxygen out of her brain one molecule at a time. Emily quickly stepped aside and let Billie tumble back down the stairs, where she would lay quietly for the next half hour.

This was Emily's in-between time. And time was suddenly important. She had a secret that she was keeping from Billie. Emily had met a man.

A few months ago, she was scrubbing floors on the fifth floor of the county jail. Billie had gotten busted, but as usual, it was Emily who had to do the time. It was all right, though. Emily had her own cell, and the work was easy, at least compared to Billie sucking fifty dicks a night. With Emily's mouth.

The fifth floor was where the county put the crazies. Most were in foam rubber rooms or chained to poles in the corridor.

But for the really strung-out psychopathic super-predators, there were the slickers. Slickers were long, slender cages with a concrete floor, one to a man.

The maniacs paced or ran back and forth ceaselessly all day long, like dogs in a kennel run. The guards slid them their food through a slot in the bars, and there was a hole in the floor for them to go to the bathroom.

At the end of the day, the water hose would be turned on them. Full blast.

That was where Emily met Leon. He didn't speak either.

She knew his name from the warning sign on his cage. Everyday he watched her, stalking her with his eyes, as she went through her chores, his fingers choking the iron bars like the necks of everyone everywhere who had ever done him wrong.

She had watched him too, but kept her distance on the advice of the chief deputy.

But one afternoon, an inmate slashed his wrists around the corner of the cellblock. The deputy yelled at Emily not to move until he got back.

She was scared. People were yelling. Alarms were going off.

She felt herself retreating backwards, like she always did when she was frightened. She was hoping that Billie would come out and save her. But Billie never even moved.

That's when she felt Leon's fingers grab her arms tightly, the way they grabbed the iron bars. She wanted to scream, but couldn't.

With one arm around her waist, Leon pulled her flush against the bars. His strength was like nothing she had ever felt. It was isometric, stiff and unyielding.

With his free hand, he ripped down her pants and with a hard shove bent her forward. He pushed himself inside her and fucked her hard, grunting and gnashing, while the other inmates shrieked and screamed in vicarious lubricity.

Emily was too helpless to fight. She always was. Billie was the bully. Emily was the scared little girl. Even now, she could hear Billie stirring in her sleep.

To her the smell of sex was like spirits of ammonia.

But she didn't wake up.

She wasn't about to come out of hibernation over a fuck. They were still in jail. And Billie didn't like jail. She might kill somebody if she ever woke up in a cell. Including Emily. So Emily just closed her eyes and took it.

The way her father had taught her to.

The frantic screeching of the inmates sounded like the aviary at the zoo. When a cat gets in. That was the picture Emily superimposed over this. The zoo.

She dreamed that she had gotten too close to the lion cage, and now the king of the beasts held her in his giant paws while her silent grace begged his mercy.

The Sins of Angels

Fantasy had always been Emily's strongest ally.

"Throw the bitch over to me! Throw her my way!"
"No, nigga! Over here! It's my turn to pound that pussy, bitch!"
"I'ma rawhide that motherfucka!"
"You gonna ride or die tonight, bitch!"

Emily opened her eyes and saw the other prisoners masturbating wildly, their arms reaching out of their cells like flailing tentacles, hoping that Leon would throw her their way when he was through.

Just then, he groaned, and Emily felt his warm wetness move into hers. She could feel the muscles in his arms relax just a little. She thought about trying to break away, but she couldn't. She was just too scared.

As usual.

She was at his complete mercy. The maniacs on the cellblock were still shouting and trying to get Leon to toss her to them. But he didn't. He released his arm from its lock around her waist and set her free.

The next week, he got shipped off to the state prison. The one that housed the death row inmates. Leon Nia Jamal had killed two people in an armed robbery. Now it was his turn to die. But what the warden didn't know was that he had already escaped.

Two months after she got out of jail, Emily learned that she was pregnant. And that Leon was inside her. One trimester away from early parole.

But now she had to be careful. Billie had been asleep while they were in jail. And soon she would be storming back up the stairs. She could hide the baby for a little while, but after that, Billie would be getting suspicious.

Emily knew Billie wouldn't let her keep the baby.

It would mean too much downtime.

She would simply pull Emily by the hair to the *Obija* lady down the street if she had to, to get the potions that would cause her to miscarry.

That's what all the other prostitutes did.

One of them, a dumb country girl named Reba, did it too late and had to leave town in a hurry after she aborted a viable fetus in the bushes behind a crack house. The police said the baby girl was alive for half a day before it died. By the time they found it, the placenta had worms in it.

Even if Billie didn't make her have an abortion, Emily didn't want to be pregnant on the street. A hooker named Michele taught her that.

CHAPTER THIRTY-FIVE
"Want a date?"

She was actually one of two prostitutes named Michele, who worked the same block. On the street everybody referred to them in the plural as "The Micheles."

The other Michele called herself Michele-A. It had a nice ring to it and helped the tricks separate them. Michele-A was a knockout. She used to dance at the Gatsby, the fanciest strip club in Atlanta. But she busted a kneecap in a fall off the stage, and ended up limping from corner to corner on the street, sucking dicks for tricks.

229

The other Michele didn't have a sob story. She was just a freak on crack who loved to fuck. She was still working her corner, when she was nine months pregnant.

It was winter and even though she wore a heavy coat Michele's stomach stuck out like a basketball. But that didn't stop her from standing around waving down cars like everybody else. The weird thing was she got more business than any of the other girls.

One day, she came staggering out of the alley toward Billie. Emily peeked out and could see her face up close. She wanted to see this woman that all the other girls were talking about.

Billie got along with Michele more than most. She was all about business, and Billie could respect that. She didn't mind other whores trying to jock her johns. After all, she'd do it in a heartbeat.

But Billie hated a whore who thought she was better than her. They all sucked dick for a living. Yet the streets were full of prima donna ho's who thought they were above the others. Like their snatches didn't stink. But Michele wasn't like that.

She was pretty. Once.

But now, her hair was matted and dirty like a dead lion's mane. Her eyes were deep-set and in a trance from the new smack in her veins. Her mouth was crusty with dried and frozen semen. She was a mess. Billie laughed at her.

"Gurl, you better eat somethin. If not for you, then for that baby."

She smiled wearily, as she wrapped her arms around her shivering body. "I eats," she stammered through chattering teeth.

"Sperm aint food, baby doll."

Michele laughed so hard that her belly shook.

Billie laughed with her then stopped suddenly.

"You leakin, sweet pea!"

"Huh?"

"You leakin."

"W-w-what you talkin about, Billie?"

Her words were slurred and heavy like they were being spoken in slow motion.

Billie pointed down to her legs.

"I think your water broke. Unless you peein on yourself."

Michele looked down. Amniotic fluid was trickling in a rivulet down her leg, into her shoe.

"Oh, shit!" she whispered, even though she had wanted to yell.

But she had her groove on, and nothing, not even the baby on board, was going to fuck that up. A car slowed down as it came up to them.

"Hey, baby," Michele purred. "Want a date?"

Billie poked her hard in the tit.

"Bitch! You better get your sorry ass to the dayum hospital!"

Then, she turned to the man in the car. "What you lookin for shoog? Hmmm?"

With that, she opened the door and got in, and the two of them drove off. Michele stood there, holding her stomach, and giggling to herself, until she fell down on the sidewalk, writhing in pain or ecstasy. She didn't know which.

CHAPTER THIRTY-SIX
"They peered out darkly like hooded clerics from a Byzantine steeple."

A few months later, Billie met up with her again. This time, Michele was pushing a baby carriage. Her face and her eyes had cleared up, and she looked like she was clean and sober. Both she and the baby were in detox for twelve weeks.

The baby was big, thirteen pounds now, and she looked perfectly normal, except that her left eye stayed rolled up in her head.

Michele said she was going to call her Left Eye after the girl in her favorite group, TLC, but that the social worker had advised her against it, since the paralysis appeared to be only temporary.

So, instead, she named her daughter T'quilla, after her favorite drink. She called her TeeKee for short.

"I wanted to thank you, Billie," Michele said with a sober smile. "I think you saved my life."

"Shit, I aint did nothin, gurl."

"You ever saw that TV show, the Flyin Nun?"

"Uh huhn."

"Well, I was the Flyin Ho! You can believe that shit, baby!" Both Michele and Billie laughed out loud.

"So what, you like straight, now? Just sayin no and shit?"

"Tryin. But every time I see a needle, girl, I get wet. It's like I gotta have it."

"How's the baby?"

"That's my angel. She keeps me doin the right thang, cause, you know, I got to look out for her now. We a family and shit."

A man walked by, then stopped, looking the women up and down. He had a gold tooth and a diamond ring. Billie smiled at him, but before she could speak, Michele lifted her skirt.

"Hey, baby. Wanna date?"

Michele and the man disappeared down the alley, like a husband and wife out on a walk with their baby. They stopped by a dumpster, where they disappeared. The stroller was parked in the middle of the alley. Billie could see the outline of Michele's back as she knelt down, to give the man a blowjob.

After a few minutes, the baby began to cry.

Michele's arm reached out from behind the dumpster and grabbed the handle of the buggy. And without missing a beat, while one hand made the baby sleep, the other made the baby lotion.

Billie shook her head and walked away, muttering under her breath. "Crazy bitch!"

A few days later, Billie bumped into Michele again, but this time, Michele was without her baby. "Where's your little girl?" she asked, kind of surprised that she actually gave a damn.

Michele tried to smile, but instead melted into soft tears.

"TeeKee's dead," she said calmly.

"What?"

"She's... dead." Billie looked deeply into Michele's eyes. They were red and weary. Michele's face tried to summon up some kind of tragic bravery but couldn't. Suddenly, her expression went totally blank. Her eyes were momentarily vacant, like someone had pulled the plug on her soul.

And then, as though it were the only thing alive on her, her mouth opened wide, and Michele screamed deep. "SHE'S DEAD!!! Omigod!! Omigod!! SHE'S DEAD!!!"

She fell in a quivering heap, hyperventilating on the sidewalk. Emily covered her with her coat, trying to calm her down as best she could. Billie was gone. She was still holding a grudge behind Michele stealing that john the other day.

Emily learned that Michele's pimp killed her daughter. They were at his house, and he said he would watch the baby while she went inside the house to get her groove on.

Her pimp was a drug-dealer named Caine who had three crazy inbred Chows that he kept in the yard. The two females were all right, but the male was totally insane. He was the husband of his mother, and the father of his sister.

He was big for a Chow and very mean. He used to growl at nothing from the bottom of his throat. From a distance he sounded like one of those crazy homeless bastards who stood on the corner talking to themselves and shouting at no one.

The females were not as far-gone. They actually used to jump on the male, feigning as though they were all playing when Caine came around.

They knew he would beat the shit out of the dog if he barked at him. And he always barked at him. It got to the point where Caine had to hit the Chow over the head with a shovel just to get into the yard to feed the dogs.

People said Caine had fed gunpowder to the Chow when he was a pup.

It was supposed to make him mean. But instead it made him an angry, canine lunatic with fangs like a wolf.

The gunpowder, which could not be digested, sat inside him for years, eating away more and more of the lining in his stomach. When he slept, he howled quietly; and as he dreamed, his feet ran an unconscious marathon, trying to escape the pain that was driving him berserk.

It was next to this dog that Caine had placed T'Quilla.

When the police came, they found the baby's bowels, a piece of her skill, and a foot. That was all. The rest of her was inside the dog. One of the policeman pulled his service revolver to shoot the animal, but Caine told the cops that the baby had crawled inside the fence and that the dog did only what he was trained to do.

Michele stumbled out of the house, stupid high. Her eyes were giddy and unfocused, and she twirled her finger through her hair absent-mindedly.

"Where's Shorty?" she giggled. That's when she saw the bloody foam around the dog's mouth. And the empty baby carriage. And the police.

As they escorted Michele to the paddy wagon, the Chow swaggered over to the blood in the grass and scratched his paws defiantly in the dirt, marking his territory.

Then, he crouched, coiling his body tightly, and defecated.

Michele woke up in a hospital, with an IV of Demerol plugged into her arm. She was discharged a few days later and charged with felony neglect.

Caine got a ticket for having a biting dog and was in the process of appealing the misdemeanor with a lawyer who charged more per hour than the fine itself. He was demanding his dog back. In the affidavit, he told the court that he loved him. He did not mention that he had to hit him in the head with a shovel to feed him.

While impounded, the Chow had thrown up bits and pieces of the baby's body. That, along with the other parts, was gathered into a wooden box and cremated. A local funeral home donated a tiny painted particle-board coffin, and the child's ashes were buried with the rest of life's lost luggage in the county's indigent cemetery.

Michele had to be back in court the day after T'Quilla's funeral. She got up early that morning and bought a teddy bear at the 7-11 to mark her daughter's grave. Then she rode the bus to the end of the line, before walking the last mile to this desolate, forgotten place.

Her feet hurt, and the red stiletto heels of her fuck-me-pumps sank into the freshly turned up dirt. She had to kick them off as she laid the teddy bear in its place. Michele stood there alone for a long time, in a dirty black mini-skirt and a ripped purple and gold LA Lakers jacket.

A rusty backhoe leaking oil stood guard over the graveyard, which was overgrown with brown grass as tall as hay.

Power lines buzzed loudly in the nearby utility right of way.

Because of the landfill that sprawled next to the cemetery, giant vultures nested in the heights of the steel towers.

They peered out darkly like hooded clerics from a Byzantine steeple, stretching their wings occasionally in the faint necrotic updrafts. They worked for the state as protected carrion-birds. And they mourned no one.

The police chaplain had promised to come say a brief requiem mass over the child but never made it. He had fallen asleep in his car at a rest stop, clutching a small bottle of corn liquor in his lap.

A cold wind made the hair on the back of Michele's neck stand up and she whispered a prayer to chase away the dread. It was the only prayer she knew.

"God is good. God is great. Thank you for the food we...."

She took a deep breath and resigned herself to the fact that she was already in hell. And that maybe she deserved to be.

Michele went back to the stroll afterward and told the other girls about the burial. She had gotten hold of herself and had stopped crying, and she looked like she had braced herself for the misery that was ahead. That was the last time anybody ever saw her on the street.

The judge sentenced her to thirty days. But he was far more lenient than she.

In the holding tank, waiting to be fingerprinted and photographed like she had a hundred times before, she took the pull string out from the inside of her coat. She tied one end to the door handle and the other in a slipknot around her neck.

Then, with her feet firmly planted on the floor, she simply sat down.

Her buttocks were only a couple of inches from the floor, and she could have lifted herself up at anytime. But she didn't. And that's how the guards found her.

Hanging.

With her feet on the floor.

And her eyes wide open.

CHAPTER THIRTY-SEVEN
"Why?"

The man was breathing heavily as he came barreling down the hallway at full speed. His feet nearly slipped out from under him as he turned sharply to enter the room. It was Luis Estrada, the Fulton County court magistrate.

"Dr. Harris, thank God you're here!"

"What is it, Lou? What's the matter?"

"A woman in holding tried to hang herself! They think she may still be alive."

"Let's go!" Jerry said, grabbing his black bag as he dashed in a sprint out of the office.

Once a week, Jerry volunteered his services at the Atlanta Pre-Trial Facility.

Many of the people brought here were mentally ill or non-violent substance abusers who did not belong behind bars. But because they were homeless or off their meds and incoherent most simply stayed locked up for weeks and months at a time.

It was Jerry's job to winnow these out.

That way, the ones with emotional problems could be released to the psych ward at Grady Hospital. At the very least, they could be placed under round-the-clock supervision in the suicide watch.

The woman lying on the cell floor down the hall had just been brought in moments earlier. Her case file was still upstairs in the courtroom, and her background was not known.

But Jerry could tell immediately that she must have been suicidal long before she had been booked into custody.

Typically, even the high-risk inmates took awhile before the grim reality of their circumstances set in. The threshold of desperation was almost always measured in hours or days, hardly ever in seconds or minutes.

The fact that they had found her hanging from a sitting position indicated that she had been extremely resolute in her desire to end her life.

One of the guards had already removed the thin nylon string from around the woman's neck, revealing a deep red ligature mark.

Jerry put on his rubber gloves before he wiped away the foamy drool coming out of the side of her mouth. The woman was not breathing.

He turned her head to the side and gingerly felt the area around her throat. She did not have a pulse. Jerry also determined that her windpipe had not been crushed and that he would not have to perform a tracheotomy.

Using an Ambu-Bag from the jail's medical kit, he began to force feed air into her lungs. He squeezed the bag in a frantic rhythm as he checked the rest of her vitals.

Conditioned by his trade, Dr. Harris automatically assessed the woman's apparent mental state simultaneously with her physical condition.

As she lay motionless on the cold concrete floor, he could still see all the classic predictors of a suicide.

Her skin was sallow, with an almost translucent pallor that made the dark circles under her eyes stand out like purple shiners.

She was abhorrently thin and malnourished.

Her teeth were covered with a foul yellow calculus. Her hair was matted and filthy. And the smell of alcohol was seeping from her pores as well as the warm puddle of urine beneath her.

These were salient physical signs of depression and addiction. She might as well have been walking around with a noose as a necklace.

"What's her name?" the doctor asked urgently.

"Michele, something," said the guard standing behind him.

The doctor smacked her firmly on her face.

"Michele? Michele? You with me, honey?"

There was no response. Jerry was afraid that the rope had cut off too much oxygen to her brain. Her lips and fingernails were blue. Her eyes were wide open, with the pupils dilated.

"I think we got here too late, doc," said Lou, shaking his head at the sad spectacle. "You want to call the ball?"

"Not yet," Jerry said as he continued pumping the bag. "Let's give it another minute or so. Michele? Michele? Can you hear me?"

Jerry still wasn't sure if the woman was beyond resuscitation.

He looked closer at the ligature line.

It ran about an inch below the jawbone. He thought it might be possible that the rope had hit the bifurcation point of the carotid artery.

If that were the case, Michele may be suffering from a severe bradycardia.

He ripped opened her blouse to put his ear to her bare chest.

He had learned long ago that a stethoscope was no match for the unimpeded biochemical circuitry of human touch. He could listen and feel at the same time with an inerrant precision that only the best EKG could duplicate.

But since the jail didn't have one of those, his ear would have to do.

There was no heartbeat that he could hear.

But there was one he could feel. Fluttering gently like a trapped butterfly against his cheek.

Jerry grabbed the jail's defibrillator and shocked Michele with 700 volts. Her body jumped.

He put his ear back to her chest. No change.

He increased the voltage to the maximum of 1700 and shocked her again. Her body convulsed in slow motion. This time her eyes squeezed shut, and she moaned.

A minute later, tears filled her eyes as she looked at the doctor and tried to speak. Her words were barely a whisper. Jerry put his ear close to her lips as she repeated the one word she was trying to utter.

"Why?"

CHAPTER THIRTY-EIGHT
"Is this young lady one of yours?"

The next day, Jerry found Michele lying on a gurney in the hallway outside the Grady ER. He often walked quickly through this area, since two of the rooms were host to his worst memories.

He grabbed her charts and ran his finger down the mysterious looking characters that passed for doctors' notes.

The woman was in serious but stable condition.

Both of her wrists were handcuffed to the metal slides of the gurney. It was standard practice for suicidal patients. And those heading to jail.

Michele was both.

She was on her fifth saline drip, and the color was coming back to her skin. She had also been given 150mg of propafenone to help correct her heartbeat.

He put the palm of his hand on her forehead. No fever. He palpated her neck and throat. The ligature line had left a deep impression in her skin that would take several weeks to disappear.

At that moment, a pack of student doctors from the Morehouse school of Medicine burst through the swinging doors to the corridor, chattering animatedly as they made their rounds.

In the middle of them was Will Thomas.

"Jerry! What a surprise! How are you?" he asked, as he gave him a bear hug.

"I'm doing all right, Will. How have you been?"

"Good, good! You look great."

"That's thanks in large part to you."

"Get outta here," Will laughed, as the hug turned automatically into an impromptu exam. Will gently compressed Jerry's chest with his hands, adroitly assessing the strength of his breathing.

"You've rebounded nicely, Jerry. I see you've been working out, too. Excellent. I couldn't be more proud of you," he said, backing away. "By the way, how's Jackie?" he asked, lowering his voice. "I heard she was having a… 'thing.'"

It was a queer euphemism, bordering on superstitious.

Why was it that nobody ever wanted to call cancer by its name? Not even doctors. It was not unlike being afraid to speak of the Devil for fear that he might appear.

Despite decades of medical erudition and a trillion dollars in research, nobody really knew what exactly caused cancer.

Perhaps it was wise after all not to invite it with words.

"Locally, at least, it appears to be in remission."

"That's fantastic, Jerry!"

"Yeah, we're pretty excited about it. Right now, we're waiting for the Darkfield and the T/Antigens to come back. Then, we'll breathe a little easier."

"If they've got to go that far to find anything, 99.99-percent of the time there's nothing to find," Will said, reassuringly. "If you want, have her come over to Emory, and I'll arrange a time for her to meet with the chair of the Oncology Department. She can go over her case with her. You know, just as a second opinion."

"Thanks, Will. She just might do that."

"Is this young lady one of yours?" Will asked, gently placing his fingers on her radial artery. As he spoke, he timed her pulse with the second hand of his beaten but indefatigable Timex watch.

"Close call, here," he murmured gravely.

"Very," Jerry seconded.

The interns gathered in a tight crowd around the woman, jostling over one another for a better view, occasionally bumping into the gurney. It was obvious that for them, interacting with real patients was a treat.

Trying to diagnose the biometrics robot back at the school was pretty lame. The only time they ever got fooled was when the software acted up, corrupting the settings. Whenever that happened, symptoms set for something as simple as an ear infection could morph arbitrarily into typhoid or malaria or appendicitis, throwing the class off for hours.

Will turned to the students, moving them back with his arms out like a goalie.

"We're going to let this young lady sleep for awhile," he said in a soft voice. "Besides, I suspect this case is a little bit outside our *oeuvre*. Jerry, I'll see you later. Have Jackie call me."

His bad French notwithstanding, Will was perhaps the best doctor Jerry had ever worked with. Tenacious as a bull when it came to saving people's lives. Tender as a kitten when it came to saving their dignity.

He knew immediately that the woman had tried to commit suicide. And the last thing she needed was a pack of overzealous doctor dilettantes violating her privacy while she struggled with whatever was silently tormenting her.

"I'll have Jack give you a call, Will. Take care."

Just then, paramedics raced an emergency patient through the intake. Will smiled and winked at Jerry. Then he and his students galloped off in a blur of white lab coats and stethoscopes in hot pursuit of the new meat being wheeled down the hall.

CHAPTER THIRTY-NINE
"Hon'in beki tachisaru!"

As Dr. Harris reviewed Michele's files, the woman opened her eyes with sudden alarm.

"Doyatsu temae? Doyatsu temae?" she babbled groggily.

Jerry was momentarily shocked. He could not understand a word Michele was saying. He shook his head sadly.

Her glossolalia was likely a sign of the brain damage he had suspected earlier.

The loss of oxygen while she was hanging in the cell at the jail could have starved her temporal lobe. That would certainly account for this queer type of aphasia.

She probably knew what she was saying.

She just didn't know how to say it.

"Michele, I know you're scared. But you're okay now. You're in the hospital, and I promise you, I'm going to do everything I can to get you back on your feet."

Jerry tore a piece of paper from his note pad. Sometimes, despite their inability to speak, aphasic patients could still read and write. As he grabbed his pen, he was startled by the redundant urgency of Michele's words.

"Doyatsu temae? Doyatsu temae?"

As he listened further, it became slowly apparent that the woman was speaking another language. Perhaps Japanese.

Before he could shrug off the absurdity of the thought, Michele became suddenly alert.

"Nani?"

Her eyes began to dart about wildly. She tried to get up and jerked violently against the restraints, making the gurney move on its wheels with the momentum of her force.

"Tetsuda! Tetsuda!" she yelled at the top of her lungs.

Jerry gently pushed the gurney back against the wall and tried to reassure her in a soothing voice that everything was all right.

"Calm down. Take it easy."

He was at a loss.

He didn't speak Japanese. In fact, the only Japanese words he knew were from the song by Styx.

"Doumo arigatou?"

The woman's face lit up.

"Douzo! Douzo!" she answered excitedly. *"Houshutsu touhou meireiikka!"*

"Hold on, hold on. I don't really speak Japanese."

"Doko hon ichi?"

"I don't know what you're saying."

"Doko hon ichi?"

"I don't understand."

"Hon'in beki tachisaru!"

Jerry shook his head with futility, trying to convey to Michele that he had no idea what she was trying to say. But as she spoke more, it became clear to him that whatever she was saying, she was saying it with an almost imperious authority.

"Sono toshiwakai ro-du korede tookarazu. Houshutsu touhou meireiikka!"

"Please, speak English, if you can," he pleaded.

"Kumi-daiko," she said softly, almost whispering.

A sense of calm appeared on her face as she craned her neck to see down the corridor. It seemed as though she was looking for something specific.

"Achira yowakusuru."

"What is it?"

"Achira yowakusuru."

Dr. Harris instinctively began to look down the corridor along with Michele. He could not see anything out of the ordinary.

"Kiku."

"I don't understand."

"Kiku. Kumu-daiko. Sono denrisha monooto."

The doctor was about to reach for the phone when the woman looked him straight in the eyes.

248

"Temae!" she said sternly, pointing directly at him.

"Me?" Jerry said, pointing to himself.

"Hai!"

"My name is Dr. Jerry Harris," he said slowly and deliberately. "I'm trying to help you get out of here. But you have suffered a severe trauma."

"Hon'in gorannasai inai temae. Goshujin kokoro houshou motte junshin."

Michele studied Jerry as hard as he studied her.

She motioned with her restrained hands toward her body. A look of sad contempt crossed her face like a shadow.

"Kono shinjou feiru. Sono fujoshi beki saikoro taishite kyuusei. Anou kono kerai!"

"Again, I'm sorry but I don't under...."

"She say, 'This body, she finished.'"

The doctor nearly jumped out of his shoes. Standing behind him was a hospital janitor. A short elderly man with a mop. Who happened to be Asian.

"She tell me to tell you, 'Your eyes sing with purity.'"

"Please, continue to speak with her. She was saying something before that I could not make out. Ask her to repeat what she was saying."

The old man moved closer to the woman but made it clear from his body language that he did not wish to get too close to her.

"Douzo, kamoshirenai Hon'in toransure-to?"
"Hai."

As Jerry looked on, the two spoke in what appeared to be conflicting dialects of Japanese, judging from the repeated look of frustration on the woman's face and the confusion on the man's.

Michele spoke with great animation and sincerity, forcing eye contact with the old man, whose head remained bowed throughout most of the conversation.

"She say she does not know how she come to this place. She must leave now. The lord is soon coming. She hear the herald of the drum. And she must go."

"Go? Go where?"

"I don't know. She not says."

Jerry did not know what to make of what was happening.

He rubbed his forehead as he thought.

There were rare cases in the literature that chronicled people who could spontaneously speak foreign languages that they had never heard before. But nearly all of them had been completely fraudulent.

"Temae kan tezawari kenshiki. Senpou tawamure motte sono hiyowai jisou."

Michele smiled as she spoke these words.

"What did she say?" Jerry asked.

"She say, you may feel great pride. He play with all the sickly children here."

"He? He, who?" Jerry asked.

"Jonathan," the woman said, smiling.

"Jonathan," the old man repeated, smiling as well.

CHAPTER FORTY

"Dr. Satoshi Tatsuro," he bowed.

"Jonathan?" Jerry said softly. "What do you mean? How do you know about my son?"

Michele continued to look tenderly at Jerry's face, despite the fact that her eyes could no longer see. It took him a minute to realize that she had died right there in front of him.

"Kyuui dzuki temae," the old man said bowing his head. "Peace unto you."

Jerry reached quickly for the phone to call for a crash cart. But the janitor gently put his hand over the receiver, shaking his head solemnly.

"She no want that. Remember her say, 'this body, she finished.'"

"Yes, but…"

"In another life, I too was doctor," the old man interrupted softly. "See much death. Much death. Some not want to die. Some ready to die. She ready. Let her go in peace."

251

Jerry thought about the old man's words for a moment then nodded his head.

He checked Michele's vitals one last time. Then he closed her eyes and covered her body with a sheet. As he logged the time of her death on the chart, he looked over at the janitor curiously.

"I didn't catch your name, Dr...?"

The old man smiled.

"Dr. Satoshi Tatsuro," he bowed. "And you are Dr. Harris."

Jerry was startled.

"You tell name to woman before she die," he reminded.

"Oh yes. That's right."

At that moment, Jerry flagged down a passing orderly to unlock the woman's restraints and take her down to the morgue.

"Tell the Medical Examiner that Doctor Jerry Harris would like to see the results of her autopsy. I'm particularly interested in his assessment of her brain, any disease or aberration. That sort of thing. My card is with her charts. Thanks."

When he turned his attention back to the old man, Jerry couldn't find him anywhere. He was still confused about what had just happened. And slightly disbelieving. He was disappointed that he had not gotten a chance to talk to the Japanese doctor further.

But as he walked around the corner to leave, he found the old man dutifully mopping the lobby floor in front of the elevators.

"Dr. Tatsuro," he said politely. "Would you mind sparing a few minutes to have lunch with me?"

"Still have many floors to clean."

"Tell you what," Jerry said, gently prying the mop free from the man's strong ancient hands, "If anybody says anything, let me know, and I'll call the president of the hospital. He's a golf buddy of mine."

Dr. Tatsuro chuckled. "Fair enough. But no hospital food."

"I couldn't agree more," he laughed. 'It's my treat. So it's your choice."

"Ahhh," he grinned excitedly. "Then we go to Farmer Market down street. Best unagi in city."

"Unagi?"

"Eel!" the old man squealed enthusiastically.

Jerry couldn't help but grimace slightly as the two of them wove their way through the crowd and out of the hospital.

The Farmers' Market had the curious smell of all Farmers' Markets. A tart redolence that wafted somewhere between a slaughterhouse and a steakhouse, depending on what side of the building you were on.

At the entrance, raw meat hung from hooks on the rafters, as butchers prowled the display cases, wielding long sharp knives that could shred paper with a twist of the blade.

Their white aprons were stained pink in the front, the litmus of their trade. Which today appeared extremely busy.

The air was cold, and you could see their breath as they toiled over the meat, turning fat red carcasses into small dinner filets. They all had the hands of surgeons. And Dr. Harris marveled at the effortless skill they employed.

As they walked to the far side of the market, where the restaurants were, Dr. Tatsuro spoke fluent Korean to one of the vegetable vendors he knew. Then perfect Chinese to a woman making soup nearby.

They stopped at a giant glass tank teeming with hundreds of fish of all types. There, he spoke with a young Japanese boy who was minding the tank. Moments later, he was laughing and pointing as the young boy set about trying to catch a long black eel with a grappling hook.

"Anna hitotsu!" he laughed. *"Choudai itto! Choudai itto!"*

The boy was getting soaked as the eels thrashed wildly about in the water. They were indeed as slippery as their reputation.

"Sousou!" the old man laughed in almost delirious pleasure. *"Sousou!"*

And just when it looked like the boy was about to give up his pursuit, he snared the fattest eel in the tank, beaming proudly as he delivered it to his father at the cutting board.

With his massive hands moving in a blur, the man wrapped the eel immediately into a tight coil. And with two or three quick cuts, he sliced it into a dozen or more pieces, some of which continued to wriggle stubbornly.

Among these were the head of the eel, whose mouth and eyes continued to move and flit, as though they did not know their mutual circumstance had changed dramatically from when the creature was inside the tank.

But a second later, all of the pieces were wriggling in a hot wok that steamed loudly with peanut oil. And a minute or two after that, they were on the plates being placed before the two doctors.

"Taste like chicken, right?" Dr, Tatsuro laughed.

"Very salty chicken," Jerry nodded. "It's good though."

"Ahhh, yes. Best in town!"

"I'll take your word on that," he smiled.

After they had eaten, the doctors leaned back in their chairs, enjoying the warm *saki* that came with their meal. Given the unsettling events with Michele, this was a splendid diversion that Jerry had thoroughly enjoyed.

It also gave him a chance to get to know more about the old man smiling contentedly before him.

The doctor in the janitor's uniform.

"Please, Dr. Tatsuro. Tell me about your self. Your 'other life.'"

The old doctor smiled. "Long story," he sighed.

"We have a little time," Jerry smiled, as he raised the empty bottle of *saki.*

The little boy quickly brought out another and refilled their empty cups.

"My wife and I both doctor," the old man began in a tired but firm voice. "Belong to *Medecins Sans Frontiers.*"

Jerry was astonished by his impeccable French accent.

"I've heard of that agency. Doctors Without Borders."

"*Hai.* Every year, during summer holiday, we volunteer. We travel world, help people. Even take our daughters with us. Cambodia. Haiti. Honduras. Croatia. Sudan. We what you call 'idealists,'" he smiled weakly.

"One year we go North Korea. My wife, her ancestors from province there. We go. Not come back."

"You decided to move there?"

"No!" he said sharply. "They keep us there. Prisoner."

"Oh my God."

"God a stranger in that country," he chided. "Police say her family name on list of traitor. Put her in jail. Tell embassy our children and I free to leave. But she must stay."

The old man paused, shaking his head. "I cannot leave her."

"No. Of course not," Jerry agreed.

"They keep her in jail five month. Until I sign paper renounce my Japanese citizenship. My children's too. Wife freed from prison. But she never same again. Never speak of what happen there. I do not know."

"I'm so very sorry, Dr. Tatsuro."

The old man sighed heavily. He looked distantly into his cup of *saki* before taking a small almost medicinal sip.

"They send us to small mountain prefecture. Tell us set up hospital for farmers there. Many very sick. Dysentery. River Blindness. Guinea Worm. We overwhelmed. Get sick too.

"But I remember, one summer, when I intern long ago, I work with Jimmy Carter Center right here in Atlanta. Learn that all over world, whole villages sick like this one. It all in water. Filter the disease out of well, everyone get better. We did same here. Everyone get better. Build fine hospital. Make good friends. Stay many year. But still prisoners."

"So how is it that you came here, Doctor?"

"My wife, Chi, she get pregnant. Another daughter," he grinned. "But Chi no care for baby. Depression killing her. My other daughters help raise child for their mother. But I know she die if we not leave soon."

All Jerry could do was nod his head slowly as he listened.

Two hours before, the old man was just an invisible janitor in a hallway at the hospital. Now, he was one of the most fascinating people he had ever met.

"Villagers know wife dying. They help us escape. Build two raft. Many of them join us. Smuggle them through Chinese border to city of Yantai. Can make South Korean coast in one day on good current.

"We leave at night. Thirty-two of us. Take food and water for two week. Also take fishing nets. If lost, we all agree it better to die at sea than prisoner. Girls scared. I tell them it all right. They believe me."

For the first time since he began his story, the doctor's voice broke with emotion. "They believe me."

257

"I'm sorry, Dr. Tatsuro," Jerry said, gently placing his hand on the old man's shoulder. "I had no idea. If this is too painful for you, please, by all means stop."

"No." the doctor said calmly. "I must set this memories free."

Jerry nodded with patient encouragement.

"It was fall. Water still warm. But night air cool. We take many blanket. Fishing boat take us out to sea. Then we all climb on board rafts. Boat turn around. And we are alone on ocean.

"It is new moon. Nothing but stars and blackness. We paddle south. Pick up current. Keep lights of coast in sight. Girls start singing lullaby to baby. Very soft. Very beautiful. I so proud of them. Li and Mai. My angels.

"Wife scared. So are we all. Hours go by. We moving well. Before dawn, fog come. Now, cannot see coast. Everyone more scared. Then, we hear boat. I tell everyone be quiet! But someone in second raft yell for help. That when shooting start.

"Now everyone screaming. We paddle away from second raft. A rocket whoosh overhead. Another one explode in sea next to us. The next one hit second raft. People screaming. Water turn red. Daughters crying. Wife rocking back and forth. Back and forth. Only baby quiet. Sound asleep. My Mimi."

The old doctor took another sip of his wine. Then he collected his thoughts once again, before taking the hard journey back to this crucible of his life.

"Can see the boat now. Floating like a ghost in the mist. Chinese. Gunship. It pull next to what left of second raft. People screaming for help. Begging. I hear voice I recognize saying there is another raft. Us. Then machine guns open fire. No more begging. No more screaming.

"Now, another rocket fly over our head. Then another. And another. And another. It raining hot metal. Two or three die from shrapnel. They still sitting upright in raft not knowing they dead.

"People jumping into sea. Raft turn over. Sinking. I grab Mimi and start swimming. I yelling for my daughters. But they no answer. My wife holding on to rubber tire. Swimming to me and Mimi. She help me put baby on tire. She stroke Mimi wet hair out of her eyes. Then she kiss her. And me. And let go."

Jerry was dumbfounded. He could barely keep from crying as he listened to Dr. Tatsuro's story. "Why did she let go?"

"She ready to die. I watch her face as she sink in the blackness of ocean. She smile. Just like woman at hospital."

"Jesus," Jerry whispered to himself.

"No Jesus!" the doctor said angrily. "My wife want only to be free again. He answer her prayer only when she drowning."

Jerry knew there was nothing he could say to dispel the doctor's crisis of the faith. Not that there weren't words. Just none that meant anything.

"Somehow I get away with Mimi. We float a long time. She cold. I wrap my arms around her on the tire to keep her warm. She is so beautiful. Her eyes smiling at me. I kiss her and hug her tight. She do the same. Then I hear singing in fog. Li and Mai. Her sisters.

"I yell out to them. 'We are here! Li! Mai! Where are you! Daddy here with sister! Li! Mai! My angels! Tell me where you are!' There no answer. Just singing. Lullaby. I swim to sound. But never find girls. I think I am crazy. And I cry more water than in ocean.

"Suddenly, the singing stop. And the fog lift. And there, a hundred yards away is coast of South Korea. I laughing and tell Mimi we going home. Look, I say. Look! But Mimi gone. Like the singing. Gone.

"I carry her to shore. The people who gather wrap me in blanket and try to take her from me, knowing she dead. I not let her go. I not let her go. I dead too. I a ghost."

Dr. Tatsuro looked up at Jerry with tears in his eyes. "I still a ghost. Just not ready to die."

Jerry took a heavy breath and looked up for a moment. The butcher and his son were standing nearby with their heads bowed. A group of women at the table next to them were weeping audibly. They had all overhead the doctor's story and could not contain their emotions.

Doctor Tatsuro stood up quietly. "Please excuse me," he bowed. "I must return to work."

Over the next several months, the two doctors met often at the Farmers' Market for lunch and light conversational aperitif.

It was here that the two established a curious but firm friendship based on a mutual respect that had little to do with their medical resumes. They seemed irretrievably drawn to each other by the sad gravitational pull of personal tragedy.

Jerry had told Dr. Tatsuro the story of the accident and his son's death, a part of his life that he had shared with precious few people outside of a psychiatrist's office.

The two of them, by every outward appearance, made a very odd couple indeed. But the bond they shared was deep and rare, forged as it was from the kind of pain that needed two doctors to heal.

But here, over exotic meals and warm *saki*, the two of them could sit at their tiny corner table and release the silent yet seismic torment of their souls.

"How did you discover this place," Jerry asked Dr. Tatsuro as he nibbled on the hard noodles that came with their soup.

"I work here when I first come back to Atlanta," he smiled.

He pulled out his wallet and proudly showed off his old employee's badge. Under his name were flags of the countries whose languages his spoke. Japanese. Mandarin. Swahili. Croat. Spanish. French.

"Where's the American flag?" Jerry asked.

"My English. Not so good," he laughed.

"Better than a lot of Americans," Jerry laughed back.

"Perhaps," he smiled.

"Why did you stop working here? It's obvious everybody loves having you around."

"Need to be near hospital. Too many years doctor."

"I can understand that."

Jerry had spoken with Will Thomas some time before and had asked him if he could find Dr. Tatsuro a job at the hospital that was better suited for him than pushing a mop.

So Will had Grady's Intake division create a position for the old man as a translator in the clinic and the ER. It was supposed to be the hospital's equivalent to a Walmart Greeter who spoke several languages.

But Will quickly discovered that the erstwhile janitor was a brilliant triage specialist. Often, before he had spoken a single word to a patient, he had already diagnosed them.

Accurately.

Nowadays, instead of the prison-gray custodian's outfit he used to wear, Dr. Tatsuro could be found ambling through the clinic in blue scrubs with a stethoscope just like any of the other doctors.

And none of them were complaining.

With the on-call residents getting two hours of sleep a night and the specialists barely coming in at all, anything or anyone who could cut down the interminable waiting list of patients was a godsend to the hospital.

Everyone simply learned to look the other way when the kindly, "unofficial" doctor was seeing a patient in the exam room.

In fact, there was now talk among Will and some of the other department heads about sponsoring Dr. Tatsuro so that he could petition the Medical Licensing Board for American certification of his old Japanese MD.

"Dr. Tatsuro, there's been something I've been meaning to ask you," Jerry said casually.

"Jonathan."

Startled by the old man's prescience, Jerry simply nodded his head.

"How the woman know about your son."

"Yes," Jerry said pausing. "I need help understanding this."

"Of course."

"I thought maybe she had read about the accident. But that was so very long ago. And frankly her profile wasn't the type to stay abreast of the news, one would think. So there had to be some other way."

The old man nodded. "The woman not know."

"How do you mean?"

"It the spirit inside her."

"Her spirit?"

"Not hers."

"Whose?"

"His."

Jerry stroked his chin absently in bewilderment.

The old doctor noticed his confusion and continued.

"He say through woman his name. Po Lin. Very old. From Chau-tun Village. Tree spirit."

"A tree spirit?"

"Yes. He trapped. Many century. Big flood come. Tree fall. He break free."

"You're pulling my leg, right?"

"No."

The old doctor's face betrayed no sign of humor.

"How did he get to be inside the woman?"

"When person die by suicide or forfeit their life in any way, spirit can climb in, like squirrel in attic. It possess them before body die completely. They already dead. Host spirit gone. Body not far behind."

"So when Michele hung herself, and I revived her, it wasn't her that I brought back."

"Correct. It like dead battery in flashlight. Sometimes, when light go out, shake it, light come on again before it die for good."

"When I asked you to translate, you seemed afraid. Why?"

Dr. Tatsuro nodded. "I know even then, woman not woman."

"How?"

"I could feel it."

"What about Jonathan? How would this Po Lin know about my son?"

The old doctor smiled. "Because he there. At hospital."

As the two got up to leave, Jerry's face could not hide his disbelief.

The two of them had returned to the Emergency Room by the time he had summoned up the courage to bring the subject up again.

"Dr. Tatsuro, what did you mean, Jonathan was here?"

"He here," the old doctor repeated. "You yourself may have seen him. In corner of eye. Reflection in glass door. Shadow in window. You just not believe."

It was true that there were moments when Jerry felt that he was not alone, when in fact he was. He had simply brushed them off as the kind of spooky déjà vu's that happen when the brain is tired, and the synapses fire randomly like bored duck hunters at anything that catches their interest.

His mind could easily rationalize this. But his heart could not. His intuition had always been strong. And there simply was no medical explanation for that.

Jerry led the old doctor into an empty office where they could talk in private.

"Dr. Tatsuro, there was something you said that makes me think you can help me."

"*Hai*?"

"You said, when a person forfeits his life in some way or another, a spirit could enter their body."

"*Hai*," he said softly.

"You called yourself a ghost. That would suggest, emotionally at least, that you forfeited your life on that beach in South Korea. That says to me that maybe you opened yourself up to certain 'gifts.'"

The old doctor nodded his head gravely.

265

"I don't exactly know how to say this, but...."

"You want me talk to Jonathan."

Jerry hesitated a long moment before he answered. "Yes."

Dr. Tatsuro looked him in the eyes.

"It true after Mimi die, I die. Inside. Not long after, have dreams. See my wife, my daughters, myself. Dreams real. But over time, wife and daughters move on. Only me left. Then, new faces come. Many new faces."

"Jonathan was among them, wasn't he?"

"Yes. When I come to hospital I first see him."

"I don't understand. How?"

"Body like open circuit. Spirit close it. All energy."

Jerry thought back to his many conversations with Ed Lee. "I've heard that before."

"When I come to hospital, spirits drawn to me. Like magnet. So many. I see Jonathan. He see me."

"He talked to you."

"Yes. Very good boy."

Jerry didn't know whether to laugh or cry.

Part of him wanted to believe the old doctor. But the other part wanted to laugh at the absurdity of what Dr. Tatsuro was saying.

He decided to see if the doctor could ask Jonathan a question that only the boy could answer. That way he would have enough proof to dispel his lingering doubts. Before he could come up with one, the old doctor spoke.

"He call himself, 'Dr. Harris.'"

"What did you say?" Jerry asked, in shock.

"The boy. He call himself, Dr. Harris. Like his father."

A lump sat heavily in Jerry's throat. "My God," he said softly.

"No God," the old doctor chided gently, just as he had that first day they met. "Boy also say that he keep his word."

"What do you mean?"

"He tell you he would be right back.

"You really are psychic," Jerry said in amazement.

"Not psychic," he grinned. "Just available."

"Available?"

"To listen."

Suddenly, Jerry was giddy with excitement. There were so many things he wanted to ask Jonathan. Tears were now welling in his eyes. He was ecstatic. The fortress he had built around the memory of his son was crumbling before his eyes.

The heavy stones of empiricism that had been set with the quick mortar of science were now lying in a heap at the foot of all the things he thought he knew.

"Could you ask him... if he knows how much I love him?"

"*Hai.* But you already have."

Jerry laughed with nervous embarrassment. "I guess, I mean can you tell me what he says?"

"*Hai*. But why you not let him tell you himself."

"Because I'm not psychic."

"Nor am I."

"But..."

"Why you think woman in hall choose *you* to speak to?"

"I don't know."

"You the one who bring her back."

"Doctors revive patients everyday. You know that."

"But not so many doctor who come back from dead. Like you, Jerry."

The thought sent a shiver through Jerry. It had never occurred to him that he too was what Dr. Tatsuro had called an "open circuit."

"Before, your fear blind you. Now, you are becoming."

"Becoming?"

"Alive. On new level."

"Jesus," Jerry said quietly to himself.

"No Jesus," the doctor said the same way.

"Satoshi, can you... see him?"

"*Hai*."

Jerry gasped. "You can really see him?"

"*Hai*. So can you."

"Where?"

"Behind you."

Jerry wheeled around in his chair.

And just as clearly as he could see the old man sitting on the other side of the table, he could now see Jonathan standing before him.

He could smell him. He could touch him. And when the boy smiled, his father embraced him. He closed his eyes deeply and wept the kind of tears that he had wept at Jonathan's birth.

And his death.

"I've been waiting for you daddy," Jonathan whispered.

When Jerry opened his eyes, the room was teeming with children. Standing next to Jonathan was the girl from the dream Jerry had had in the Emergency Room after the accident that killed his son.

The old man smiled.

"Everyday I search among these faces for my girls. Mimi. Li. Mai. One day, they will find their way to me. Of this, I am sure. Until then, these too are my children, Dr. Harris. And I will love them. And when the time comes, I will join them. And we will all find our way to other side. Together."

Jerry nodded his head and closed his eyes as he continued to hug his son.

"Jonathan!" he whispered with complete joy.

Just holding the boy in his arms lifted every care and vexation out of his soul.

He could feel his son's weight and the familiar way his callow muscles twitched as Jonathan hugged him back. Sixty-eight pounds was what he had weighed at his last wellness check.

Jerry believed he weighed every bit of that now.

"I love you, daddy. Tell mommy I love her too."

"Oh, I will, I will. How I've missed you! My son! My beautiful son!"

When he opened his eyes, the boy was gone, though he could still feel him in every nerve in his body. Jerry was stunned and looked wildly around the room.

All of the children were gone.

"They will be back," Dr. Tatsuro assuaged. "For some reason I do not understand, the children never seem to stay in one place for long. It almost like it is forbidden. They say 'hide and seek.'"

"Hide and seek? Some kind of a game?"

"Perhaps game," he said solemnly. "Perhaps not."

CHAPTER FORTY-ONE

"Mannitol. Sodium Bicarbonate. Benzoylethylecgonine."

To the untrained eye, the graph read like the angry scribbling of a child. The jagged peaks and valleys ran up and down with a quixotic fury that mirrored the painful contractions of the woman lying between the stirrups in Exam Room Number Four of the Grady Hospital Maternity Ward.

Without success, the interns had tried repeatedly to get the woman to tell them her name. At first they thought that she might be mute. But every time they left the room, they could hear her shouting expletives at the top of her lungs to no one.

That's why Dr. Harris was finally called in.

The first thing he did was order a series of blood tests to tell if the woman was strung out on drugs, a common enough condition among the indigents who showed up at the Grady ER.

Her only known malady was not a malady at all. She was simply one of a couple dozen women in the ward who were about to have a child.

As he waited outside her room, Dr. Harris could hear her railing on hysterically about being "knocked up with some dead man's bastard!" She appeared to take a queer delight in calling herself a "fucking street cunt!" And she repeatedly told someone that she wished "you would fucking die already!"

It was entirely normal for many expectant mothers to vent with the occasional swear word. But this woman spewed an acid rain of non-stop obscenities that made the staff blush and cringe as they walked quickly past her door.

When the preliminary blood tests came back later, Dr. Harris went over them thoroughly, nodding his head as he recognized each of the salient chemicals with an almost predictable ease.

Mannitol. Sodium Bicarbonate. Benzoylethylecgonine.

It became immediately apparent to him that the woman in the room was a crack head.

Dr. Harris shook his head heavily.

Despite the medical mythology, crack babies were a relatively rare phenomenon. Most mothers addicted to coke or crack generally stopped using once their pregnancies were confirmed.

Only the hardcore drug abusers continued getting high. Like the zombie prostitutes who turned tricks for two or three dollars a pop. But even they generally resorted to back street abortions. That way they wouldn't lose any of the money they could make on the stroll.

Perhaps one in a hundred junkies actually carried their fetuses to term. Which in Georgia was a felony.

It was a good law. That's because every time the mother took a hit of crack, the fetus took the equivalent of a thousand. The drug would immediately deprive the growing embryo of oxygen, suffocating it in a slow macabre ecstasy that could be described as a form of in vitro erotic asphyxiation.

And once the crack entered the amniotic fluid, it stayed there for weeks at a time, polluting the baby's sentient dreaming with blind hallucinations that caused the fetus to scratch and claw and run in place for its very life until near-death fatigue finally, mercifully, put it to sleep.

Such torture certainly rose to a Class Three felony. If not higher.

For their parts, the mothers got off much easier.

Most of the time, they were sent to jail or rehab for a few months. Typically, they were using drugs again within days of their release.

The child, on the other hand was given a life sentence of learning disabilities, growth disorders, and mental illness. Factor in the ordeals of revolving foster care, poverty, truancy, and a lack of proper medical treatment, and most of them would end up in jail or living in destitution on the street.

Either way, chances were excellent that they would return to the very same drug that had become a part of their DNA.

"You stupid fucking bitch!" the woman yelled, just as Dr. Harris opened the door.

In the short time he had been monitoring her from outside the room her vicious diatribes were becoming increasingly more virulent and frequent. These bizarre paroxysms of verbal violence reminded the doctor of the "kindling" effect usually seen in schizophrenics or people with bipolar disease. People who flagellated themselves with angry words into a heightened emotional state.

So, despite the fact that her outbursts appeared to coincide with the strength of her contractions, it was certainly possible that the woman was also severely mentally ill. And the pain was very likely pushing her over the edge.

He would not know this for sure until after she had delivered her child. Indeed, at the moment, there was little he could do for her medically. Prescribing an anti-convulsive might calm her down, but it might also interfere with the birth and certainly with the other drugs the on-call doctor had prescribed.

There was also still the question of how many street drugs remained in her bloodstream. It was already a potentially fatal broth. At the risk of exacerbating her condition, there was little he could do for her now other than wait.

As he approached her, the woman turned with a start.

"Goshujin kokoro houshou motte junshin."

Jerry Harris stopped dead in his tracks.

Not again, he thought to himself. This could not be happening. Not again.

"I'm sorry," he asked timidly. "What did you say?"

"Huh?"

"You said something. In Japanese, I think."

"I did?" the woman said. She was clearly confused.

"Goshujin kokoro... something," he stammered.

"Go... where?" she said groggily.

"Uh, never mind. Must be my mistake. I'm Doctor...."

"Harris," the woman interrupted.

She had a curious look on her face that suggested to Jerry that she too was surprised that she knew his name.

He looked down to see if he was wearing his badge. He wasn't.

"Do we know each other?" he asked with obvious hesitation.

"I don't know," the woman responded. "Ever hang around Dill Street or Stewart Avenue?"

"No, I'm afraid not," he grinned with embarrassment. "Your chart doesn't have your name on it."

"Emily. My name's Emily."

CHAPTER FORTY-TWO

"The baby's tiny fingers began to knead dough."

Emily suddenly reached out and grabbed Jerry's hand tightly, letting out a scream that had the nurses running into the room.

"She's crowning!" one of them said loudly, as she looked between her legs. "Call the O.B. on duty. Now!"

"Hope you remember how to birth them babies, Dr. Harris," the other nurse chuckled in a mock southern drawl. "Last I heard the O.B. was still in the O.R."

Jerry sighed heavily. "Great."

As Emily moaned in pain, she clutched his arm with both hands, making doubly sure that he would not leave her side. As he gently patted her hand, he became surreptitiously aware of a multitude of scars on the inside of her arm.

Some were old. Others were new. Some were deep. Others shallow.

Emily was a cutter.

Dr. Harris had seen a few of these in his career. But they were few and far between. And all of them had been women.

It was well known that men typically acted on their angst by lashing out at others. Women, on the other hand, often internalized their aggression. And some of them turned to self-motification.

With a little time, the scarring on Emily's arm, and presumably other parts of her body, could be read by an expert, not unlike the rings of a tree by an arborist. It wouldn't be too hard to determine how recently she had been depressed, how often, and how far back her disorder had begun.

Self-mutilation was not a cry for help. It was a whimper.

The people who did it were usually too afraid of death to kill themselves. And too afraid of life to live it head-on. So, they simply existed in the private purgatory between the two. For them, release could only come at the sharp end of a knife or razor or pair of scissors, a few millimeters at a time. It was a queer affliction.

Technically, cutting was not in itself a mental illness. But it was almost always symptomatic of some other type of personality disorder. Oddly, the impulse to do it often went away on its own after about a year.

But Emily's cutting appeared to have lasted for much longer than that.

"Is she one of yours, Dr. Harris?" one of the nurses asked.

He looked into Emily's eyes. They were desperate and starving for compassion. Her hair was matted with sweat to her brow, and she was breathing hard in that feral way women breathe in the terrifying seconds before giving birth.

The last time he had witnessed this spectacle, it was his own wife lying before him. He smiled.

"Yes," he told the nurse. "She's one of mine."

At that moment, the resident obstetrician sauntered into the room. "Sorry, I'm late, gang," he said merrily as he pulled up one of the rolling stools.

"Had a Caesarian down the hall. Mom had twins, but only one of them took. Had to scrape out one last tablespoon of baby before we could close her up. Whatchu gonna do?" he shrugged.

He snapped on his rubber gloves with a loud pop, oblivious to the grimaces all around him.

"And who do we have here?" he mused, reading over the woman's chart. "Ah. Emily, eh? Well, by the looks of things Emmy, you'll be outta here in no time flat."

The O.B. looked over to Jerry. "Dr. Harris, how are you?"

"Good, thanks."

"She one of yours?"

"Yes, she is," Jerry reiterated.

"Awesome. Emmy, between the two of us," the doctor said loudly into her widely dilated cervix, "I'd say you're in pretty good hands."

Twelve minutes later, Emily delivered an eight pound six ounce baby boy. Baby Doe seemed to be in perfect health. He was well above the healthy weight index and responded on cue to all the stimuli he was supposed to.

He had curly black hair and pecan-colored skin. The nurses immediately wrapped him up in a blanket and took his foot prints. Then, they gave him to Emily, who cried with joy, stroking his hair and instinctively counting his fingers and toes. It was a beautiful sight to behold.

But that was the problem.

Dr. Harris simply could not reconcile the image of the woman cradling the newborn in front of him with the foul-mouthed crack harlot he had first encountered earlier in the day. There was something profoundly wrong with this picture.

"He's quite beautiful, Emily," he said.

"Thank you, Dr. Harris."

"Do you know what you're going to call him?"

Emily thought for a moment then smiled weakly. "Leon. After his father."

"Oh. Will he be here soon?"

"No," she said absently. "He's dead."

"I'm very sorry."

"It's okay," she said. "It's probably better that way."

The doctor instantly took note of the afterthought.

There was clearly more being said in the space between the words. But that was something he could chase down later. For the moment he was infatuated by the loving scene in front of him.

As Emily and her child snuggled together, the baby's tiny fingers began to knead dough and his mouth began to purse rapidly in a sucking fashion. Without missing a beat, Emily pulled down the front of her gown presenting a swollen breast for the baby to nurse.

For an instant, Dr. Harris thought it might be prudent to stop them, given the residual crack cocaine in the woman's bloodstream. But ultimately he chose to do nothing. The baby had already been exposed to the drug for the past nine months. A few minutes more would certainly not do any great harm.

Indeed, preventing the union might have a longer-lasting negative impact on the boy psychologically.

After all, this was one of God's true gifts.

The Mother and Child archetype was sacrosanct in every known religion and tribal ritual in the world. The reason why could be seen on the faces of the people in the room. Each and every person here wore the very same unconscious expression of almost narcotic beatitude.

The female nurses licked their lips unknowingly in a silent frenzy of endorphin release. The male doctor's face mimicked the expression of the little boy's every time their eyes met. And a palpable happy silence barricaded the mother and her child from any intrusion other than the necessary business of ordering the room and documenting their vital signs.

"Emily, I'll check back in with you in the morning. You and Leon try to get some rest tonight."

"Thank you, Dr. Harris." Emily took the little boy's hand gently and waved it at the doctor. "Bye-bye, Dr. Hawwis," she giggled, imitating a baby's voice. "Bye-bye."

Jerry Harris smiled as he turned to walk away.

But once he was outside the door, his expression changed darkly. Things here were definitely not as they seemed, he thought to himself.

And far more importantly, the baby would soon begin the withdrawal process.

Later that night, he decided to stop by the maternity ward to look in on Leon personally. He wanted to make sure everything was being done to comfort the boy if he was in distress.

There were nineteen sleeping infants in the viewing room.

Jerry did not have the little boy's identification number, but thought surely that he would not be hard to find.

Crack babies were usually loud and fitful insomniacs.

Their little bodies shook with the jitters, and they sweated pools. Despite that, they were often wrapped tightly in their little baby blankets to keep them from touching themselves. Their own fingers could send them into easy hysterics with disconsolate shrieking that could keep the entire ward awake.

Cold turkey seemed a harsh remedy. But for now sedatives were too dangerous to use. Hugging and cradling weren't much of an option either. Many of the newborns did not like to be touched, even by the loving hands of the nurses and volunteer Rocking Chair Grandmothers.

Simple warm water baths worked the best to ease their physical suffering. But the soothing effect was often short-lived, and within minutes they would return to their frenzied states.

It was a ritual that would continue until the agony of detoxification was complete.

But looking through the giant window pane, Dr Harris could not find Leon. The babies were all sound asleep in the collective repose that is one of the signatures of social animals.

Perhaps they had moved him, the doctor speculated.

He had passed Emily's room on the way, and he knew that the baby was not with her. He prayed silently that the boy had not had some sort of physical setback.

He went to the nurse supervisor and asked her what had happened to Leon.

"Nothing, Dr. Harris. The baby's asleep," she said nonchalantly.

"Where?"

"In the viewing room. Crib number 14, on the end of the row. I'll show you," she said leading the way.

Just as the nurse said, baby Leon was sound asleep in Crib 14. A nearby desk lamp shone on his face with a soft orange hue that softened the old-man wrinkles etched around his eyes.

"That light's not supposed to be on," the nurse fussed quietly to herself as she went inside to turn it off.

When she got to the desk, she stopped with a curious look on her face.

"That's odd," she murmured.

The light switch was already in the off position.

As Dr. Harris watched from the window, she flicked the switch back and forth. Nothing happened. She gently tapped at the base of the lamp, and the light bulb exploded with a loud pop into a shower of sparks.

With a start, she jumped back. Instantly, all the babies in the room woke up in a loud crescendo of crying. All but one.

Baby Leon.

Jerry watched the spectacle through the glass, shaking his head in disbelief. Two other nurses rushed into the room, turning the overhead fluorescent lights on. For a second, the change in light shifted the reflection on the viewing window.

From the corner of his eye, Jerry could see a chorus of children standing behind him.

"Jonathan?" he said turning quickly around.

But there was no one in the hall except for a confused-looking orderly who happened to be passing by.

"Nah, I'm Mike. You know, the guy who runs the charts and stuff? You all right, Dr. Harris?" he asked.

"Oh, uh, yes. Just talking to myself."

"Sounds a little crazy, for a psych doc," Mike smiled as he continued walking."

The doctor chuckled, thinking about it for a moment.

"It's only crazy when you answer yourself back," he advised with a grin.

Even though Jerry hadn't seen Jonathan and the other children in the hospital for many weeks, he could still feel their presence every now and then.

It had become both reassuring and unsettling.

Occasionally, the empiricist side of the brain would try to convince him that he was hallucinating. He had even been tempted more than once to schedule a confidential CAT scan at Emory University Hospital to see if there were any abnormalities in his temporal lobes or hippocampus.

He had also considered a blood test could to determine whether or not his serotonin levels were deficient, which could potentially short-circuit the amygdale.

And if that were the case, his brain could be tricked into deciphering otherwise meaningless neural noise into a finely-woven tapestry of events and people that his subconscious could easily manufacture.

The Sins of Angels

The psychiatric literature was replete with case studies of people who saw and heard ghosts, saints, demons, and angels. They were always either schizophrenics or people with chemical imbalances that could massage their minds into seeing anything it wanted to.

Such phenomena could even be contagious.

He could be having a delayed memetic response to Dr. Tatsuro's tormented life story in which he was haunted, curiously, by the *absence* of the ghosts of his own children.

The tale had touched him deeply. And that kind of resonance could certainly generate a convergent wave of emotion between the two men. Rather like two waves in the ocean coming together to form one bigger wave.

In their case the ocean was an ocean of grief.

At one time Dr. Harris had thought that Ed Lee could be suffering from one of these disorders. That was until he realized that Ed was perfectly healthy and, by every known measure, entirely sane.

These days, Dr. Harris knew that he could not with absolute certainty say the same thing about himself.

All he had left to convince him that he was fine was his faith.

And that made him laugh out loud.

He had often derided faith as the poor man's sextant of the soul. An absurdly impractical tool in the hands of people who still oafishly thought the world was morally flat.

The acumen of science was inarguably superior. Or so he had once thought. Before Ed Lee. Before the Vitruvian Man. Before Mars.

Lately, nothing was as clear as it once had been.

Jerry had begun to realize that he had spent half a lifetime studying the brain, only to discover that he was a maestro of an instrument whose music he could not even play.

CHAPTER FORTY-THREE
"Phrenology."

The fish tank purled softly with an upward cascade of bubbles while brightly colored fish swam in a slow-moving portrait of serenity. The walls of the room were painted beige and dotted symmetrically with prints of vintage maps and 19th century sketches of long-extinct flora and fauna.

The design was right out of Therapy 101. Nothing in the office could distract the patient from the invisible work of the counseling session.

But it was not always a hard and fast rule.

On the desk, next to an old brass banker's lamp, sat the bust of a bald head. It was mapped out precisely like an intricate three dimensional jigsaw puzzle, illustrating the various regions of human behavior. Etched into its base was one word.

"Phrenology."

Just a hundred years ago, the phrenologist and the psychiatrist held equal seats on the pantheon of mental health sciences.

But eventually, as the shrinks liked to joke, the Id had won out over the Idiots.

Some of the psychiatrists on the ward had advised Dr. Harris to get rid of the bust, given the fact that it was little more than a fetish of the quackery that made people suspicious of all so-called head doctors.

But he had decided to keep the relic as a reminder that sometimes science and buffoonery are kissing cousins. Indeed, only the psychiatrists' prerogative to prescribe drugs had given them their ultimate advantage over their Victorian rivals.

Despite this, even today there were thousands of New Age charlatans who still professed the ability to diagnose severe mental disorders by simply reading the bumps on a person's head. And while they were widely lampooned, these self-proclaimed "organic" therapists argued that at least their diagnoses and treatments didn't require turning the patient into a drug-addled zombie.

And that, with no small measure of irony, was true.

As the Windsor chimes pronounced the hour, the door to the office opened slowly. Emily was escorted into the room by an attendant.

"Good morning, Emily. How are you?" Dr. Harris said cheerily.

"Not so good, Dr. Asshole!" she grunted.

Jerry tried in vain not to betray how absolutely taken aback he was with Emily's bizarre outburst

As she stood before him, her head twisted and her face contorted in visual staccatos that made her entire body lock and convulse.

The attendant shook his head as he helped her into her chair.

"You gonna be all right, Doc?" he asked with a hint of warning in his voice. "Want me to stay?"

"Fuck off!" she spat, as she shook her arm loose from his grasp.

"No. No. It's okay, Mike," the doctor said cautiously, never once deviating his gaze from Emily's eyes.

"I'll be right outside if you need me."

"Thanks. But I'm sure we'll be fine," he said with meretricious optimism.

With that, the attendant reluctantly closed the door behind him as he left the room.

"Emily?" Dr. Harris said gently.

"What do you want with that bitch?" she sneered. "I got what you want right here," she said lasciviously, lifting her hospital gown far enough for the doctor to see between her thighs.

The doctor noted that the way she opened her legs suggestively back and forth, rubbing her crotch obscenely, Emily seemed oblivious to the trauma of having given birth just a few days before.

"We can do it right here," she whispered, looking at the door.

"Emily, I don't…"

"Fuck Emily!" she said angrily. Then, laughing, she sneered, "No, really. Fuck Emily."

Smiling obscenely, she grabbed the doctor's Phrenology bust.

"How bout we start with a little head?" she laughed, as she tossed the bust menacingly from hand to hand.

"Emily, I need you to put that back on the desk, okay?" the doctor said patiently.

"W-What?" she said in obvious confusion. "Dr. Harris? What's going on?"

"It's okay, Emily. Just put the statue back on the desk."

"Huh? Oh, sure. I'm sorry," she said leaning forward to return the bust to its place on the desk. Her hands shook as she cradled it carefully, making sure she didn't drop it.

"Thank you, Emily."'

"Oops! I think I just changed my mind," she roared laughing.

At that moment she jumped out of her seat, holding the bust over her head.

"Maybe I'll just smash your fucking brains out with it instead!"

With that, she kicked Jerry hard in the balls. He doubled over in pain. But as she lunged forward to hit him, strong hands grabbed the statue before it could crash down on Jerry's head.

"Damn! It's a good thing you called me, doc."

"What?" Jerry groaned.

Racked with pain and nausea, he couldn't remember calling the orderly to save his life. Literally.

"Fuck off, bitch!" Emily screamed at the man.

With a single motion he had pushed her back into her chair with one hand, while gently giving the doctor his bust with the other.

"Doc, I strongly recommend you restrain this one," Mike warned. "Please."

The doctor nodded gravely, as he struggled to catch his breath and recover his composure.

"Hold her down," he wheezed.

The attendant locked both of Emily's arms with one of his own and pushed her head to one side, exposing her carotid artery. The more she tried to struggle, the harder it pulsed visibly through the skin.

Dr. Harris quickly filled a hypodermic needle with 25mg of Loprazolam and injected it directly into her neck. Thirty seconds later, Emily sat dazed in a semi-conscious state with her legs splayed out and her head leaning heavily to one side.

Occasionally, she made hard grunting sounds, like a person with Tourette's Syndrome. Finally her eyes fluttered upward into her skull and her mouth curled at the end with an indelible smirk.

The dosage should have been enough to knock out a man as big as Mike. But Emily was not completely unconscious. She was merely suspended in a quasi-soporific state. She panted agitatedly, and occasionally her fingertips moved as she tried to will her body out of its forced sleep.

The doctor sat down on the edge of the desk in front of her. He was momentarily dumbstruck. This was most certainly not the Emily he had befriended in the delivery room.

This was the vicious snarling harpy that had spoken only when everyone had left the room.

It was now obvious that the personality paradigm had shifted.

Violently.

As Dr. Harris contemplated this sudden change of events, it dawned on him that Emily had perhaps inadvertently diagnosed herself.

"I think I just changed my mind," she had said as she was about to smash the bust over his head.

Changed her mind indeed, he thought. Emily was suffering from a very clear multiple personality disorder.

In most cases, patients with MPD had suffered some form of trauma in their lives that caused them to dissociate their intrinsic identities.

Child molestation. Rape. Torture. These were the Big Three, and the odds were overwhelming in every case that at least one, two, or all of them were involved in a patient's past.

The doctor shook his head.

He had wrongly focused too much on the drugs in her system as the reason behind her erratic episodes that day in the hospital.

It was true that he did acknowledge the possibility she might be profoundly mentally ill. But at the time, her crack addiction had eclipsed all the other possible problems she might be having. As it now appeared, her crack use may have been the least of her problems, nothing more than self-medication.

He had made a rookie mistake.

The MPD should have been easy to see. Self-destructive phobics are classic candidates for dissociation behavior.

He had misconstrued the signs; and that wasn't like him.

But he wasn't the priority issue here. Emily was.

He studied her carefully. Her state of mind had not changed appreciably since he had given her the sedative. He wondered as he took her pulse, how she could have morphed so completely into the monster sitting before him?

But it was the next thought that sent a shiver down his spine.

Was this the Emily in front of the looking glass?

Or the one behind it?

It would be hard to tell.

Jerry was well aware that many doctors thoroughly dismissed dissociation as a canard, a pseudo disease that had all but disappeared during the medieval era of electric shock therapy.

Psychiatrists had discovered back in the 1930's that pain was a pretty good cure for crazy.

The logic was certainly barbaric. But in many cases it was also inerrant.

The indisputable fact was that once such treatments were outlawed, certain disorders began to make a remarkably coincidental come-back.

MPD was one of these.

These days it had found itself rooted firmly back in favor.

In fact, it was considered far more commonplace than most people might think. Dissociation could be as harmless as daydreaming. Or as severe as chronic amnesia. But left to the inventions of a creative mind, it could morph into a full-blown case of MPD.

Just like Emily.

"You soil yourself with doubt," she suddenly snarled.

"What?"

"You're quite pathetic, doctor," she mocked.

"Emily?"

"The cunt is gone.

"What do you mean, 'gone'?"

"Gone," she repeated ominously

The doctor stood up and backed away slowly.

"Who are you?" he asked with noticeable trepidation.

"I am Beleal."

"Beleal?"

"Daughter of Lilith and nemesis of Solomon. The keeper of this bitch."

"I don't understand. What does all that mean, Bileal?" Doctor Harris probed gently, trying to manufacture as much patience as he could under the circumstances.

"Fool! My name is written upon the ages!"

"All right," the doctor offered weakly.

Bileal smiled condescendingly.

"Ecce meus nomen intra ille magnus volumen de angelus exercitus. Ille cantus de Clavicula Salomoni et il Magu Honorius exsilio meus non! Meus potentia et regno terror imperium! Praecipito ad tuus genubus servus de ille Fictus Unus!"

Dr. Harris breathed in deeply as he contemplated what he had just heard. This was the kind of Latin that went way beyond what Rev. Hamm had taught in eighth grade, and it was spoken with a conversational ease that should not exist in modern times.

Bileal spoke quickly, but Jerry was able to pick up the gist of what she was saying.

There was something further about Solomon and a wizard. She had also called him a slave and had commanded him to fall to his knees. But one thing in particular stuck out from everything else. The Great Book of the Army of Angels.

"Sicut erat in principio, et nunc, et simper, et in saecula saeculorum. Amen. Sicut erat in principio, et nunc, et et simper, et in saecula saeculorum. Amen."

At first, Dr. Harris thought his ears were deceiving him. Bileal was praying. Indeed, every good Catholic acolyte knew the words she spoke. "As it was in the beginning, is now, and ever shall be, world without end. Amen."

But it soon became apparent that Bileal was not praying to God. She was praying to the Devil.

"Gloria Lucifere!" she shouted. *"Et Bileal et spiritui maloso!"*

Dr. Harris decided it would be best to feign as though he had no idea what Bileal had said. Perhaps, that would lull her into revealing more.

"I'm afraid my Latin's too rusty to understand what you were trying to say."

Bileal laughed, turning her head queerly as she peered deeply into his eyes. The look made the down hairs on the doctor's neck raise. He felt a shudder rise through the length of his body that felt like a sustained current of low voltage.

"Id videor fortasse tu solum simulo sum ludificor," she smiled.

The doctor could not translate all of the words, but he nonetheless got the unmistakable impression that his ruse did not work. Her words meant something to the effect of "Perhaps you are not as stupid as you pretend to be."

"Fair enough, Bileal. But tell me, why Latin? Why not plain English? Why go to all the trouble and complication of such a tedious, not to mention dead, language?"

"Ego loquor ille lingua de meus expergiscor."

292

"The language of your awakening?"

"Ego affero ille praenuntius de lumen!"

"You? The harbinger of the light?"

Dr. Harris found himself laughing out loud, another of the cardinal sins during therapy. No matter how absurd the patient's words or acts became a psychiatrist always had to give the appearance of being in complete control of his or her emotions, at least ostensibly eloigned from the viscera of the discourse.

But before he could stop, Jerry found himself laughing even harder and going so far as to insult Bileal.

In the tongue of her "awakening."

"Vos perditus belua! Undique vos ille lumen serpo in fastidium!"
(Vile monster! The light crawls from you in every direction in disgust!)

It was at this point that the doctor found himself spitting on Bileal, who suddenly recoiled in transparent fear.

Dr. Harris looked up and saw the attendant Mike staring at him with his mouth agape.

"Now, that's what I'm talkin' about, doc!" he laughed. "I don't know what the fuck you just said, but I'm gonna leave and let you handle your business. I'll be right outside if you need me."

The doctor nodded his head slowly, unsure of what he had just done.

As he opened the door, Mike looked back at the woman squirming nervously in the chair.

"Crazy bitch," he muttered, as he shut the door behind him.

"She fears you, Jerry."

The doctor wheeled around. The voice was as clear as if the person speaking were standing right behind him. But there was no one there.

"Take her hands," the voice commanded. "Now, before it's too late."

Suddenly, Jerry understood. The voice belonged to the caretaker at The Vitruvian Man.

Just then, Bileal began to chant. Urgently.

"Bagabi laca bachabe. Lamac lamec bachalyas. Lamac cahi achababe...."

"Grab her now!" the voice commanded. "She's invoking the spirit of her Master! You must act quickly!"

"Samahac et famyolas...."

Before Bileal could utter another word, Dr. Harris grabbed her hands. A hot charge of static shot between their fingers. The woman let out a scream. And then a moan. Her eyes rolled up in her head, and she began to shake violently.

As he continued to hold her hands, every muscle in the woman's body relaxed at once, and she appeared to fall into a deep trance. The doctor's mouth opened wide.

In silent screaming.

CHAPTER FORTY-FOUR

"Fear."

The handle was made of fruit wood. It was sturdy, water-tight and unyielding. A design so perfect for the job that it had not changed in ten thousand years. The only distinguishing mark was a military emblem with the rank of general carved into it.

As the man tightened his grip around the polished crescent, the friction from his palm made a noise not dissimilar to someone cracking his knuckles. The faces of those who stood before him winced with every subtle pop and creak.

He smiled at the littlest one in the line. She in turn smiled back innocently. He knelt down to her level and genuinely admired the beauty of her face.

It was the color of a roasted almond, with hazel eyes that in the sunlight glowed like raw African honey.

She was tall and strong for her age. And her hair was full, black and curly, the unmistakable signature of both her Moorish ancestry and her family's wealth.

Many of the children in this part of the country had red hair and rickets. It seemed that half were orphans, and that the other half were going to be. But in this community, where the merchants and the bankers lived, the children flourished.

At two years old, the little girl thought that her family was playing a game with the men who had loudly entered their home. One by one, her brothers and sisters, her mother and father, her grandparents and cousins, her aunts and uncles were all led into the front yard of their villa, where they now stood.

295

There was shouting and squealing and crying.

But these were the very same devices that she herself had employed to win candy and kisses and other goodies from her "*Mamangu*" and "*Abu*," her Mother and her Father.

The only time she had seen this much commotion was when Papa Nick had visited her daycare at The International School. He was much bigger than this man, with a very large belly. He wore a red and white suit, had a fluffy white beard, and bore a curious resemblance to Father Jeremiah, the French missionary who held mass at the school.

The children had cried and shouted there, too, until all of them had been given a toy from Papa Nick's big bag.

It had not escaped the little girl's attention that the ones who cried the loudest had gotten their gifts the quickest. That's why she was angry at her mother for hysterically begging the man to come over to her instead.

"Greedy *Mamangu!*" she thought petulantly.

"Me! Me! Me!" she exclaimed with one of her favorite and best articulated words. "Me! Me! Me!"

"Yes! You, you, you!" the general pointed, laughing aloud as he stood back up.

He looked around at the others wearing red berets behind him. They grinned in unison, nodding their heads at the exchange.

He patted the girl on her head and stroked the fullness of her cheeks. With his forefinger on her chin, he gently tilted her face so that their eyes met. He noticed with amusement that her two front teeth were just beginning to come in.

With an exaggerated smile, he showed the little girl his own teeth. They were white and glistening. The brightest she had ever seen. Proudly, she smiled in the same exaggerated way, just before he raised his machete and cut her head off.

Simultaneously, the family squeezed shut their eyes in horror and disbelief and the false hope that what they had just seen somehow was not real. How could it possibly be real? Little girls in Sunday pinafores did not get their heads hacked off. It defied all that is human. Even in the seething hell of Rwanda.

And yet, there she lay on the lawn, her head separated from her body, with tiny flecks of grass sticking in the curls, the same way they did when she rolled down the hill at the back of the villa playing with her big brother.

The relatives stood frozen and dumbstruck, glued to the ground with a force stronger than gravity.

Fear.

The man had seen this picture a thousand times before. To him, it had become a visual platitude. He knew from experience that the first one to act would not be the father. It would most certainly be the mother. Just like a lioness on the plain.

Her attack would be swift. And she would kill.

If she could.

Except for the husband, the others would try to run away, scattering in every direction, at first fleeing in scared silence until they realized it was futile.

Then would come the begging. After that, the bartering. Then, the betrayals. The pointing of fingers to condemn your favorite cousin or nephew or auntie in exchange for sparing your own life.

Somewhere in the middle of this chaos, the husband would inevitably awaken from his impotent stupor, torn between joining his wife in the fight and rushing to his slain child. This was hard to predict. And for that reason alone, the platoon would go after him immediately.

Indeed, the men and the boys were always the first to be slaughtered. Not because they were stronger or would fight harder. That was most certainly not the case.

They simply had no purpose. They were completely irrelevant and useless extras in this human drama.

From above, the fifty-five swinging machetes were a rhythmic symphony of mayhem and gore. The platoon moved like some terrible threshing machine with tines that turned the dirt into mud with blood. Torsos lay separated from their limbs and heads in a macabre landscape of distorted reality.

After circling her prey for several minutes, the little girl's mother fell to her knees in shock and exhaustion. She was light-headed from the adrenaline overdose, and now she panted with her mouth and eyes wide open, watching the little boy in the general's grip.

And the machete at his throat.

Her mouth was too dry to speak. But it was easy for him to read her lips. After all, he had been called the name many times before.

"*Dubwana,*" she croaked hoarsely.

Monster.

In weak supplication, she raised her arm, pointing at the boy. She didn't feel the blade as it sliced her hand off at the wrist, fingers still twitching in the dust at the general's feet.

As the little boy watched, the soldiers tore off his mother's clothes and gang-raped her while she bled to death.

And thereafter.

Her daughters and sisters were thrown into trucks and taken back to the barracks where they too would eventually be raped until they died. As for the boy, the general showed a measure of mercy by releasing him. But not before sodomizing him and burning his corneas with a lit cigar.

The boy would wake up every day of his life in a gray plasmic darkness. The images of torture and slaughter would remain forever a stark pentimento beneath the drooling infected translucence that had replaced his vision.

He would never forget the general's face, however, or the patches his men wore on their sleeves. Each one emblazoned with the screaming face of a *shaitani*, a demon. Beneath it, words he could not yet read but could spell from memory. *Kikuli kivosi.*

The Ghost Platoon.

Jerry felt nausea welling up in every cell of his being. Though he could see the horrific events playing out before him, he had no sense of where he was, only who. And even that was vague. It was as though he were witness to someone else's nightmare. Except that he was actually in the nightmare.

He could smell the blood and the stench of death all around him. His could feel the clothes sticking against his skin with sweat, and he reeked of ammonia-strong body odor. He burned beneath the oppressive heat beating against his arms and face. And he could taste the queer bile of sadistic lust lingering in his mouth.

"Bileal," he thought.

Instinctively, he released her hands and staggered backwards like a beaten fighter against the ropes. He steadied himself against his desk.

"Don't let go, Jerry!" the voice of the old man boomed in his head. "She's trapped. Now, you must continue to follow her before she dies."

"Follow her? I don't understand," Jerry said aloud. "Follow her where?"

"To the beginning."

Jerry looked at the clock on the wall above the door. Though it felt like hours, less than a minute had actually passed since he had begun this… this… whatever it was. A delusion by proxy. An hysterical hallucination. There had to be some clinical diagnosis that he could cling to. Something more than a bizarre rubric of dangerous magic and reverse demonic possession.

It was with profound reluctance, yet surprising resoluteness, that he grabbed her hands once again.

The white hallway stretched for what seemed to be a quarter-mile. The tiles gleamed with immaculate cleanliness as sunlight poured in through the transoms that lined the top of the walls just below the ceilings.

Every fifty feet or so a uniformed custodian slow-waltzed a wet mop and a bucket over the floor. They were careful and deliberate.

They had better be.

Failure at this the most menial of tasks would sweep them off the corridor and into one of the many rooms along it. These were marked only by plain white doors, small windows, and the mournful wails of torment coming from inside.

Unit 731 sprawled for five square miles in the Pingfang District of Harbin, a city in Manchuria known for the primal beauty of its sprawling silver tundras and its complete compliance to the Japanese invaders.

During the long winters, the complex was hard to see by air, which made it hard for the Allied Forces to find and bomb. The desolation was perfect to hide the forsaken hordes of POW's who were brought in by the truck load.

It was they and a few dozen Chinese civilians who now spent their nights howling in agony behind the white doors. Soon they would join the thousands of others lying forever silent beneath the deep snow drifts at the rear of the facility.

General Shiro Ishii strode dispassionately down the hall, stopping at each of the doors to peer in on his subjects and take meticulous notes.

The four year-old twin girls in *Seru Ichi* were responding nicely, he thought. Three days ago they had been vivisected at the torso and sewn together with thick surgical twine to replicate an experiment to conjoin twins. It was a novel procedure suggested in a letter from his dear friend and distant colleague, the peerless Dr. Josef Mengele.

The Sins of Angels

The girls had still not regained consciousness, but they were still alive. And that was more than could be said for any of the other previous sets of twins.

In *Seru Roku,* the American soldier presented more ominous symptoms. He was pale and clammy, too weak to move without help. His breathing was shallow, and the chart hanging beneath the window noted that he was extremely hypotensive.

General Ishii nodded his head as he read.

This is what one might expect, he concluded quietly, when five milliliters of PMU is injected into the kidneys of a healthy adult male over a period of several weeks.

The soldier's muscle tone had noticeably softened, and his facial hair had all but disappeared. Small breasts were beginning to grow beneath the large green anchor tattooed on his chest.

Why he was now is such grave distress was a mystery.

Did he have some underlying medical condition? They would doubtless have to resolve this question during his autopsy.

Next time, General Ishii thought, he would try the PMU on a female subject. After all, pregnant mare urine is full of conjugated estrogens and medroxyprogesterone.

The applications for regenerative fertility were limitless.

Future scientists would surely thank him for his pioneering studies, he smiled.

Seru Go was sealed with a special leaded tape around the door. Behind it was another door, this one made of steel. It led to a chamber that was less a room than a furnace.

Or to be precise, an incinerator.

Flames would shoot down from three vents in the ceiling and up from a line of burners beneath the metal grate floor. Whatever was inside at the time would be turned to ash in a matter of minutes.

At the moment, that was a young Chinese woman and her two small sons.

Beneath the wooden bench they were huddled on sat a spring-loaded box containing approximately half a kilogram of fleas. Each one of them had been contaminated with bacillus Yersinia Pestis.

The Black Plague.

The General looked at his watch. A cheap clock inside the box would trip the spring any moment now and voracious fleas by the tens of thousands would leap and crawl over the unsuspecting family in a biting orgy of pestilence and pain.

Death would be slow.

Their lymph nodes would swell like balloons and fever would incapacitate them within hours. Their lungs would soon fill with fluid and then cease to function.

But the prognosis was not assured for everyone. That is exactly why tests like these were important.

A third of the infected patients managed to survive the plague. But through careful engineering, the bacillus being used here had been bred and distilled to a staggering ninety-seven percent lethality. And those who did survive will wish they hadn't.

General Ishii tapped gently on the glass, waving and smiling at the little boy staring at him.

"Kaitsuu sono bokkusu!" he teased, gesturing with his hands.

"Open the box!"

In an instant, the scene in front of Jerry changed. Then changed again.

All over time.

All over the world.

And, it seemed, all at once.

The air was now warm and redolent with expensive perfume.

The woman fanned herself furiously with an ornate *eventail* made of crimson silk and ivory. Gilded Chinese characters were woven into the fabric and filled the screen when the fan was fully extended. It was the favorite affectation among the Ladies of the Temperance Council, who often passed it around, fondling it admiringly, not knowing that the words belonged to the poet Li Po.

"I can love wine, without shame before God."

The ladies did not know that their friend had commissioned the embroidery during a missionary trip to Shanghai many years ago. Nor did they know that the trip itself had been less concerned with converting the savage souls of the Orient than about spending days of delirium and lubricity in the city's opium dens. Indeed, that is where the fan had been acquired.

But regardless of its dubious history, the fan did its job exceedingly well, both in the front pew during service and now outside on the well-manicured esplanade of Mount Calvary Baptist Church.

It was a beautiful Sunday afternoon, and the church bells pealed their iron homily for miles around.

A crowd of hundreds had gathered for an early supper of fried chicken and ham, fish and coleslaw, snap beans and squash, cornbread and cake.

The smell of the feast wafted higher than the steeple itself, and as the preacher blessed the food and those about to consume it, the Ladies of the Temperance Council whispered giddily among themselves.

"I heard that he fought like Mighty Ajax himself!"

"Yes, and that it took four strong men to bring him down."

"You don't say."

"Oh, yes, dear. Such strength!" the woman with the fan opined. "I mean... *for a Jew.*"

The cluster of women nodded together somberly.

"Who would have thought?" one of them snickered.

"Yes. I've seen him in his store. Meek as a gelded mule."

"Meek, yes. Gelded, no," another chuckled. "He's got five sons!"

"His poor wife," sighed one of the women, with specious compassion. "Can you imagine having to knit all those little beanie caps."

"Four boys now," the lady with the fan corrected.

"What?"

"One of them was killed when the Knights came for their father."

"Oh, my!"

"How awful."

"My husband told me that it was most unpleasant," she sighed piously.

As they walked across the street to a large gazebo in the park, the ladies coalesced in a swirling pastel collage of crinolines and bonnets.

The Sins of Angels

When they stopped, they stood out from the crowd like a very large bouquet of spring carnations.

Children raced about the park, laughing with gentle mischief, as their parents watched with proud amusement. It wasn't long before the littlest of them were quietly lined up, taking turns at the hand crank of Miller Sweeny's ice-cream churn.

A small band with a banjo began to play a hymn that everyone here knew by heart. Soon the crowd began to sway and hold hands in singing. The lady with the fan had the most beautiful voice of them all and led the chorus using her *eventail* like a conductor's baton.

> *"Must Jesus bear the cross alone*
> *And all the world go free.*
> *No, there's a cross for everyone*
> *And there's a cross for me."*

As the crowd sang, and the children made ice cream, a small group of men made their way to the giant elm for which the street bordering the park was named. Moving the Sparkin' Swing out of the way, one of men hoisted a thick rope over the large branch that hung over the pavement.

The others tightened the noose at the end of it around the neck of Manny Schoenberg.

His face was red and blue and horribly disfigured. His eyelids were the size and color of bruised lemons, and his nose was broken and twisted in an asymmetrical portrait of agony. His front teeth were missing, and his lips were grossly engorged with ferocious swelling.

The singing grew louder and more energized, as the men wrapped a heavy metal chain around Manny's ankles and threw the other end over the limb next to the rope.

"The consecrated cross I'll bear
Till death shall set me free.
And then go home my crown to wear
For there's a crown for me."

With one great movement, the men pulled the chain and the rope together, till Manny was hanging prostrate in the air, gasping for breath, bubbles of blood and mucus wheezing from his twisted nose and shattered mouth.

"O precious cross! O glorious crown!
O resurrection day!
When Christ the Lord from Heav'n comes down
And bears my soul away."

Suddenly, the singing and the music stopped. On cue, the crowd surged forward and began punching and kicking Manny as he hung over the sidewalk. The children picked up sticks and poked at him like a corpse that hadn't yet died.

Women jabbed him viciously with umbrellas and hat pins, drawing blood. And when the men tired of beating him with their fists and kicking him with their boots, they picked up shovels and ax handles and anything else they could grab.

The Sins of Angels

The frenzy lasted no more than five minutes. Manny, unfortunately, lasted longer than that. So, the men hoisted him higher, by the neck, until the tendons and bone stretched and snapped like a wooden pin on an overloaded wagon wheel.

Somehow, in the twilight of asphyxia, Manny had managed to open his swollen eyes for one last pathetic look at the world.

There before him stood the men who had frequented his shop, panting and foaming at the mouth like mad dogs. The women whose groceries he had bagged, their faces and elegant dresses now stained with his blood. The children who once had free reign of the penny candy in his store, had now innocently returned to their laughter, drooling their melting ice cream all over their Sunday best clothes.

A nearby photographer didn't need to tell the crowd to smile as he took their picture with a polished wooden camera. The tray of magnesium powder flashed a brilliant white light that blinded Manny for a moment, erasing the images before him, but not hiding the horror even for a second.

Across the street, his wife and four sons stood out as the only white people amid a sea of frightened black faces. The High Sheriff had ordered them here to remind them what happened to uppity niggers and nigger-loving Jews who had the effrontery to accuse a white lady in this town of anything. Especially stealing.

And especially the white lady with the fan.

When the carnage was done, the men and women lined up politely to wash their hands and faces in the fountain in the middle of the park.

Chatting jovially, they returned to the church across the street to sit down and eat their Sunday supper.

Before joining them, the lady with the fan walked up past the men at the tree to take one last look at Manny Schoenberg. She stared deep into his eyes, which were now pale with the vague patina of impending death.

"Look what you've gotten yourself into, Shoog," she smirked, jingling in his face the sterling bracelets that she stole from his shop.

"Even your wife called you a liar, after they killed your boy, of course."

The lady with the fan drew even closer and whispered.

"Don't worry, when it goes up for auction, I'll buy your store. Then, I'll make your wife my maid. She'll press my underwear and lick me with her tongue like a Siamese whore whenever I wish it.

"Then, after she's murdered by some nigger scoundrel, I'll sell your sons to a flesh broker in Morocco, where they'll sit on pegs and learn to pleasure men for money."

The lady with the fan smiled and spit on Manny as she turned to walk away.

Across the street his wife fainted. An elderly black man caught her in his arms, as his wife stroked her brow. Another cradled Manny's sons against her breast.

The first black woman looked at the lady with the fan and gasped in horror.

"That woman got the devil in her," she whispered to her husband.

"They all does," he answered, surveying the crowd as they ate supper on the lawn.

"No!" she said sharply, looking him in the eyes. "That woman has got the devil *in* her. I seen it just now, when she was talkin' to poor Manny. The Lord tell me, she gonna come for dis woman next. And them boys after that. That's why we got to get them away from here. Right now."

The men left Manny's body hanging from the tree overnight.

In the morning just before dawn, the town mortician, who was also the county coroner, came out to file an official and sealed report.

"Death by hanging. Probable suicide," he wrote by the light of his lantern.

With much coaxing, he backed his horses up, parking the wagon beneath the body, where he could cut it down. It fell with a loud and undignified thud.

As he wrapped the body in burlap, the coroner saw something moving in the mist out of the corner of his eye.

At first, he thought it was a phantasm. But as it moved closer, he could see that the shifting silhouette belonged to the woman with the fan. But here, she had no fan. And she had no clothes. In the dim glow of the park's gas lamps, she appeared to be completely naked.

The coroner squinted.

The woman was breathing hard, and her face was distorted with rage.

"Miss Anne? You all right?" he yelled tentatively. "Miss Anne?"

The woman clenched her fists at her sides and screamed like someone had run her through with a spear. The horses in front of the wagon reared up, and the man grabbed hold of the reigns with all his strength to keep them from bolting.

A moment later, he looked back toward the park. But the woman was gone.

He had no idea what to make of what he had just seen. Perhaps it *was* an apparition. He sat there mouth agape for a moment while he collected his thoughts. Shaking his head, he finally turned back to finish his grim work.

That's when he saw the woman sitting in a crouch, mere inches from his face, staring at him curiously. He did likewise. Even as she tore into his flesh with her teeth and nails, which were sharp as talons.

As the life drained from him in a stream of blood, the coroner watched mutely as the woman stood up. Her sweat made yellowish streaks as it dripped in rivulets through the blood spattered on her body. His blood.

With his spine snapped in several places, the coroner could only move his eyes. He looked down at the gaping hole in his chest, and thanked God that he could not feel. Suddenly, his vision grew blurred, and his eyelids blinked furiously as he looked up to see the woman urinating on his face.

Grunting loudly when she was done, she jumped from the wagon and disappeared, running into the mist.

Once again, faces and scenes blurred past Jerry's eyes, spinning through the centuries…

The Sins of Angels

The waves crashed over the rails, and the water hissed as it poured over the hot metal latches. Such was the unrelenting heat of the sun on the open sea.

The tumescent stench was brutal and filled the lungs the way the wind filled the giant white sails.

The foulness of the air was cut weakly by a thin haze of smoke from the cheap Portuguese cigars that the crew favored on these long voyages to and from the Colonies.

The only one who didn't smoke on this ship was the captain.

He preferred to chew on thick pieces of *Yohimba* root. They were extremely bitter and somehow that eased the terrible smell. But the *Yohimba* was also a potent stimulant that made him hallucinate and inconsolably mean.

As he paced the forward deck, he inhaled deeply the salty spray. Tiny droplets formed on his beard and cooled his face.

The ship was making excellent headway. But the captain appeared angry. Even at a distance he could be heard ranting agitatedly in Flemish. No one knew what he was talking about, other than the bastardized French swear-words that surfaced every now and then.

Such bizarre antics were why the crew had taken to calling him *Feiticeiro Frenetico.*

The Mad Wizard.

When he had had his fill of invective, he strode down the stairs to the third sub-deck of the hold and unlocked the biggest and strongest African male in the stowage.

The Songhai warrior towered over the captain by nearly a foot.

His legs were weak from days of bondage. But somehow they managed to automatically spring firm and solid now.

312

In the dim light, the warrior's body shone like a statue of polished anthracite, and his muscles twitched with magnificent power. He looked around at the eyes watching him in the darkness. They glowed white and stared with unblinking fascination.

Suddenly and without hesitation, he fell low to the ground, sweeping his long right leg into the hinge of the captain's knee, knocking him squarely to the floor.

In an instant, he was on top of his captor, with his hands tightening around his quarry's throat. He could feel the beating of the captain's arteries pounding with a desperate futility against his unyielding fingers. He watched his face as it slowly began to turn blue, his mouth opening and closing silently like a fish out of water.

The great warrior slave smiled as he looked into the evil man's eyes. He knew that soon they would roll back into his head and grow darker and darker with *kifo*.

Death.

"*Adhimia Mtukufu!*" he yelled. Praise God!
"*Tasbihi!*" the other slaves rejoiced in unison. Halleluja!

The women spun themselves madly in howling ululations, as the children danced in feral glee. Someone kicked over an oil lantern and liquid fire spilled in a flaming cascade over the deck and into the hold.

In the growing frenzy, the crewmen could not arm themselves. The captain kept the keys to the armory around his neck, which was now firmly attached to the massive hands of the slave. The other slaves could sense the crew's fear, and the sailors braced themselves for the violent unknown as the ship cut through the breakers at an ungodly speed, riding on the invisible adrenaline of a screaming gale.

All eyes were now on the slave who held the captain in a death clench. In seconds it would all be over.

His eyes rolled back into his head where only the white flesh of them could be seen. Tiny jaundiced capillaries pulsed weakly as tears began to well up involuntarily in the sockets. His eyelids fluttered, and he gasped, letting out the most horrific shriek. It filled the hold with a palpable terror that infected the others with instant docility.

The blade of the *estilete* had sliced through the soft collagenous tissue of the slave's testicles, and, with a twist, had castrated him instantly.

As the warrior lay clutching his torn genitals, the captain slowly regained his composure and hoarsely ordered the ship's surgeon to stitch up the man's grave wound. Walking through the blood rapidly pooling around the slave, he looked at the others locked up in the hold and at those peering down from the deck.

"Sera o meu cadela," he sneered derisively, commanding his translator to tell the other slaves what he had said.

"He is now my bitch!"

The captain left large bloody footprints on the stairs as he returned to his cabin. Behind him, there was complete silence except for the pitiful screaming of the mutilated warrior.

Below decks was the place the men called the catacombs. The tombs. And they were full to bursting.

With the living.

In about a week that would change.

The slaves lay in their stalls, weeping and screaming, writhing and gnashing their teeth like wild animals. When it was feeding time, the din was awful, and sounded every bit like a colony of ravenously mad baboons.

Even though the slaves spoke in many foreign tongues simultaneously, the crew could always tell when they were praying. They murmured together in low, soft doleful voices in the cadence of what could have been a Catholic Novena.

In the beginning, some of the men would take off their caps as a sign of respect to the unknown God of these dark and beaten beasts. A few even believed that they had souls. But after many days at sea, none of that mattered.

The prayers had become so incessant and so desperate as to offend even the most Christian sensibilities. And that's when the men began to take it upon themselves to answer the prayers.

With whips.

The cargo was lined up all along the circumference of the hull, lying in scores like mummies in a crypt. Then, in the center of the vessel, hundreds more would be arranged in symmetric rows, shoulder to shoulder, feet to head.

Upon them, a second tier of stalls was locked into place, and upon that a third. These were mostly for the women and children, who were often allowed to roam the ship freely, in exchange for comforting the crewmen at night.

The captain of the Carnelian always stuffed his ship with more than twice the reasonable limit of slaves. He knew from experience that half would die on the journey, and half of those left would fetch less money than their original worth.

To him, the black faces were nothing more than black decimal points on a ledger.

Dozens of the *escravo* committed suicide as they lay in the hold, refusing to eat or drink the spare rations provided for them. Some would bite their tongues off and drown in their own blood. Others would take advantage of the serendipity of finding an exposed nail with which to slit their wrists.

Then there were those who set their minds on rebellion, whispering to the women or young boys to set the ship ablaze with the stores of rum and oil. They reasoned that it was better that they all perish here and now in a floating inferno than be taken alive to the land of the devils.

Broken bones, torn ligaments, starvation, and disease would take a heavy toll on the rest of the purse, perhaps as much as a quarter million dollars, truly a treasure lost at sea. The carcasses of the dead would be thrown overboard to the sharks that trailed the ship in a blood-red wake.

At times they could be heard angrily bumping the bottom of the hull, jarring the lamps that hung from the oaken futtocks, demanding more in the insatiate orgy of white teeth and black flesh. Indeed, they shadowed the Carnelian all the way across the Atlantic from the Cape of Good Hope right into the turquoise sea of the West Indies.

The sharks only turned back when the ship arrived in the frigid waters of the American eastern seaboard, though some of the hardier species were known to swim north of the ports of Charleston, where once, a great white had been harpooned by a local fisherman along Cooper's River.

When he cut the shark open, human limbs and torsos fell out onto the pier in piles. A sketch of the horrific event was published in the Charleston Courier, prompting the town's aldermen to ban shark hunting during the spring and summer months, when the slave trade was at its most robust.

The Carnelian was a fifty year-old Danish sailing vessel. The captain had won it in a duel of cards that had turned into a duel of pistols at the previous owner's plantation in Saint Croix.

The schooner boasted five masts and was larger than most of its contemporaries. With the cannons and ammunition stored in the aft chamber, the hold could fit more than four hundred slaves.

Inevitably, such excruciating confinement led to uncontrolled disease, dysentery being the most common and most lethal of the contagions.

The slaves were so closely piled upon one another that halfway through the voyage they would be covered with the paste of each other's excrement. Add to that infected skin ulcerations, parasites, and rat bites, and the death toll was often catastrophic.

 In fact, there were many instances where ships had found their way into ports, despite the fact that no one on board was left alive.

Sailors knew that if the rudders were lashed in place, the shrieking winds of the middle passage would do the rest. These gales were known as *Aguardente de Africa.*

The Ghosts of Africa.

The captain had come across more than one of the abandoned vessels, adrift far from shore. The law of the sea allowed him to commandeer such a ship if he so pleased.

He had only made that mistake once, with a schooner called The Eidolon.

The above decks were completely empty, and the rowboats were all gone. He should have known from that alone that whatever the ship carried, the crew had wanted no part of it. They had risked certain death to flee in tiny skiffs that could not possibly withstand the fury of the ocean.

Nonetheless, he and a handful of mates had boarded the ship to investigate. Corked carafes of port wine and loaves of molded bread lay untouched in the captain's quarters. His pistol was missing, but his sword and scabbard remained on their shelf above his bed.

As he looked about, the captain heard a curious humming. He touched the floor and could literally feel it vibrating subtly beneath him. Slowly, he walked to the hold. Here, the humming grew louder.

As he unlocked the hatch, millions upon millions of flies exploded through the opening. The force and fury were so great that the captain was knocked on his back. In a second, the flies covered him in a thick blanket of quivering black sepsis. He screamed at the top of his lungs. But the flies invaded his mouth until he choked.

When he awoke, he was in his bed on the Carnelian. The ship's surgeon stood over him mixing a foul-smelling medicinal unction. He could see through the portal that the Eidolon was ablaze. She drifted indifferently on rolling green swells, burning incandescently like a twin sun floating on the horizon.

The crew had set torch to the ship after discovering nearly a thousand cadavers in the belly of the vessel.

The smoke burned with the acid smell of death. His lungs heaved in involuntary distress, and nausea hit him like a foaming wave of putrescence.

Dr. Harris opened his eyes suddenly, panting as sweat poured from his brow. He squinted downward and saw the woman in his grip. She had stopped squirming violently and now lay before him like she was comatose.

Her eyes darted back and forth as though in deep REM sleep. Her mouth was open, and she drooled slightly. He could feel her pulse. Barely.

"Release her," the old man whispered in his mind. "Do not let her die in your grasp."

Instantly, Dr. Harris let go of Bileal. He staggered over to the door and got Mike to help him load her into a wheelchair.

"Please take her back to her room, Mike," he said softly.

"You sure, doc?" Mike asked.

Dr. Harris looked at the attendant, not quite sure how to respond to his question.

No one would ever understand what had happened in the session that left her so weak and near death. There would most certainly be questions and perhaps even a formal inquiry if she were delivered to the emergency room in her present state. There would be no way around it.

Drugs had been used. Bruises had been inflicted.

And all anyone would see is a helpless and troubled new mother who may have been beaten and over-medicated by an overzealous psychiatrist.

"Yeah, Mike. Take her to her room," Dr. Harris repeated dourly. "I'll check in on her later."

Jerry sat down heavily on the couch in his office and rubbed his brow. He picked up a pen and paper to record the events that had just taken place. But even he had trouble believing what he had just seen. Where would he begin?

Each vision he had seen only lasted a few minutes. They had gone on all afternoon and well into the night. He was physically spent and decided instead to lie down and close his eyes for a few minutes.

"The Allais Effect," a voice whispered through the fog of sleep. The doctor knew he was dreaming. And he knew the voice.

Ed Lee.

"In two days there will be a lunar eclipse. During that time, the laws of the universe will be suspended. Gravity will retrograde, and the magnetic precession will open a portal in time.

"Seek the newborn."

Dr. Harris opened his eyes. The office was dark. It was night.

He looked at his watch. *Fourteen* hours had passed.

He jumped to his feet and raced out of the room.

The hospital corridors seemed to stretch out further with every step he took. Only the nurses stations were lit, and dimly at that. He had not seen anyone as he made his way to the maternity ward.

As he slowly opened the door to Bileal's room, he could see the woman's sleeping form in the darkness. She was curled on her side and breathing peacefully. Monitors beeped softly, and the light of their screens bathed the room in a fuzzy green hue that reflected off the windowpanes.

Dr. Harris grabbed the chart at the foot of the bed. Blood pressure was good. No fever. Arterial blood gases fine. A notation at the bottom showed that she had just finished nursing her twins an hour ago.

Twins?

The doctor checked the name hidden under his thumb. *Dolores Marsh.*

Oh, no, he thought.

He ran to the other side of the bed. The woman was definitely not Bileal. He looked around the room wildly. He ran to the door and double-checked the number. He was in the right place.

He looked down the hall toward the nurse's station. A security guard had shown up and was leaning against the counter talking to someone Jerry could not see.

He took a deep breath. There was no avoiding it now. He had to take his medicine, he thought, wincing at the terrible pun. But something had happened to Bileal. And all he had were questions.

Questions he had to answer for.

He closed his eyes and steadied himself. When he opened them, Mike the orderly was standing in front of him.

"Relax, doc," he said smiling. Not moving his lips.

Did I see what I just thought I saw, he wondered.

Mike smiled. "Walk with me, Doctor."

As they made their way down the hall, Dr. Harris looked over at Mike.

"I'm almost afraid to ask. But what happened to Emily?"

"You mean Billie?"

Jerry nodded. "What happened to her, Mike?"

"What should have happened to her a long time ago."

"Is she… dead?"

"Evil can't die, doc," he said nonchalantly.

Dr. Harris thought about that for a moment. He could keep asking questions, but it was clear that the attendant wasn't going to settle this mystery. And that was probably for the doctor's own good. But there was one more mystery that he might be able to resolve.

"Why didn't you tell me you were one of… one of…"

"Go on, doc, it's all right to say it," Mike grinned. "One of *us?*"

One of "them" is the word he had wanted to use. But ultimately it was Mike who was right.

Two days later, Emily was listed as a "walk-away," someone who leaves the hospital of their own volition. More than twenty-thousand patients did the very same thing every year at Grady. It was a routine occurrence that would not raise an eyebrow. Half the surveillance cameras were broken, and there was no money to fix them. People left all the time, completely unnoticed.

An annoyed administrator had taken a hasty report, misspelling the young mother's name. She later entered it into a police database, following the hospital's standard protocol.

The result returned a "zero" match.

And just like that Emily had become a ghost in the machine, her life deleted and forever lost in a purgatory of uncaring petabytes.

Dr. Harris leaned against the viewing window where the babies were kept. Leon was sleeping peacefully as usual. He was a bona fide miracle. Who was now an orphan.

Jerry walked into the room and asked the nurse if he could hold the boy.

"Go ahead, Dr. Harris," she whispered. "He's a complete joy. By the way, how did they screw up his diagnosis?"

"What do you mean?" he asked cradling the boy in his arms.

"Well, if he's a crack baby, I'm the Queen of England."

The doctor could only shake his head. He had no clue what had happened either. In fact, the most recent blood work showed that there were no signs of the drug whatsoever in the boy.

He sat down in the grandmother rocker and studied him.

His skin was scrunched up around his chin like a Shar Pei puppy. He had a full head of hair. And a mouthful of tiny teeth. *Remarkable,* the doctor thought.

As he brushed a tiny fleck of sleep from the infant's eyelash, the boy opened his eyes wide, capturing Jerry's gaze like a foot in a bear trap.

CHAPTER FORTY-FIVE

"Apollyon would close his eyes and squint past the millennia."

The moon passed before the sun, occulting its light into tiny molten beads. These slowly blended together in a glowing bulge, not unlike a cornea in the side view of an eyeball.

The Sins of Angels

The superstitious often worshipped this type of eclipse, believing it to represent the awakening of the Eye of Horus, who would now look down upon them in judgment.

But Appolyon knew it was more than that.

He removed a golden Phaistos disc from the bag on his hip, gently fingering the hieroglyphic seals like Braille. He then held it to his eye, so he could watch the celestial beads as they tumbled over one another in slow motion.

He could feel the magnetic rotation of the earth shift ever so slightly. Suddenly, the sky flashed red and blue, shimmering like a prism in the shower of ions. Time would soon shift enharmonically, opening up entire worlds and dimensions to anyone who had the vision to see beyond the opaque.

And this was the true magic of the eclipse.

Atoms would now reorient their collective spin by millionths of a fraction, making the heretofore invisible completely visible. At least to those who could see.

He sat cross-legged on a perch of black marble that jutted out queerly from the side of the mountain. A shepherd's path had found this place a thousand years ago, and ever since people would come here to rest and to look out over the desert below.

The mount was green and full of trees on all but the eastern face. This is where the rock had pushed itself free of the granite and lava-stone, back when the desert was an ocean. Even today, violent gusts from the desolate land below splashed upward like great crashing waves, scorching this side of the mountain so that nothing here ever grew.

But not even the wind geysers could get past the black rock. And everything above and beyond it was lush.

A team of geologists from American University in Lebanon had done tests on the rock and discovered that it was primarily Precambrian with abundant traces of obsidian. But the molecular analysis could not begin to explain to them how it had gotten here. It was like finding a sunken ship.

In the ionosphere.

Villagers in the area say a shaman in need of an altar had pulled the marble free with his magic, and those who believe this will not go near the black rock. But others say that it's just a story. An old wives' tale. And everyone knows that old wives spin tales the way a loom spins wool.

Apollyon liked to sit here at night. And smoke opium.

He liked the way the drug flowed downward from his lungs and rubbed his Hara. It made his skin flush with warmth and sentience.

He liked the way the smoke poured from his nostrils and played about his temples and lingered in his hair like a sweet-bitter perfume. It brought him the closest to sleep he had ever come. With opium, time was a cat poised to pounce.

Interminably.

In the moonlight, he could see ripples of heat still rising off the ground in the distance, thermalling so high over the horizon that the desert could, at times, become a mirage of itself.

But it was real. Painfully.

The sands burned with invisible fire. The lizards ran and the animals howled from the heat locked in the dunes.

The Sins of Angels

Apollyon would close his eyes and squint past the millenia.

He could still hear the heavy bronze camel bells ringing faintly across the centuries, as the spice caravans made their way in a line to the markets in Jerusalem.

Just as they did today.

The black rock was his throne over the world. A God-forsaken world.

There were carvings in the rock. Letters from an alphabet long-dead. And a language only whispered about in secret rabbinical cabals.

It was quite a controversy among the great Jewish scholars. Many scoffed at the myth of a language older than man. But others claimed it was real. And that it was not the tongue of man at all. But of angels.

More than one child, born of the veil, had spoken of hearing the words that sung like musical notes. Words spoken to them in their dreams by spirits with wings of white light.

The rock held the secret. On its underbelly.

Apollyon knew this. After all, it was he who had carved the letters there in the first place. A thousand, thousand years ago. When this iteration of men were monkeys.

To him, the black rock was little more than a blackboard. And the carvings a primer on the divine idiom for anyone smart enough to figure it out.

Sofar, that was no one. No one human.

Few even braved coming here for more than a minute or two at a time. And no one ever climbed over its edge, to see what was there. Or who.

There were other places on Earth that bore witness to the language of angels. Many places in fact. And some were not at all hidden or arcane. Some were just etched so large in the ground that the only way to see the letters was from thousands of feet in the air.

Others were carved into mountainsides above the cloud-rims, or far beneath the face of the ocean in the abyssals that remain even today unexplored by men.

All of them, however, were merely Kilroys, signet graffiti, left by other angels who wanted to taunt Apollyon with the fact that they had come and gone into his territory without him ever knowing.

Apollyon was pariah among his peers and was left to dwell in this place alone, estranged from their company and the old way of life. A gentle sneer crept across his face. That was the arrogance of angels, he thought: to construe *him* as being alone, despite a world full of people within his reach.

But deep within he knew they were right.

Apollyon did miss speaking in the old way and pined for it.

He had always hoped that man would learn the secret tongue and become fluent in the language of his Father.

But it was just a dream. As old as Eden. And just as far away.

Sometimes, he would hear an errant noise carry in the wind. A whistling made by a bird or bat or perhaps even a whale that, in the delicate corruption of time and space, arrived to the ear a weary traveler of sound, stripped of its corporeality and its animal ancestry.

Then and only then could it come even remotely close to a letter or maybe even a poorly-formed syllable from the divine alphabet. But nothing from man's lips could ever utter something so pristine. Except for one simple contrivance.

Music. Pure and beautiful music.

Apollyon loved the flute. And the lyre. Both played in the soft voice of a child singing to itself. These sweet sounds were the closest any human had ever come to truly speaking to God.

And to him.

After all, they spoke with one voice. At least, all of God's legitimate children did.

Man was His most prodigal and prolific bastard, always groveling at the knees and begging for favors. To the angels, man was a devious victim of the laws of primogeniture, a step-child who, only in death, could aspire to see God.

And that was from a distance. Like a by-stander.

The angels themselves were siblings of mischief and insatiate fetish. They were the jealous first-born, who often ranted to The Father with divine loathing that man should be expunged and erased from His will. Hastily.

It was Apollyon who had interceded on man's behalf.

His seat at the right hand of God was coveted by the sycophants who courted The Father's rage toward man. Their parliament voted to execute Apollyon, but God, who loved him above all others, made him instead a king and "banished" him close by. That way He could always look upon him in admiration and longing.

He anointed him sovereign of this place, this savage paradise of pain and profligacy.

Apollyon called it New Heaven.

The angels called it Hell.

God called it Earth.

CHAPTER FORTY-SIX

"The necromancer from the slums of Bethlehem."

Holy men had taught their flocks and minions that God wanted them to pray.

But Apollyon knew that to God praying sounded like the braying of hungry mules. And that if He ever responded it was simply to shut the loudest of the faithful up.

After all, it was well known that God lamented man. Because giving man a soul was like giving a flightless bird wings. Indeed, these would have been mistakes.

Had there been a divine word for mistake.

So God left man to his own device and hoped for the best. The best actually being the worst.

Presumable, the clay souls of the earth-bound wretched would return quietly to the dust from whence they came. Following into oblivion the gargantuan footsteps of the dinosaur.

The Sins of Angels

There was a time when God loved man; but with a enforceable caveat. Man would be without knowledge. A prisoner of ignorance.

For eternity.

In the end, or the beginning, depending on who tells the story, it was not God who set man free. It was Apollyon.

The beautiful one. The most adored. The most abhorred. Depending on who tells the story.

It was Apollyon who whispered the song of seduction in Eve's ear. Who put the apple to her lips. And made her know Adam.

And it was for knowing, and only knowing, that God had sentenced man to death.

The smell of olives was heavier than the wind and fell in soft, aromatic cascades from the orchards to the west. But it was not heavy enough to blanch out the odor of death, which sat like a vulture on the black marble perch.

Apollyon stood up, and the corpse he had sitting propped up against his back fell over like a sleeping drunk.

They had sat there in that way together, for many hours. Or was it many days? He could not entirely remember how long the two of them had been there.

He and the Magician.

All of the Western World from Persia to Egypt had heard of The Great Illusionist. The necromancer from the slums of Bethlehem, who ran with a tight mob of local thugs and thieves and prostitutes and others of ill-repute.

He was a young man, enamored of sweet wines and cheap Egyptian gold rings, which he wore in different weights on every finger like a usurer.

Women fought each other to wash his feet with their hair and massage his brow with their breasts.

Curly black hair dangled loosely down his back and a callow beard grew in light patches on his face. Dark tattoos were inked around his eyelids, and from a distance he had the soft mien of an adolescent girl.

The Magician lived a plush, albeit itinerant life out of a tent like a troubadour in a circus. Except, his tent was bigger and sturdier and fancier than most homes made of stone and wood.

A small mobile city of other tents were always erected around it so as to accommodate his entire entourage and their attendants and animals. Other rings of tents surrounded these in concentric order and were reserved for the thousands of worshippers and revelers and merchants who followed the Magician wherever he went.

Giant banners of red and saffron silk blew gently around his compound and announced his arrival for miles, even when the giant *doundounbas* weren't playing. When they were, they drummed with a cadence of licentiousness and smarm and drove the mob mad with lascivious wanting.

Wherever the Magician went, crowds of adoring devotees followed and made camp with him. And on any given night, you could see them in large groups, singing and dancing naked in front of the giant torches that lined the path to the tent.

Some nights, the guards would take a few of the revelers into the Magician's sleep chamber so they too could perform.

The Magician was the greatest showman in all the known lands. No amphitheater could hold his audiences. They would spill over into the streets by the thousands and crowd precariously onto the nearby rooftops for a better view.

Sometimes, as the drums and the wine mixed, the people would hoist women atop their shoulders and pass them around the crowd, stripping them of their garments while they were aloft. And then of their inhibitions when they were back on the ground.

They worshipped The Magician and screamed his name like lovers in mid-thrall.

"*Jesus! Jesus! Jesus!*"

And Jesus reveled in the narcosis of it. For he was at where his life was supposed to be.

The priests in the temple of Judah initiated him early into their secretive enclaves.

His parents had always paid their taxes and tithes on time, and did all the proper things that showed loyalty and homage apropos of their faith. And when they petitioned to have their first-born son admitted into the synagogue school, the chief rabbi himself made the decision to accept the boy, even though his examiners weren't sure whether Jesus was a child prodigy or simply vexed with bouts of bizarre behavior.

He was often plagued with visions and petite fits. But his mother had worked hard to guarantee his destiny early on in the cleverest of ways.

After all, it was she, fourteen year-old Mary of the Nomads, who had contrived the Great Story. The parthenogenesis.

The virgin birth.

It was the ancient and forgotten story of the Egyptian god Horace that her great-grandmother had once whispered to her as a child. But Mary was keen. And used the story to her own end.

CHAPTER FORTY-SEVEN
"Mary."

She was a beautiful swarthy woman of Abyssinian blood, small, with ample breasts and the full lips and hips of her African ancestry. She was also very dark-skinned. But that alone made her an embarrassment. She was eschewed by her own parents. And they did not object when she ran off in the night with a minor actor and musician named Joseph.

Mary's sister, Jalil, knew her to be pregnant at the time. Two maybe three months. Her belly was still small, but her breasts were fuller, and her nipples were dark and wont to swell and ripen at even the slightest chill in the air. Mary could not stay here for long.

It was known that her parents had been approached by a marriage broker, who told them that a traveler, believed to be of Nubian blood, had seen Mary from his encampment and was smitten by her "raw beauty," as the broker put it.

Normally, Mary's father would have been offended by the suggestion that his daughter marry a black-skinned *Mauros*. But to his credit he was also an *Edot HaMizrach*, an African Jew. That meant they prayed generally to the same God. Besides, the Nubian was also a wealthy stonemason and was prepared to offer more than a modest sum of money for Mary's hand.

There were conditions, however.

The broker said that since the Nubian was thrice-married already, Mary would be forced to defer in rank and privilege to the wives before her. And to their twelve children. And to their children as well.

Also, Mary would have to undergo some sort of purification ritual that involved the minor circumcision of her clitoris. The broker assured her parents that this was not particularly painful. Indeed, the Nubian insisted that it heightened his wives' pleasure during love-making. Hence their many children.

A tribal *Mufti* would oversee the procedure. As would the Nubian's eldest wife, who would closely inspect the new bride's genitals and then direct the surgeon where to cut her bulb. Her intimate knowledge of her husband's lovemaking made her the best one to oversee this.

But Mary had heard about circumcision from other nomad girls who had traveled to the tips of Africa. She had actually met one whose sister had been circumcised. She said the day after the girl's eleventh birthday, the midwives came to their tent and made her drink a special wine that was supposed to dull the pain and put her to sleep.

They sat around her in a circle and burned incense and prayed. Slowly and softly at first, but then more fervently and demonstratively, as the smoke turned everything into a haze.

As the men played music outside the tent, some of the women danced, spinning in place in wild vortices of ecstatic passion. Others continued to kneel, but wheeled their heads violently in concentric jerks that threw the bangles from their hair and the veils from their faces.

The sitar and bells sang with the same glossolalia as the frenzied women inside, until the tribal doctor entered the room. In an instant, the hysterical clamor ceased and only the low whimper of the frightened girl in the middle of the crowd could be heard.

As the doctor unfolded a blanket of knives, the midwives hurriedly poured more wine into her.

The women held the girl down while the tribal doctor cut out the nub of her flower. She said the girl screamed until she passed out. She continued to weep in her sleep.

After the operation, the doctor sewed up her vagina almost until it was closed completely.

On the girl's wedding night, she passed out again because the pain of sex was excruciating. The nomad told Mary that the girl bled almost constantly, not just during her time. And worse still, when her sister bore her husband a child, the birth ripped her genitals so badly that now she often defecated from the resulting fissure in her vagina.

The girl remained in a constant state of sickliness and infirmity. Her husband all but discarded her, treating her like a slave and kicking her around like a dog when he got drunk. She had to beg him for food to feed herself and her baby, and he never gave her any money to buy clothes or trinkets in the market, though she knew he was saving as much as he could.

To buy another wife.

The Sins of Angels

The girl who told Mary the story said that in another year, she would have to be circumcised herself. That is why she was preparing to run away to the Sudan, perhaps to become a whore.

Living on her back, she said, was far better than crawling on her belly.

Mary's mother, Amira, was excited about the idea of marrying off her daughter.

Many times in the past, whether at dinner or the laundry stone or the marketplace, Amira would lament about the wan prospects of finding a husband for Mary. Not an unattractive girl, she would say.

Just dark as dirt.

But Amira was that way. She was a poisonous shrew, soured by her repeated inability to conceive a son for her husband. She spared no one the rod. When the girls were still babies and her dugs were dry, she would beat them for crying in their hunger.

As they grew older, her daughters made fun of her behind her back, often pointing their fingers down at the mouth like fangs, as though she were a monster. Which she could certainly be.

It rained like a monsoon the night Amira bore her husband a third daughter.

Jalil and Mary raised the canvas of their tent and watched secretly as their mother took the newborn into her arms. After the midwife and her attendants had gone, Amira lay for many moments quietly with her daughter, gently caressing her face and smoothing her thick black hair with her fingers.

With great care she placed the smiling infant lovingly into a coracle she had woven for her over the weeks of her pregnancy. She had covered it in a goatskin brightly painted with dancing *shabti* to welcome her daughter into the world.

Then she cradled the basket in her arms, covering the both of them with her shawl as she walked outside. In a few minutes, she returned empty-handed, having placed the basket beneath a deep crease in the overhang of the tent.

It was here that the rainwater drained in buckets, filling the basket in seconds and drowning their sister soon after.

Mary never forgot that night.

She knew her mother would demand her death, if she ever learned that her dark-skinned, unwed daughter was pregnant without the benefit of wedlock and dowry.

Besides, it was the law.

During the family's long journey to Basra, Mary befriended a girl named Sephyr of Syene. She was beautiful and dark like Mary, and they spoke in a similar tongue. Enough to laugh and steal sips of wine together, which was easy to do since Sephyr was betrothed to a successful wine-maker's son, who made sure her family had plenty to drink. A trick of the trade to lower the cash dowry.

Sometimes, the girls would steal away at dusk and wash each other's hair or lay about naked in the cool night air, talking about their secrets and their dreams and their loves. Which for young girls like Mary and Sephyr were always one in the same.

The Sins of Angels

The last night they would do this was the night before Sephyr was to be wed.

On that day, Mary watched as Sephyr's sisters and mother wept in happiness and threw flowers at her feet during her marriage. She wished that she and her own mother could be that close and cried silent tears.

The next day, she and Jalil were awakened by loud shouts and crying in the street. They ran with their mother outside and saw Sephyr running from her husband, but blocked at every turn by a large circle of on-lookers that included her own parents and relatives.

She was pleading for adjudication. She wanted the law-givers to decide her guilt or innocence, not her husband and his family.

Her husband was a short, portly man, with wine-stained teeth and thinning hair. Sephyr had told Mary that she did not particularly like him but that she was anxious to marry him, as he had money and position that would help her family get ahead.

The man she really loved was an apprentice wheel-maker, whose parents had died of plague when he was a boy, leaving him destitute with dim prospects for the future.

Sephyr's marriage to the wine-maker's son was brokered by an old crone named Hedia, who was now standing among those in the growing circle of agitators. Hedia had done well for Sephyr's family, securing for them an admirable wage for the matrimony.

Though not part of the original deal, she had even gotten the groom's family to sprinkle tasty flecks of gold and silver on the large servings of goat and lamb at the wedding feast.

Hedia studied the bed-sheet hanging outside the wedding tent. There was no blood. She shook her head slowly. It was now obvious to all that Sephyr was no virgin. She had lied and now had to pay the price.

The dowry was not refundable and most of it had all ready been spent, paying off traders who had extended credit to the girl's family during the trip.

Hedia mused to herself that if the girl had told her the truth, for a little extra, she could have planted a small pig bladder of blood inside her, to give the groom a new maidenhead to break, as he consummated his marriage.

But that too may not have worked, as his family was rich enough to hire a conjugal practitioner to inspect the bride properly after that first night. Sadly, there was nothing at all she could do now to help the frightened girl groveling in the dust before her.

The old crone walked away. She knew what would come next.

The first stone hit Sephyr on the knee, making her curl up in a fetal ball in pain. She held out her hand to her husband, but he smacked her and tore off her gown, so that now she lay naked before the crowd.

The groom's brothers and uncles grabbed her and carried her screaming back into the wedding tent. There, they raped and sodomized her, brutalizing her like a cheap desert whore.

This time when they hung out the sheet it was soaked in blood. And they laughed and patted each other heartily on the back.

The men then brought Sephyr out with her hands and legs bound. Her naked body was horribly bruised, and her face was swollen. Her hair had been torn out in handfuls.

The Sins of Angels

Mary was hysterical and called out to Sephyr, but Amira smacked her so hard in the mouth that she fell backwards to the ground. Jailil helped her back to her feet and held her in her arms as they watched their mother carefully select the biggest stones to throw at the disgraced new bride.

Jalil tried to muffle Mary's wailing as the crowd stoned Sephyr. Even Sephyr's mother and sisters, who the night before threw flower petals at her feet, now threw rocks and mud bricks at her face and arms and legs as she lay in a ball, moaning like a slaughter-calf that's been hit with a maul.

Sephyr's husband waved his arms and told everybody to get away from her.

Mary looked up and breathed a hopeful sigh of relief, as the mob moved back. Then, she saw Sephyr's husband pour a large urn of lantern oil all over his bride, who was too unconscious to even writhe in agony.

The man walked over to his brother, who gave him a torch. And as Mary watched wide-eyed, he threw the flame on Sephyr and immolated her.

Mary stopped crying. The adrenaline flushing itself through her made her eyes dart about, back and forth from Sephyr to the faces in the crowd surrounding her. She watched the flames melt Sephyr's beautiful dark skin, boiling it first in clear bubbles the size of grapes that burst in sickening little pops. At first, Sephyr awoke and screamed in pain, but suddenly she stopped and cried aloud only for her mother.

The woman stood before her, breathing hard, as though she had just run some great distance in haste. She put her veil over her face to keep out the smell of her daughter's cooking flesh.

Her eyes looked like unpolished rocks that could not see the atrocity before her. Sephyr's eyes never blinked before they burst. When they did, her sisters ran away screaming for God to forgive them.

When the fire had turned Sephyr black like the trunk of a burned tree, the crowd dispersed back into their tents or back to their chores. From a distance, her body lay twisted and frozen in agony. Only her skull stood out as something remotely recognizable.

Mary, still in shock, moved closer to her friend. She put a hand over her mouth to try and quell the nausea. Yellowish folds of fat steamed in protrusions from Sephyr's thighs and hissed like meat on a spit, the way Berbers roasted rabbits.

Mary studied every inch of the smoldering corpse before her.

Not from ghoulish fascination, but in a vain attempt to somehow find Sephyr, to discern the funny girl with whom she had sneaked sips of wine just a couple of days before.

She looked at her left hand and saw the ring her husband had given to her. Melted into a trickle down her blackened fingers. She wanted to touch her, but Jalil pulled her away, and they quickly walked back to their tent.

Sephyr stayed there in the street all day, as everyone went about their business all around her.

That night, jackals stole quietly into the caravan and pulled her corpse into the desert with the wild dogs, where they devoured it together, growling and howling in the hills.

Mary thought hard about Sephyr and knew from what she had just witnessed that she could never tell anyone the truth about her pregnancy.

But after many nights of deep calculation, she invented the Great Story.

She took her sister aside and tested the tale on her. But while Jalil enjoyed the fantasy, she did not believe it for a second. She told Mary in a whisper that she had seen her run off one night many weeks before with the Damascan shephard's son. A boy named Sytun.

Jalil swore she would never tell anyone the truth, but warned Mary that their mother would also never believe the lie.

So Mary had to find someone who would.

CHAPTER FORTY-EIGHT

"Women and men screamed in pain and ecstasy."

She met Joseph at a party, a drunken loud convivial around the Well of Sinai. The well was a rest stop for traveling merchants, complete with bordellos and saloons and vices of every imagining.

Here you could pay to watch women or men have sex with each other or with trained beasts. You could look through a silk screen and purchase for a night, one of the mute young boys. Or for the same price, you could buy two little girls. Maybe even three.

On this night, half a dozen caravans had converged, and the revelers made merry, few speaking in the same tongue but all speaking the same foul language.

The smell of sour mango wine filled the tents and thick clouds of hashish hung in the air like dark spirits.

Women and men screamed in pain and ecstasy. Music of every instrument pierced the night, and even the animals swayed and bucked in their yokes as though drunk themselves. It was in this place of salaciousness and sin that Mary and Joseph first laid eyes on one another.

Joseph came from a wealthy Jewish family, though he himself was a man of little means or ambition. He liked to spend what money he could make on opium, katt, hemp, hashish, and the other fruits of delirium.

But he was a handsome and stout man of great physical prowess. And women were drawn to him. It was said that he had fathered many children in many cities. Under many different names.

But Mary would captivate him. And more.

CHAPTER FORTY-NINE

"The hair of boars but the beauty of gods."

She had stolen away from her tent, as her parents and Jalil slept, making her way quickly past the drunken camel-lice and ruffians who littered the road to the well.

Strange colors glowed incandescently in the fires that lined the rest stop. And in the flickering shadows, whores and seers, wizards and barkers, chided the passers-by to sample their wares and their magic.

Mary eased cautiously into the tent of a woman selling potions. Inside, tables were lined with scented candles and stone phalluses and wooden sculptures of couples having sex in every way imaginable.

Behind an ornately crocheted cloth partition, a naked man was being massaged by a naked little girl who pulled the blind completely closed, as she smiled knowingly at Mary.

The warm, musky redolence of the shop told Mary that she had found the place she was looking for. The woman at the entrance, whose face was hidden behind a *pardah* of tiny silver bangles and a black silk veil, now stood inside the parlor, next to a shelf of bottles and vials and mortars and pestles, both large and small.

There were all sorts of lotions and powders and perfumes. There were also pebbles, tiny and smooth, the kind that were inserted into the vaginas of cows. As well as women who did not wish to conceive a child.

Like most women, Mary could not read. But she could smell that some of the jars on the racks contained sweet and bitter spices.

She could see that some contained the bodies of small animals or animal fetuses or the parts of either of these. Each jar bore an inscription upon its label that she could not understand, but beneath these words were the simple cuneiforms and hieroglyphs that she could read.

Snake. Lion. Baby. Penis. Coin. *Heart.*

That was the one.

The woman removed her veil and hood and stood next to Mary. She had the thickest black hair Mary had ever seen. It did not dangle lazily down the back or shoulders like most other women's hair. Instead, it pushed itself wildly out in a puff of dark curls, that shone with the settling humidity in the air.

The woman's lips were thick and painted black with the same dark make-up that highlighted her eyes. Mary thought her perhaps to be a Spartan or some such other Greek, as men say they have the hair of boars but the beauty of gods.

The woman spoke in a tongue unknown to Mary. She offered her a vial of red liquid that she had already had in her hand. Mary shook her head politely and pointed to the bottle with the heart on the label.

The woman smiled and waved her hand over that bottle, as she shook her head back to Mary.

The woman then touched Mary softly on the cheek, tracing the flush that the candlelight seemed to enhance. She looked down at Mary's belly and put her hand over it, moving it in a circular pattern. Then, she brought her arms up to her breasts, rocking them gently as though cradling the baby inside Mary's belly. Once again, she pressed the vial into her hand.

Mary stood with her mouth agape, as the woman brought her hands together and, in a blur, produced a silver drachma out of thin air. Mary giggled as the woman then took her hands and brushed them through Mary's hair, where she found a second and then a third silver coin.

She held them up, and pointed at the vial in Mary's hand.

Mary winked and held up two fingers, and the woman grinned, showing perfectly white teeth, that came to sharp points at the incisors.

The Sins of Angels

She nodded her head and held up two fingers, as she pushed the vial toward Mary, who gave her two *drachmas* and quickly left the store.

Joseph and his minstrels had performed for the caravans on several occasions to perfunctory applause and a few coins that would buy them dinner for the night. He played the lute and sang. He had a sweet tenor's voice and eyes that could find the women with loose coins and loose morals.

It was his eyes that were his true instrument, because he could play them for all they were worth.

He stood over six feet and had large, delicate hands, well-matched to the lute. As he moved in time to his singing, Mary could see that, beneath his tunic, his body was a mural of tattoos. She could not make them out. But she could see that he was covered in them.

Such was the way of musicians, she thought. Everyone she had ever seen had at least one tattoo from each village they had played in. Joseph's read like a world tour.

Sumeria. Babylon. Canaan. Israel. Egypt. Greece.

She studied him thoroughly. And she calculated. Deeply.

Joseph had dreams of playing before kings and noblemen. But so far his aspirations had stayed just beyond the reach of his fingertips, as they danced between the taut strings of his lute. He was getting older and life in the desert, with its easy temptations, had begun to take a toll on him physically.

He was older than many of those in his troupe and was starting to feel out of place. And there were feelings he had never had before.

Feelings of fatherhood. For the first time in his life, he wanted a child. With someone he could love.

He often sang songs of love and lament, sometimes even going into the crowd and serenading the women one on one. But lately, he noticed, as he sang, his real feelings were beginning to slip through the fraud of his lyrics. The meretricious ballads were suddenly desperate cries for love. That Mary could hear.

And this was why she chose him.

She came upon him sleeping beneath his wagon, his head lying on a plump goatskin of wine, his knees up, giving her a glimpse of the nakedness beneath his tunic. She giggled to herself. There was something about this man that made her breathe deep and look long. As she studied him, he awoke.

He rubbed his eyes and looked carefully at her, up and down her body. She knew that he was looking past her clothes, and she did not blush.

Instead, she sat next to him and stroked his face. Joseph was taken aback by this and lifted himself until he was sitting as she was.

He was confused and needed a drink. He brought the wine sack to his lips and took a giant swig. When he had finished, he offered Mary a drink, as well. She did not hesitate, and when she had taken a sip she gently loosed the top of her sari so that it fell below her breasts.

At this, Joseph stood up and took Mary by the hand to a private place where they could lay by the well.

As he disrobed, Mary quickly poured the contents of the vial into the goatskin jug. She too took off her clothes and lay purposefully beside him. His strong arms reached out to bring her near him, but she played coy and acted like she needed another sip of wine, which she then offered to him.

Joseph drank greedily, and almost instantly he began to reel. He felt like he had just stepped off a ship after a long voyage over rough seas. The earth continued to undulate beneath him as Mary climbed slowly astride him.

And then, looking Joseph in the eye, Mary made love to him in the soft silt that traced the edge of the well. Afterward, they lay there beneath the stars, listening to the wind play gently against the water and the night birds splash about in its shallows.

Joseph could hear the blur of loud music coming from far, far away. Inside his head.

Mary rested against him and put her mouth close to his, making him breathe her air, making him smell her flesh, making him love her beyond his control as the potion spread through his blood.

And that night, as the black became indigo, they stole away in Joseph's wagon and eloped to Bethlehem.

As they steered down the rocky paths and roads along their journey, Mary became suddenly afraid and unsure that her bold plan would work. Many would doubt her and perhaps even stone her. In some tribes, mendacity from a woman was also punishable by death.

Her heart beat with real fear, because in truth she was little more than a little girl. Part of her wanted to run back home to her mother and confess her sin and throw herself on Amira's mercy. Surely, there must be some particle of maternal loyalty within her mother's breast. Some tiny spring of warmth to assuage her daughter's terror.

But that would never happen.

The wagon rolled into the saffron dawn, and Joseph gently stroked his new bride's hair, which was wet from the sweat on her brow. And as Mary swayed with the wagon's girth, she let herself be rocked to sleep next to her new husband.

And in the mirage between sleep and waking, she could hear the jackals fighting in the distance of the desert.

She thought of her friend Sephyr. And herself.

She thought of the fire. The stones. And Amira.

Throwing them at her.

CHAPTER FIFTY
"His interest in Jesus was genuine."

Many months later, Mary bore a son. Jesus.

After considerable council, the elders within the tribe, weighed the veracity of her story and agreed in a unanimous ballot that there was evidence of its truth. Most notably, her good and devoted character.

And, of course, the cosmic circumstances of the birth.

No less than a new star was born on the very same night.

Despite this omen, some of the older women in the tribe giggled under their breath at the Great Story. But since the elders' word was law, punishable by death, and women were nothing more than birth-vessels with no vote or say in anything, few ever spoke of what they suspected.

Besides, Mary was far more cunning than any of them and plied their husbands with unctuous words of flattery and cajoling that sat in their heads like the sweet medicine of wine. And after a time, even those most suspicious of the women sought to be in her favor.

The elders adopted the family and gave them a house and cattle and gifts of all kind.

They became remarkably popular. Posters with their likenesses were hung in all the major cities of the region, and people would make hajj's just to see the boy born of God.

Great seers and minor kings. Pundits and paupers. The strong and the infirm.

Large crowds would sit outside their home, waiting for Mary to come to her balcony and hold the babe high in her hands. She surprised herself with how much she had taken to her celebrity. And her influence.

And with every passing day, rain or shine, as the boy grew, so too did Bethlehem. In wealth and importance.

Vendors prowled the faithful hordes like wolverines upon loose chickens. They sold everything from magic beads and anointed water to brass charms of Mary and whalebone sculptures of the baby Jesus.

They sold roasted pigeons and sugar-glazed cakes. There were even kiddie-rides on the backs of baby camels. And for every three coins collected, one went to Mary and Joseph, another went to the temple, and the rest went to the vendor for him to split with Caesar.

A special audience could be had with the family but only for a gift commensurate with the honor. For an additional incentive, a commissioned portrait-maker could paint your visage next to that of the baby Jesus and sign it with the official stamp of the Bethlehem Temple.

Among the many who came bearing magnanimous gifts was Apollyon.

He brought young Jesus a chest constructed of gold so heavy that it could only be supported with a custom-made mantle built of thick Egyptian nehet and ebony from the Sudan. It took six strong men to heft it into the home where it sat prominently over the stone fireplace in the family's dining room.

After that, Mary and Joseph personally invited Apollyon to visit as often as he liked. And he did.

In many different guises.

More than they knew, he had dined across the table from them. He always engaged the family in the same manner, with heartfelt toasts and sincere flatteries.

His interest in Jesus was genuine. He would clasp the boy's hands in a fatherly, almost prideful way, watching him grow over the years from an awkward youth to a beautiful young man.

And each time he came, he brought with him another gift.

Queerest among them was a life-sized bronze statue of a Nubian warrior, cast with giant eyes of pink sapphires. In his hands he clutched a golden *tanto* from the Far East with a sheath covered in perfect diamonds that burned brighter than any light shining upon it.

He also presented them with three mastiff pups sired in the house of the Roman Emperor himself, their collars bearing the special-minted coins that identified the holders as diplomats of the realm.

The Sins of Angels

The years passed, and the family, led by the ceaseless cunning and craft of Mary, became wealthy and well-positioned. But eventually they were forced by their own good fortune to move.

On three separate occasions, thieves and mercenary kidnappers had broken into the home to abduct Jesus for ransom. But in each attempt, the boy had been spared only by divine intervention.

One villain had gained access to the home, only to slip and fall, impaling himself in the throat with the golden *tanto* of the bronze Nubian.

Another had the bones in his neck crushed by the heavy statue after it fell on him when he apparently tried to steal it. And a third was torn to shreds by the three now-grown mastiffs, which slept outside the door to Jesus' room.

CHAPTER FIFTY-ONE

"Anywhere beyond the Red Sea, Jesus had to be careful."

Mary chose to move her family to the larger city of Nazareth. It was there that Jesus had wished to become a journeyman carpenter after his bar mitzvah.

But he was besieged to no end by all manner of young women, some of whom had sold all their possessions and cashed in their dowries to travel there and propose marriage to a mere boy who had barely reached puberty.

The Sins of Angels

Jesus eventually had to leave home and seek sanctuary within the temple of the Nazarene high priests. It was there, alone within the quiet stone warren of prayer chambers and rooms of ritual, that he could live unperturbed by his own prodigious fame.

His room was four levels below ground, and sometimes he felt that wasn't deep enough. The walls of hand-chiseled rock were cool to the touch. A spring dripped through a conduit above his bed, and many nights he would divert the water with a rock so that it fell upon his brow in a soft cascade.

Often, when he was here, he would blow out the reading lantern next to his bed, strip off his clothes and kneel in prayer in the pitch-black darkness.

It was here that he would also practice his magic.

Apollyon loved this.

He could tutor the boy invisibly from the shadows on the many nuances of sleight-of-hand. True magic only dwelled in the meniscus between heaven and earth. And the only way to find it was with the help of someone who had been to both.

On many occasions the rabbis would not see Jesus for days at a time, and all the food left outside his door, would go untouched, except by the mice that skirted along the wooden beams and crevices.

The Pharisees did not understand why Jesus would want to live in this place and in such a way. But it added to his already strange and mystical presence. And that could only be good. And profitable.

They were the ones who spread the gossip about his bizarre behavior and whipped the frenzy of a mob already starving to catch just a glimpse of him.

353

Long after he had put down the tools of carpentry, Jesus would be known for building Nazareth into a cross-road of political repute and financial influence.

And that's why here, just as in Bethlehem, the holy men took an extraordinary interest in him, mentoring him personally in the ways of mysteries and theosophy.

When they let the youth oversee the worship service, the crowds quadrupled, mostly with squealing girls and boys, but all of them with money. It wasn't long before Jesus was preaching every week. They called him a rain-maker. And when he started incorporating magic into the sermons, he became a miracle-maker as well.

One of his first miracles was for a woman who had been run over by the heavy wheels of a lumber cart.

Her back was broken in many sections, and pieces of her spine pierced the skin like shards from a broken pot. By the time they brought her to the temple, blood was filling her mouth and nose, and she was near death.

Unsure of what he should do, Jesus washed her wounds with the sweet mulsum wine that the rabbis kept in an urn near the door. And as she screamed in agony, he pushed her vertebrae back under the skin with his hands. After many minutes, when it appeared that the woman was dead and the crowd was stunned to silence, she suddenly gasped, and her eyes opened wide.

Jesus grabbed her by the hands and lifted her to her feet, leading her as she walked in baby steps back to her family. Even he was shocked, and very relieved, having improvised the treatment on the spot.

Many months later, she returned and offered herself as payment. She was escorted to his room and allowed to stay the night. When she and her parents left town many months later, her back was strong. And her belly was swollen

But despite his growing fame for magic, it wasn't Jesus making the miracles. It was Apollyon. And when the boy-evangelist decided to take his show on the road, it was Apollyon, who had in fact made the decision for him.

Jesus and his enclave traveled all along the Great Sea. From as far north as Damascus to as far south as Mizraim.

His bodyguards were with him at all times.

They were loyal to a fault and were rumored to have killed many people in their zeal to protect their master.

The meanest of them was a brutish man whose name was almost as well known as Jesus', but for the opposite reasons. He was called "John the Bastard," an unrepentant criminal who had served many years of his youth on a slave ship. He had huge muscles and the strength of a stud bull.

John had been recruited by Jesus himself to help collect the money owed to him by unscrupulous promoters, and other would-be merchants of his fame.

As it turned out, he was a distant cousin of Mary's on her father's side. She remembered her grandmother speaking of him when she was a girl. She said he was ferocious as a lion. But to those he loved, he was completely harmless.

And so she had sent for him to watch over her son as he set out to embrace his destiny.

One of John's responsibilities was to set fire to the kiosks belonging to vendors operating without permission from Jesus or his agents. These were forbidden to set up shop within a radius of 300 royal cubits. This ring of dominant influence and was strictly patrolled by John.

He had met Jesus for the first time in a tavern along the Great Sea. He had heard of Jesus and his penchant for miracles even before Mary's letter but had been skeptical, despite their kinship.

He had sought to challenge him with the only kind of test he trusted. A test of strength, in a wrestling match.

At first, Jesus' guards drew their bows and were ready to execute John on the spot, but Jesus told them to put away their weapons. With a hearty laugh, he agreed to the contest, going so far as to wager that John would not even be able to touch him.

John laughed at first, but then he ran toward Jesus with his fist pulled back in a furious charge. Yet at the last minute, according to those who witnessed it, he stopped in his tracks and stood frozen mere inches from the young Magician.

It was as if he had seen a monster, instead of the handsome young man who stood before him with his arms out to his side and his palms up.

John wept as Jesus put his hand upon his shoulder and led him to the shallows of a nearby river. There, Jesus pulled the hair out of John's eyes and whispered into his ear. And then holding him close, Jesus lowered him into the water to cleanse him of the vision that had harrowed him so.

From that moment on, John rarely ever left Jesus' side. And never did he utter a word of what he had seen that day.

Anywhere beyond the Red Sea, Jesus had to be careful.

The Egyptians despised him, because his mother had plagiarized the long-dead yet still holy gospel of the Pharaohs. And the Egyptians were a vengeful people. The king had vowed to kill Jesus personally if his footsteps ever dared to desecrate the sacred dunes of Giza.

The Jews on the other hand loved Jesus.

He was one of them, and he took care of his own. He brought jobs, money, and respect into their cities. And because of that he was treated like a monarch.

Very often in ghettos everywhere, terrible, bloody fights would break out between the Jews and the Egyptians because of Jesus.

But no matter where Jesus was Apollyon always saw to it that he was never harmed, no matter how many times he was targeted for assassination, by any of the different factions, including a few from within the Jewish kingdom.

But most people curried his favor. And it was nothing for him to spend days or weeks at a time in the barricaded seraglios of the mayors or governors of the Roman prefectures.

Despite his seeming wanton and wicked ways, Jesus could be at times a true ascetic, given to private moments of self-flagellation and mortification. He would secret himself away in a dark cave or dungeon and pray. In pain. During these times, Apollyon left him alone to his own bizarre devices.

Jesus was not one of those insane thanatomaniacs who believed that they had to die to inherit the kingdom of God. He knew that Heaven was here and now.

Just like Hell.

It simply depended on your circumstance.

But he did have one great and growing weakness, Apollyon began to discover. Jesus was beginning to believe his own propaganda.

One night, after the caravan had stopped on its journey to Jerusalem, Jesus rose from his bed, neither awake nor asleep.

As though in a trance, he slipped past John and the bodyguards and wandered alone, deep into the desert. The light of the moon illuminated a small goat path that wound circuitously up the side of a steep hill.

To the Black Rock of Apollyon.

Here, the two would meet face to face for the first time without deception. But it had not gone the way Apollyon had planned. Jesus was disconsolate with terror. He had snapped awake from his daze and was running about the rock, breathing heavily and waving his hands frenetically.

Apollyon was captivated by this.

He watched Jesus screaming the prolix of his conceit to the heavens, holding his hands high in the air, as though conjuring some great spirit from the sky.

But the trumpet of his words had brought only the mournful response of the jackals prowling the empty inferno below. He nonetheless persisted with his ranting until finally, reluctantly, it had brought Apollyon out into the open.

As Appolyon stepped slowly from the shadows, the Magician recoiled in absolute terror, rebuking at the top of his lungs this *deiwos* of the night. He held his arms out in front of him as he spoke to keep the spirit at bay both with words and hands.

Jesus frothed at the mouth and babbled in the Hebraic tongues of legerdemain that he had been taught in the temple, drooling a foolish hubris about kings and constellations and God's great plan.

For him.

The sermon entertained Apollyon. He was genuinely amused.

And for the first time in an epoch, he had actually laughed. Out loud. But the Magician grew angry and fierce, demanding that Apollyon repent his sacrilege and bow at the knee before him.

Whispering softly, soothingly, Apollyon moved forward slow and deliberate as smoke, wrapping his arms around the magician, who seemed startled and not wanting of this great gesture. But the more Jesus fought, the more Apollyon began to squeeze like a Burmese python, tightening his grip with every breath the magician took. Until he passed out.

When he regained consciousness, he was laid out on his stomach, splay and naked on the black marble. He rolled over groaning to see Apollyon standing over him, naked as well.

The Magician stood up, slowly. Apollyon smiled at him. But Jesus grew wild in his fear and sense of violation and tried to run away.

Apollyon reacted instinctively, grabbing him by the neck and sweeping him in an instant off his feet onto the hard ground.

His eyes opened wide as he lay on his back. He could see the clouds shimmering like veins of silver in the moonlight. He could even feel them deliquesce with a fragile electricity, as his spirit moved through them, swirling into the frigid vortex of space.

Apollyon lifted Jesus' body and laid it tenderly on a sward of high grass in the olive orchard near the Black Rock. He gently laid his hands over the open eyes and closed them as he spoke soft words of contrition.

He studied the shape and contour of the Magician's countenance until his own face took on those very characteristics, cell for cell, molecule for molecule.

His hair grew thick and curly and hung below his shoulders, and a soft beard filled out in patches on his face. He could feel his torso stretch and the muscles grow tumescent with the strength and vigor of youth. His eyes turned brown as they squinted toward the distant fires of the camp in the valley below.

It was then that he donned Jesus' tunic and sandals and walked down the Mount to join the assemblage that had begun to despair in their leader's absence.

As he approached, the crowd cheered wildly.

The Magician looked as strong and sure as the day he had left. He smiled reassuringly at the faithful as they surged forth in a churning human tide of noise and chaos.

Apollyon-- now Jesus --raised his arms and roared at the mob with a commanding voice that emanated from deep within his lungs:

"Peace!" he exhorted. "Be still. For we have much to do."

CHAPTER FIFTY-TWO

"Remember your Einstein, Dr. Harris."

Dr Harris awoke from his trance with a shudder. The baby stared at him in the same curious way that he stared at the baby. They sat there in that manner for several minutes.

"Daddy?"

Dr. Harris looked closely at the child.

"Daddy?"

The doctor wheeled around. It was Jonathan. And the children.

"Jonathan," he whispered with surprise.

"I have to go now, daddy," he said quietly. "*We* have to go," he said looking over at the others.

"Go where, son?"

The boy walked over to his father. He smiled as he looked at the infant in his arms. Then he wrapped his arms around his father's neck and hugged him like he used to before he left for school in the mornings.

Dr. Harris used his free arm to pull the boy close. He breathed in his smell and rubbed his cheek against his son's face.

"It's time for us to leave this place," he whispered.

"But... I don't understand, Jonathan," he said softly as tears began to well in his eyes.

"It time to go, Dr. Harris."

It was another voice. One that the doctor knew well.

"Dr. Tatsuro," Jerry said as he opened his eyes. "What's going on?"

"The children. Their work is finish."

"Their work? What work?"

"Always in movie, when someone about to die, they says 'Don't go into light.' But they wrong. When you die, you become the light. Energy. The children are good energy. They needed here. Now, needed no longer."

Jonathan smiled as the old doctor spoke. He touched the baby's forehead with his fingertips. The infant smiled back and looked directly into Jonathan's eyes. It was obvious that he could see him.

The doctor was confused.

"The children here to protect Baby," Dr. Tatsuro explained. "Their good energy needed to repel the bad, like magnets turned against each other. They have done well. And now it is time to go."

Jerry had no idea what his friend was talking about. All he knew was that he didn't want his son to leave.

"Don't worry, Daddy," he said cheerfully. "We'll see each other again. Besides…" he said looking over at the baby, "He needs you. You can be his daddy too."

"But…"

Jerry wanted to speak. But he was overwhelmed by the emotions pouring into his heart and head all at once.

"Remember your Einstein, Dr. Harris," Dr. Tatsuro said patiently.

Jerry looked at him, unsure of what he meant.

"For energy, time stop. No time pass for boy. He energy now. Even if you live to be a hundred years old, to him, less than a nano-second will pass. Same for other children. Same for all who die. And wait for the living."

"*Mokka, Otokooya!*" squealed two little girls in the group of children. One of them carried a smiling infant girl.

"Li! Mai! Don't be so impatient!" Dr. Tatsuro scolded playfully. "I almost done."

Dr. Harris looked at the girls. Then at the elderly physician.

"*Li? Mai?*" he thought. Those were the names of Dr. Tatsuro's daughters. The girls who had drowned.

"Your daughters?" he asked, almost to himself as he looked at the girls. "They are beautiful."

"Yes, they are. And soon Mimi will come too. My daughters. My angels."

"You found them!" Jerry grinned happily.

"No. They find me."

"How could…"

Suddenly Jerry understood.

"Yes, Dr. Harris," his friend smiled. "No time pass for me too."

Jerry looked at the old man. "Oh, my God… Satoshi," he stammered sadly.

"I was wrong Jerry. There is God. He is love. I feel it now. I happiest ever been," Dr. Tatsuro said, wrapping his girls like a bouquet in his arms. "Do not worry for Jonathan," he continued. "He my son. Till you come."

Jerry wept as he squeezed Jonathan. "I love you so much, son" he said tenderly, pressing his face against the boy's. "You've given me more than any father deserves."

"I love you too, daddy. I always will. Forever."

"Remember, Jerry," Satoshi's voice said fading. "I was wrong. There is God. He is love. Good-bye my friend."

Dr. Harris smiled, even as he opened his eyes and realized that his son, the elderly doctor, and the other children were all gone.

Leon smiled with his full set of baby teeth. Dr. Harris couldn't help but to smile back. He knew that Jackie would be thrilled to have another baby in the house. It had been he who had resisted the idea. But now, as he looked at the infant, all that melted away.

Somehow, their separate paths had brought them here through the mysteries.

With many more promised.